Someone Is Killing the Gay Boys of Verona

by
Mark A. Roeder

Writers Club Press
San Jose New York Lincoln Shanghai

Someone Is Killing the Gay Boys of Verona

Copyright © 2000 by Mark A. Roeder

This book may not be reproduced or distributed, in whole or in part, in print or by any other means without the written permission of the author.

ISBN: 0-595-09113-X

Published by Writers Club Press, an imprint of iUniverse.com, Inc.

For information address:
iUniverse.com, Inc.
620 North 48th Street
Suite 201
Lincoln, NE 68504-3467
www.iuniverse.com

URL: http://www.writersclub.com

This book is a work of fiction. Names, characters, places and incidents are products of the author's imagination or are used fictionally. Any resemblance to actual events or locales or persons, living or dead, is entirely coincidental.

Dedication

This book is dedicated to all the gay boys that have died because others do not understand, to those that must struggle against the prejudice and hate of others, and to those wise and courageous enough to help them.

Contents

Dedication iii
Preface vii
Acknowledgements ix
Chronology xi
Chapter 1   My Best Friend Marty 1
Chapter 2   Graymoor Mansion 7
Chapter 3   The First Loss 15
Chapter 4   A Puzzle Where No Pieces Fit 23
Chapter 5   The Truth Revealed 31
Chapter 6   A Bizarre Idea 37
Chapter 7   Ghosts 101 45
Chapter 8   Kindred Spirits 53
Chapter 9   Calling on the Dead 59
Chapter 10 Uncovering the Past 67
Chapter 11 The Second Loss 79
Chapter 12 A Perfect Night for a Séance 87
Chapter 13 History Repeats Itself 101
Chapter 14 First Contact 111
Chapter 15 Hatred and Lies 119
Chapter 16 Marshall's Makeover 125
Chapter 17 Contact from Beyond the Grave 133

Chapter 18 Skater Boy	139
Chapter 19 The Murderer Unmasked	145
Chapter 20 Back to Square One	151
Chapter 21 The Third Loss	157
Chapter 22 A New Boy in My Life	167
Chapter 23 Ghostly Encounters	175
Chapter 24 Going Nowhere Fast	183
Chapter 25 A Real Date?	187
Chapter 26 A Message from Beyond	193
Chapter 27 Nick and Kyle	203
Chapter 28 Terror in Graymoor	209
Chapter 29 The Return of Friends	239
Chapter 30 A Boyfriend at Last	245
Chapter 31 Wounds of the Past Healed	251
About the Author	255

Preface

This is the third of a series of novels that take place in Verona, Indiana. Each novel stands alone, but is best read in order, beginning with ***Ancient Prejudice Break To New Mutiny*** and then proceeding with ***Someone Is Watching*** and ending with the present novel ***Someone Is Killing The Gay Boys Of Verona***. This current novel introduces some new characters and revisits some familiar faces, now twenty years older. Readers will also find a couple of characters from previous novels that they won't be expecting to see. This novel is an entirely new story, but wraps up a lot of loose ends from the other novels. ***Someone Is Killing The Gay Boys Of Verona*** delves into new areas and even into the supernatural. It is part mystery, part ghost story.

The main character, Sean, is a departure from the featured characters of my first two novels. Where Mark, Taylor, Ethan, and Nathan were all rather athletic and handsome boys, Sean is more ordinary; a little pudgy, not quite so good looking, and a little more interested in reading than in playing soccer. He represents yet another type in the endless variety of gay boys in the world.

Someone Is Killing The Gay Boys Of Verona deals with some very real issues in this day and age of hate crimes against gays. It also demonstrates the power of friendship and love and gives hope for a better future. Things have come a long way in the past few years, but there is still very far to go. If we all keep working toward it, the world will someday be a place where no one need walk in fear.

Acknowledgements

I'd like to thank Ken Clark for his suggestions and criticisms of early drafts of S.I.K. I'd also like to thank all those who have written me with their comments and ideas.

Chronology

Historical Note: This novel takes place 20 years after Ancient Prejudice Break To New Mutiny and Someone Is Watching.

Chapter 1

My Best Friend Marty

I glanced to my side and in that fleeting moment I could read the tension in Marty's youthful form. Every muscle in his body was strained as if he were struggling against some great weight. I knew what it was that was bearing down upon him so. We'd spent hours discussing it the night before, and many an hour before that over the preceding weeks.

I knew the difficulty of the path he was treading. I had trod upon it myself barely a year before. Admitting to the world that you are gay is not an easy task. Walking among your friends and class-mates the day after coming out is even harder. Just entering our old familiar high school was without doubt a tremendous task for Marty, as it had been for me.

I knew Marty had to be wondering what awaited him beyond the doors before us. Would his friends stick by him, or draw away? Would the other boys at school hurl cruel taunts at him, or let him be? These and a thousand other worries were heaped upon Marty's young shoulders, just as they had been loaded upon mine. Even though I was there to support him, even though I'd talked him through it all, I knew that

Marty had never faced a greater challenge than simply walking through those doors.

I never really thought we'd reach that moment in time. I never thought that Marty would be able to summon to courage to admit what he was to the world. We'd talked about it certainly. Marty had made the decision to come out over and over again, and yet he'd never been quite able to own up to the task. All that had changed the night before, he'd come out in no uncertain terms.

My mind raced back to the dance. It was like so many other school dances, and yet, somehow, I knew it would be different. I loved to dance and had just finished a rather wild and crazy one with Zoë Peterson. Zoë was a pretty good friend and loved to dance as much as I. We often danced together when she was between boyfriends, sometimes even when she wasn't. Her boyfriends didn't mind, they knew she was safe with me. They knew I certainly wouldn't be stealing her away. There were a few advantages to being a known gay boy.

I took my usual place beside Marty and sipped on some punch. Marty wasn't much on dancing. He mainly went to dances to just hang out and talk. I was doubly surprised when he took my hand and pulled me out onto the dance floor. I didn't resist, just followed in amazement. I knew exactly what he was doing, but I still couldn't believe he had the balls to do it. Dancing with me was his way of letting everyone know he was gay.

It was a slow dance and Marty wrapped his arms around me. I must admit I was more than a bit nervous myself. Everyone knew I was gay, but I'd never dared to dance with another boy in front of everyone before. I could feel the eyes upon us. Everyone was looking at us. My discomfort was eased by the knowledge that they were looking at Marty more than me. I don't think anyone had ever guessed that he was gay.

Despite the awkwardness of the situation, something felt right about it. I smiled at Marty, trying to put him more at ease. I could tell by the look on his face that he was scared to death. He needed me. He needed someone who had already withstood the battering that came with being gay and open.

No one taunted us, but we drew plenty of stares. There were quite a few glares from the boys in the gym too. I heard more than one of them quietly mutter "faggots" under his breath. I'm sure Marty heard it too and that made it all the more difficult. We'd discussed that before however. The world was not known for making things easy on gay boys.

My head was spinning in amazement. After so long Marty had done it. He'd come out to all his friends. Little did I realize that he wasn't finished however. Marty intended to leave no doubts.

Marty stopped and looked into my eyes. He leaned forward and pressed his lips to mine. He kissed me, right there in the middle of the dance! I was astounded as his lips met mine, even more so as he slipped his tongue into my mouth. Our dancing together had drawn stares, but nothing compared to our kiss. The whole dance practically stopped as Marty gave me the most passionate kiss of my life.

Our lips parted and Marty took me by the hand once more and led me from the dance floor. Eyes followed us and I heard "fucking faggots" issue from the lips of more than one of the boys around us. Marty and I stood to the side for a few minutes more, then departed. Marty had done what he had come to do.

My mind snapped back to the present. We walked inside and I could feel eyes upon us. There were hateful glares to be sure, but most seemed merely curious. I was happy to note that Marty's friends greeted him as they did every day. I could tell that some were a bit uncomfortable, but even those seemed to go out of their way to say "hi" and thereby let Marty know that he was still their friend. I knew that Marty had a rough road ahead of him, but I had the feeling that everything would be okay.

One thing I definitely noticed was that Kyle went out of his way to talk to Marty. Kyle's family had only moved to Verona a few weeks before from Colorado. Neither Marty nor I knew him well, but we'd both taken note of him. Kyle was a real cutie. He looked like he'd stepped straight from the pages of XY Magazine (one of my favorites because of all its photos of cute boys). Kyle had short dark hair and dreamy brown eyes. His lips were definitely kiss-able. He was so sexy my heart beat a little faster near him. He wasn't paying much attention to me however. His eyes were on Marty.

I couldn't quite read what was on Kyle's mind, but I had the feeling that he had more than casual interest in my friend. I must admit I was a little jealous. It didn't bother me that another boy showed interest in Marty, we were friends after all and nothing more. That kiss on the dance floor was the sum total of our sexual contact. We'd never so much as hugged one another before. It had just never seemed right. We were more like brothers than boyfriends. I was jealous because Kyle had eyes for Marty and not me.

I knew I was reading too much into the situation. True, Marty had just come out, and true, Kyle had never paid much attention to him before, but all Kyle did was ask to borrow Marty's calculus homework. That wasn't exactly what I'd call putting the moves on someone. No doubt my overactive imagination was once again causing me to read more into the situation than was there. Then again, there was something in Kyle's eyes...I tried to just be happy for Marty, but I couldn't quite force the jealousy from my heart.

Kyle wasn't the only one giving Marty the eye. I noticed Ken looking him over too. I knew what was on Ken's mind without a doubt. Ken was one of the handful of openly gay boys at our school and he was a lot more vocal than most. He didn't take crap from anybody and he wasn't afraid to make a scene. If someone called him a fairy or something he just got right up in their face and asked them what their problem was. I had quite a bit of respect for him, but sometimes he took things too far. He was kind of militant and acted as if all the straight boys in school were the enemy. He didn't seem to realize that non-gay guys could be cool too.

I wasn't exactly happy about Ken taking an interest in my best friend. Marty was a bit naïve and innocent, Ken definitely was not. He was a nice enough boy, but he'd definitely been around. I knew he wouldn't hesitate to pounce on Marty if he got the chance. I knew he wouldn't do anything to hurt him, but if he was interested, and he certainly was, he'd do his best to get into Marty's pants. I made a mental note to talk to Ken about it. I knew that if I explained the situation to him that he'd back off. He'd even help Marty as I was. Ken had helped me back when I was coming out. Just talking to him about things had really helped when I was letting the world know I was gay. I knew firsthand how nice a guy he could be. I also knew firsthand that he was anything but innocent. I definitely had to talk to him before he went after Marty.

I walked Marty to his first period class. I felt like his bodyguard or something. When some boy glared at him, or made an unkind remark, I was there to support him. I was like a shield that protected him.

I knew Marty would be especially vulnerable in his first few days as an out gay boy. During that time he'd be an attractive target for the anti-gay crowd. He'd also be inexperienced at protecting himself. I'd already experienced all that. I'd dealt with it. I'd fought with words and fists. I still had to do so now and then, but nowhere near as often as I had to in the beginning. Until Marty got his bearings and grew a little stronger, I'd take care of him.

That task was upon me, even as I was thinking about it. I saw Alex coming down the hall toward us. I knew he'd have something to say. I wasn't wrong.

"Faggots." he said in greeting, as if it were his version of "good morning".

"Bite me Alex." was my reply. I knew immediately I'd chosen my words poorly.

"You'd like that wouldn't you Sean?"

"Fuck you Alex."

"Yeah, you're just dying to aren't you faggot?"

I shouldered past him. There was no reason to continue. Alex was a total ass. Neither Marty nor I put much value on his words, Alex did little more than cut down everyone he met. He was one of those guys that thought it was funny to greet girls with "bitch". Everyone thought he was a total creep. Everyone was right.

Before going in to class, Marty stopped and looked me in the eyes.

"Thanks for helping me through this Sean."

"No problem." I said.

He smiled and turned away. I knew that Marty was going to be just fine.

Chapter 2

Graymoor Mansion

That night I was supposed to meet Marty at our usual haunt, a little burger place not far from the school. He said he'd be there about eight. I was still waiting on him at eight-thirty. I couldn't stand waiting. I was pissed. Marty, and all my friends, knew I got all bent out of shape if they were late. It was something that really set me off. I called Marty's house, but no one was there. After another twenty minutes had passed I gave up and walked home.

It wasn't a good night for a walk. I'd been depending on Marty to drive me home, he was the one with a car after all. It was early spring and a great thunderstorm was rolling in. Already the black clouds overhead blotted out the light of the moon. The wind got up a bit and it started to rain. As if that wasn't bad enough, lightning streaked across the sky, creating a distant rumble that grew ever closer.

Actually, I was rather fond of storms, but not when I was caught out in them. I liked to watch them all comfortable and cozy from inside, or take long walks in the rain carrying a great umbrella. I was without protection as the rain fell down with ever greater intensity however. I didn't enjoying being cold and wet.

The lightning created odd shadows as did the wind blown branches of the trees. I kept thinking I saw something moving off to one side or another. There were some weird noises too. It kind of creeped me out. Walking alone, in the dark, in the rain, spooked me more than I care to admit.

Things went from bad to worse as the lightning fell closer and the rain pounded down harder. I began to run. The lightening and thunder frightened me as it blasted down with blinding flashes and deafening roars. I ran on and on and finally made it home.

When I looked up and saw the great house before me, a part of me wanted to just stay outside. No one was home and all the windows were dark. The whole place gave me the creeps. We'd moved into the old Graymoor Mansion only two days before. I was uncomfortable there in the daytime and at night it could be downright terrifying. In the raging storm it looked like something right out of a horror movie.

I was dwarfed by the house. It was enormous. I looked up at the roofline, four stories above, and saw the gargoyles staring down at me. They looked about the size of a dog from where I stood, but I knew they had to be huge. They looked almost alive as the rain and wind whipped around them. I almost felt like they would swoop down upon me.

The lightening rent the air so close by I was temporarily blinded by the light. The loud clap of thunder that followed made me jump. That made up my mind for me and I rushed inside. I grabbed a flashlight I'd left for myself near the door and walked through the large parlor toward the staircase. Parlor didn't seem the right name for the room. Like everything at Graymoor, it was huge. There was enough room in there for a basketball court.

Every shadow seemed like some horrible monster just ready to reach out and grab me. My parents had to be out of their minds buying that old place. It was literally falling apart and no one had lived there for more than a hundred years. It would take another hundred years to make it a decent place to live.

I jumped as the grandfather clock on the stair chimed the hour. It was so loud it startled me in the darkness. That old house was full of stuff that startled me. I wasn't exactly a coward, but I wondered if I've ever grow accustomed to that place.

When I reached my room on the third floor, I closed the door behind me and lit the oil lamp that sat on a stand by my bed. There was no electricity yet and wouldn't be for some time. The whole house had to be wired from the basement up. I'd never heard of a house that didn't have electricity before, but Graymoor had never had it. There were candle chandeliers and gas lights everywhere.

I was soaked to the skin and my breath came in gasps. I wasn't exactly a runner and having to dash so far in the lightning and rain was less than fun. I stripped. It was hard getting my clothes off, my shirt and boxers clung to my clammy skin. I hung them on the back of a chair to dry.

I caught sight of my reflection in the full-length mirror and gazed upon my own body. I wasn't all that happy with the way I looked naked. I looked pretty good in clothes, but out of them was a different story entirely. I needed to drop a few pounds, maybe more than a few, and I definitely needed to put on some muscle. I'd been making some progress in both those areas, but I had a long way to go. I guess not everyone could look like those guys in fitness magazines. I wasn't even close.

Actually, I wasn't much interested in looking like those over muscled guys in some magazines. They had too much of a good thing. They almost didn't look human. My goal was a firm, well-muscled body with flat abs and no fat. That's the kind of guy that got me excited, just an ordinary, in shape boy. That was my goal and I was slowly working my way toward it. I sometimes wondered if I'd ever get there however. It was a long, hard road.

I slipped into some dry clothes. The flannel shirt felt good against my naked skin. The room was a little chilly, Graymoor was always chilly. I guess that was to be expected from a house that was heated by fireplaces. I hoped my parents would get a good furnace system installed by winter. I could just imagine how unbearable the house would be if they didn't.

I sat on the edge of my bed and looked around the room. The whole place creeped me out. Everything there, except for myself and my few belongings, was just like it had been for more than a century. Even the furniture was older than the hills. The bed I slept in, the dresser I kept my clothes in, everything was from another age. I felt like I was living in a place where time had stopped.

My dresser especially creeped me out. There were little sphinxes on the handles that reminded me of evil little faces. I could swear their eyes followed me as I moved about my room. At night, I felt like they were staring at me, watching me, waiting their chance to do something to me.

The whole house had a very strange feel to it. Not exactly a bad feeling, just odd. When I say that everything there was exactly as it had been for more than a hundred years, I'm not exaggerating. The day we moved in I opened the drawers of an antique cylinder desk downstairs and found letters and post cards from the 1870's. There were all kinds of receipts, one was for a year's subscription to the local paper, it was dated June 23, 1871. Throughout the house, it looked like the Graymoor family had just left and could be back at any second. I felt like I was sneaking around in someone else's house, instead of my own.

Even my own room felt like it belonged to someone else. The day I moved in, I had to take a bunch of clothes out of the wardrobe and dresser. There were shirts and pants just hanging there the way one would expect, except that they'd been hanging there for more than a century. The clothes were about my size. I had a feeling a boy my own age had lived in that room. I wondered what he was like.

Even my bed had been untouched for a hundred years and more. Except for the layer of dust, it looked like someone had just made it and walked out of the room. I knew however that the last person to sleep in that bed had done so in the nineteenth century!

I didn't know what my parents were thinking when they bought that place. Well, that was not quite true, I knew why they wanted it. They were obsessed with old things. They were always dragging home some old antique that they displayed with great pride. They spent most of every weekend looking for their little bits of junk. I knew they had to love that scary old house, it was stuffed from top to bottom with just the kind of ancient crap they loved. My parents' obsession with the past seemed a harmless enough pass-time until they went off the deep end and bought Graymoor Mansion. Everyone knew it was haunted and no one dared to go inside. It had been up for sale for more than twenty years and not one person had bothered to even look at it. Anyone with any sense at all stayed far away. And what did my parents do? They bought it!

My parents were totally obsessed with restoring the old mansion to just the way it was in the 1870's. I wasn't even allowed to take the clothes out of my wardrobe and dresser until dad had photographed everything. My father was an archaeologist and he was treating our house like it was one of his excavations. Everything had to be recorded in its exact location. Whatever my parents restored, it had to be exactly like it was before, even the wallpaper and color of the paint. Like I said, they were obsessed.

I would much rather have stayed in our old home. It wasn't nearly as big, but it was from the right century, and it had cool things like electricity and television! Our old house was only four blocks away, but it might as well have been a million. I wasn't even allowed to bring the furniture from my old room. My parents said it wasn't right for Graymoor. They were forcing me to live in the past. I wasn't one bit happy about being exiled to that old mansion.

Graymoor gave me the creeps. I'd already been hearing weird noises at night, sounds like footsteps and distant voices. I even thought I'd seen someone walking down the hall, but it was probably only a trick of the light. One thing that really creeped me out was the cat I saw running down the hall. I didn't think much about it until I remembered we didn't have a cat. When I looked back at it, it was gone. I ran down the hall looking for it, but there was no sign of it at all. I had the feeling I'd seen a ghost cat.

Who knew what horrors lay waiting in that old house? Everyone knew it was a murder house. Even if it had happened more than a hundred years before it didn't alter the fact that old man Graymoor had went nuts and hacked his entire family to bits with an ax. That's why the house had sit empty all those years. No one dared to live there after the murders, not until my family took up residence. I didn't exactly feel honored to be the first. The thought of those ax murders scared the shit out of me. If I ever found out old man Graymoor had murdered someone in my bed I was going to be sick.

I don't think Graymoor would have been quite so scary if it wasn't so damned huge. I'd being doing a lot of exploring, but I hadn't even been in most of the rooms. Some of the halls had some really weird turns in them and it was easy to get lost. Whoever built that place was one bizarre guy. There were doors where there didn't look like there were doors, and there were doors that didn't go anywhere at all. I found one room with some really cool old toys in it. There was a train and even a miniature carrousel that still worked. I didn't have time to even begin to explore that room. I intended to get back to it, but when I looked for it again, I couldn't find it. It was like it was just gone. I knew it was there somewhere, but I just couldn't figure out where. I guessed I'd just have to wait until I stumbled upon it once more.

I wouldn't have been surprised one bit if there were secret rooms and passages in that old house. It was so big that it just wasn't possible to figure out where everything was. I don't think anyone would have had any trouble at all with hiding entire rooms in there. Who knew what was in that old mansion?

Where were my parents? They knew that old house freaked me out and they'd promised to stick around as much as they could. I knew I'd be abandoned however. I had pretty good parents, but they were both way too busy for their own, or my, good. Sometimes I felt like an orphan. I could actually go for days without seeing them. That could be pretty cool sometimes, but I didn't like it so much after we moved in that old haunted mansion.

I looked out the window and watched the storm rage through the streets. The rain came down in sheets and the wind blew it along the street like waves on the sea. I still had a chill from being soaked to the bone. I didn't appreciate being abandoned to the storm one bit, when I saw Marty the next day there would be hell to pay.

Chapter 3

The First Loss

I didn't see Marty the next day. I never saw him alive again. I waited for him to meet me to walk to school, but he never came. I looked for him in the halls and at lunch, but he wasn't there. I even called his house just before I left school, but no one answered. It wasn't until that evening that I found out what had happened, and why I'd never see my best friend again.

I was working out with my weights, attempting to force my body into the shape I desired, when the news came on my little battery powered TV. The lead story was about a boy who'd been found dead in the woods behind the school. My barbell went crashing to the floor when Marty's picture came on the screen. I just stared at it in horror while the news anchor announced that it had been a suicide. Marty had put a bullet in his own head.

I sank to my knees and watched the screen. Tears streamed from my eyes as the reporter told how Marty's body had been found by a couple of hikers in the woods just a couple of hours before. He'd been there nearly a day. I looked away as the screen showed a body bag being loaded into an ambulance. I just couldn't bear to look at it, knowing my friend was inside. I just kneeled there and cried, shaking.

I spent most of that evening crying, and that night. I'd never lost anyone before. Marty was my best friend. He could be a jerk at times, but that didn't change how I felt about him. I didn't even have anyone to help me through his loss. Without thinking, I started to leave my room, but I stopped myself when I realized I was going to see Marty. That just made me cry all the harder. I felt like I'd never be happy again.

Marty was gone. It seemed so unreal. I knew that people died, everyone died, but to have him suddenly missing from my life just didn't seem right. Part of me was in a state of disbelief. Part of me expected him to come walking through the door, or be at school the next day. Marty was only fifteen. His life was just beginning. How could it have ended so soon?

I lay face down on my bed and cried for the longest time. Eventually I fell asleep, but did not rest easy. I cried even in my dreams. As I lay there I felt a hand running through my hair, the way my mom had petted me when I was a little boy and was upset about something, or sick. I opened my eyes, expecting to find her there, but the room was empty. I had a lot of odd dreams that night.

The next day the halls at school felt like a funeral home. Marty had quite a few friends and everyone was stunned to lose him. It was just such a shock. We all saw him every day and then suddenly he was gone forever. I kept expecting to see Marty walk around the corner, or come up to me at lunch, but he was gone. I'd never see him again. That knowledge kept hitting me like a sharp jab to the gut.

I felt horrible for being angry with him for standing me up two nights before. There I was thinking he was such a jerk while he lay dead in the woods with the rain falling down on him. Perhaps he was pulling the trigger right as I was thinking such terrible thoughts. I knew it wasn't right to torture myself with that, Marty would have agreed that he was a jerk, but it still didn't feel too good to know I'd thought that as he was taking his own life.

The school brought in counselors to help people like me deal with Marty's sudden death. I talked to one of them. It helped a little, but it didn't really take away the pain. Marty's death hung over me like a black cloud. I just didn't understand why I hadn't seen it coming. I hated myself for not being smart enough to read the signs. If I'd been paying more attention he wouldn't have been dead. I was Marty's best friend. I was the one who should have seen it coming. I was the one who should have stopped it. I'd failed him.

* * *

The media didn't help matters. I knew I lived in a small town where nothing much ever happened, but the news people really drove Marty's suicide into the ground. I couldn't turn on the TV without being reminded of the death of my friend. They always did that shit, running the same story over and over until the very sight of it made me sick. This time it was far worse however. Seeing Marty's picture over and over again, and the film of his body being taken away, was like a dagger plunging into my heart. The media latched onto the fact that he was gay pretty fast and soon the story was all about that. There were related stories on the suicide rate of gay youth. That wasn't a bad thing in itself. Maybe if people realized just what their attitudes caused they'd be a little more careful. The suicide rate of gay boys (and girls) was obscene.

I'd been trying to conserve the batteries in my little television by not watching it too much, but I kept it off even more right after Marty died. I didn't want to be reminded of his death. It preyed upon my mind too much as it was. Before Marty died, I had been using the television as company, as a way to fend off the other-worldly noises of Graymoor. Without it, I heard more than I wanted to hear. There was always some creaking or groaning going on in that scary old place. The worst noises were those that sounded like voices, or footsteps. Occasionally I even heard what sounded like moans. That kind of thing might have been fun in a haunted house at Halloween, but it was no fun at all in my very own home.

Other weird shit was happening to, at least I thought it was. I'd light oil lamps in rooms then leave them. When I returned later they were out. I guess that wasn't all that odd. I guess the lamps could have gone out by themselves. It happened all too frequently however. The same thing happened with candles. What really got to me was when I was alone in the house and walked in a room to find a lamp or candle lit, that I knew I hadn't lit. Lamps and candles might go out by themselves, but they didn't light themselves.

That wasn't all either. Stuff was always disappearing, only to reappear a short time later. I set my shoes on my dresser for just a moment one day after school. I pulled off my shirt and turned back around to find my shoes gone. I was alone and only had my back turned for a moment, but they had disappeared. I looked around for them and moments later they were back where I'd left them. At first events like that freaked me out, but they soon became all too frequent to bother about. I was left with an uneasy feeling all the time. I felt like I was never really alone in that old house. I missed the television. Without it, I heard more than I wanted to hear. I didn't want to turn it on however. If I did so, I'd only be reminded of my best friend's death.

* * *

Marty's funeral and burial were on Saturday. I attended with Zoë and several of Marty's friends. During the funeral I kept looking over at Marty's mom. She was crying steadily and my heart went out to her. Marty's dad just held her, his own eyes filled with tears. I knew what they were going through. I shared their pain, or at least some part of it. I'd lost my best friend, they'd lost their son.

I didn't know what Marty's parents thought of him being gay. The truth was, there hadn't been much time for them to react. I knew that Marty had planned on telling them after he got home from the dance. He knew word would get back to them pretty fast and he wanted to be the one to tell them. I went home with him that night, but he would have had plenty of time to tell them after I left. I'd even asked him if he wanted me to stay while he told them, but he'd said no, it was something he had to handle by himself. He hadn't mentioned it to me the next day as we walked to school, but then I was busy talking him through what was about to happen. I thought there would be plenty of time to talk about everything. I thought we had years ahead of us. I was wrong. I hoped he had told his parents he was gay. I didn't want to think about them learning about it from the TV.

Zoë held my hand as I walked up to the open casket. Marty had shot himself in the head, but the mortician had been able to arrange him in the casket so that it was impossible to tell. When my eyes saw his face, tears ran down my cheeks. I just couldn't take seeing him lay there like that. He didn't even look quite like Marty. He was so pale and quiet. Marty had been such an active and loud boy, it just didn't seem like him at all lying in that casket.

I noticed that he was dressed in a nice tee-shirt with an open flannel shirt over it. That was the way he always dressed. I was glad his parents didn't put him in some damn suit.

I stood there looking at him for a long time, even though the sight hurt me. I felt a flash of anger at him for leaving me. I couldn't understand why he had done that. I couldn't understand why he hadn't come to me if something was bothering him so much it was driving him to suicide. My anger passed quickly. He hadn't killed himself to hurt me. He must have been out of his mind with pain. I cried because I'd been unable to help him when he needed me the most.

After the funeral, both his mom and dad hugged me tight. They knew I was gay. If they had any problem with Marty's homosexuality they didn't show it. It put me a little at ease. At least maybe his last night at home had been peaceful. At least he'd died knowing his parents loved him. A lot of gay boys weren't that lucky.

* * *

As the long line of cars pulled up to the graveyard, I felt sick to my stomach. I simply could not believe what I saw through the window. I prayed to God that Marty's parents didn't see it, but I knew there was no way they could have missed it. Across the street was a small group of people holding signs. Someone was actually picketing Marty's funeral!

And the signs! What horrible things they said. If I had not seen them myself, I would not have believed it. As it was I could not believe my eyes. It just didn't seem possible. A few men, women, and even some guys my age were carrying signs that read "God Hates Queers", "Marty is Burning in Hell", "No Fags in Heaven", "Fags Die, God Laughs", "Thank God for Aids", "No Tears for Queers". I turned my head away. There were more signs, but I just couldn't take it. Marty was such a kind, loving, wonderful boy. I couldn't begin to comprehend how anyone could be so evil as to hold up such signs at his burial.

There wasn't one person among the sign holders that I recognized. Not one of those people even knew Marty. I wondered if it would have made a difference however. I wondered if it would have made a difference if they knew Marty went to church every Sunday; that he was a choir boy; that he mowed his next door neighbor's lawn every week for free because she was too old to do so and too poor to pay anyone; that he'd given his own coat away to a boy at school because that boy didn't have one and his family couldn't afford one. I could have gone on for hours thinking of all the good things that Marty had done. I knew however that the sign holders would not have cared. It didn't matter to them that Marty had done more good than all of them combined. It didn't matter to them that his death had left a hole that no one could fill.

People like that were so filled with hate that they couldn't see past their own narrow beliefs.

I must admit that part of me hated them for what they were doing, and what they were, but I pitied them as well. In a way, being what they were was its own type of punishment. I could not imagine a life so filled with hatred. I was glad that I was not so. I would certainly not have envied them when God had his say. I had a feeling that God would read those signs differently. The man holding the sign reading "Marty is Burning in Hell", might as well have been holding one reading "I Do the Work of Satan, Damn Me". I would not let them shake my faith however. I knew that God would forgive even them.

The funeral party turned its back on the hosts from hell and ignored their evil. We had come to say goodbye to our friend. No matter what those holding the signs might have wanted, we knew that Marty was with God in Heaven.

I looked at Marty's parents weeping and my heart went out to them. What must it be like to lose a son? I realized only then that tears were falling from my eyes. Saying goodbye to Marty was much harder than I'd ever guessed. I just couldn't bear it. It was just too horrible to be true. I kept hoping it was all a nightmare and that I'd wake up in my bed. It was real however, and I had to deal with it. I kneeled down, laid a handful of flowers on Marty's grave, and bid my best friend farewell.

Chapter 4

A Puzzle Where No Pieces Fit

I sat at home that evening, thinking. I could not forgive myself for the death of Marty. I could forgive others, even the horrible people holding the signs, but I could not forgive me. I was Marty's friend. Why hadn't I seen it coming? What had I missed?

I turned it all over and over in my head. Marty had showed not one sign he was intent upon ending his own life. I'd read the booklets. I knew the signs. Marty didn't show any of them. Sure, he'd been concerned about coming out, but he'd done it and all went well. There were problems to be sure, and problems ahead, but nothing that would have driven him to take his own life. He'd already done the hardest part. When I'd left him that last morning, he'd smiled, he was happy. He even had Kyle interested in him, and Ken. There was just no reason for his death. Could there have been something going on that I just knew nothing about?

I was so worked up over the whole thing that I even went over to Kyle's house that evening. I'd never been there before, but I knew where he lived, it was just a few blocks away. I asked him about the last time he'd seen Marty and what he thought of his mental state. Kyle told me he hadn't seen him since lunch the day he died and that he seemed fine then. All Kyle could think of was that maybe coming out had been too much for him after all. That didn't seem to explain it to me.

My mind turned it over and over as I walked back home in the growing darkness. It simply didn't make sense. There was no reason for Marty to have committed suicide, not one sign. Marty was a deeply religious person and we attended the same church. He knew as well as I did the church's view on suicide. That view had been troubling me a lot. What if it was right? What if suicides really did go to hell? The prospect terrified me and I knew it would have terrified Marty even more. It was a puzzle where not one of the pieces fit. I thought and thought and the more I did, the more sure I became that Marty could not have killed himself. He just could not have done it, would not have done it. It just was not him.

That night as I lay in bed, I felt a cold draft. I sat up and peered through the darkness. I could feel more than see something coming toward me. My heart raced, my eyes grew wide. Slowly I could make out a form approaching me, all gray and billowy. It wasn't until he was standing right by my bed that I recognized Marty. He sat on the edge of my bed and looked upon me with great sadness. He spoke to me but I could not hear the words. I reached out to touch him, but he disappeared into nothingness.

I awoke with a start, having jerked to a sitting position in my bed. I looked at the edge of my bed, but there was no Marty there. I'd been dreaming, at least I thought so. My heart pounded in my chest. It had seemed so real, but then again most dreams did. I lay back down. It was a good while before I could get back to sleep. I was edgy and uncomfortable.

*   *   *

"So what's it like living there?" asked Marshall as he followed me down the hall at school. Ever since my family had moved into Graymoor, Marshall had taken a real interest in me. Marshall was one bizarre boy. He was forever carrying stacks of monster magazines and books on ghosts and all kinds of supernatural stuff. Every single report he ever did for English was on some weird other-worldly topic. Even his appearance was a bit bizarre, but not entirely unattractive. Marshall had dark, kind of long hair with bangs that obscured his eyes more often than not. He always had a distant look as if his mind was elsewhere. He dressed a lot in black and it gave him a mysterious look. He would probably have been very good looking, even cute, if he didn't look so damned weird.

Despite his strangeness, he seemed to be fairly well liked. At least no one seemed to dislike him. Everyone thought he was kind of queer, but no one really bugged him about it. Marshall pretty much kept to himself. He was in his own little world and didn't seem to take note of everyday events around him. He didn't seem to take notice of anything unless it was quite out of the ordinary. He'd never taken notice of me until my parents bought that creepy old house.

"You seen any ghosts yet?" He asked, intently looking at my face in anticipation.

"No." That wasn't quite the truth, because I had indeed seen something walking down the hall near my room. It wasn't quite a lie either as I suspected it was just some kind of reflection or something. Either way, I didn't want to encourage Marshall at just that moment. I had other things on my mind and he was being a pest.

"Are you sure? There's got to be ghosts in that place!"

I don't think I'd ever seen anyone so excited about something before in my life. I was a bit cross with Marshall for pestering me, but I couldn't help but like him.

"I'll tell you what Marshall, if I see one, you'll be the first to know."

With that I slipped into my third period classroom, escaping from Marshall at last.

"Thanks Sean!" he called to me and went back into the twilight zone. I wondered what had made that boy so weird.

* * *

I could not let the matter of Marty's death rest. I gathered up every single newspaper article on it that I could get my hands on. It was not a pleasant task, but I read and reread each one. Most of the articles said pretty much the same thing, but not one of them gave me reason to believe Marty had committed suicide.

I needed to be more direct. One day after school, I stopped by Marty's house. His parents were gone. I knew they would be. They'd taken off for several days just to get away from everything. I felt a little odd as I went in their house when they weren't home, but I knew they wouldn't care. It was easy to get in. Marty's parents were like many people in Verona, they never locked their doors.

I went to Marty's room. As I walked in it hit me. The last time I'd been there, Marty was still alive. We'd talked, listened to music, and wrestled on this bed. Being alone in that empty room brought the pain of his loss to the surface and tears filled my eyes.

I searched Marty's room, looking for something that could give me some clue to his death. I checked out all his hiding places, his dresser drawers, his closet. There was nothing out of the ordinary.

I found his journal. I felt like I was invading his privacy when I opened it, but I knew it would have been okay with Marty. I read through the last entries. They were mainly about his coming out, and about me. I smiled when I read that I was a great kisser. I was a little surprised when I read that Marty was attracted to me. He was thinking about approaching me. He was thinking about sleeping with me. That was his last entry. He'd written it the night he'd kissed me at the dance. I wished I'd known about his attraction to me. I wondered what would have happened if he hadn't died.

I found nothing that gave me reason to believe Marty had committed suicide. If something had forced him to commit suicide, it must have happened quickly. There was just no evidence of it at all.

I put Marty's journal away and left his room as I found it. I gazed at his room for a few moments before leaving it for the last time. We'd had a lot of fun there. I couldn't even begin to count the nights I'd stayed with Marty. We'd been friends since we were little boys. A deep sadness bit into me. I'd never see my best friend again.

The pieces didn't fit. There was something very wrong about the whole thing. I was convinced that Marty had not killed himself, but I needed to know for sure. For my own piece of mind, I had to find out what had happened, and why. I knew the one person who might be able to help me. As I stepped out of Marty's house, I headed out to see Ken.

Ken Clark had helped me before, when I was struggling with coming out. I had no doubt he'd help me out again. Marty was gay and if the suspicion growing in my mind was true, then Ken would definitely want to be in on what I had in mind. Ken was a bit too radical and outspoken for my taste, but he was someone I could count on. He'd always been there for me in the past.

His mom showed me into his room. Ken looked up from his computer screen. He was hard at work editing the newsletter he wrote for gay youth. Ken was quite involved with helping other gay youth and even had his own internet site. Back in the days when I lived in a home with electricity, I'd checked out his site often.

"Hey." said Ken in greeting. "This is a surprise."

I'm sure that it was. I spoke to Ken often at school, but rarely went to his house. He made me a bit uncomfortable at times. As I said before, he was very outspoken, and I got the feeling he thought I should be more involved with gay rights and all that. I was always afraid he'd push me into something. I was openly gay, but I wasn't quite ready to change the world like Ken seemed determined to do.

Then there was the little matter of what had happened between us in the past. Not too long after I came out, Ken and I had sex. It was the one and only time I'd ever done anything like that. Ken didn't have a problem with having sex with someone just for fun, but I wanted sex to be something special, something I did only with someone I loved. I liked Ken, but I didn't love him. He just wasn't the type that I wanted as a boyfriend.

What we had done together was incredible, a little too good in fact. I found myself wanting more. What boy wouldn't? I limited my contact with Ken because I knew how easily he could seduce me. I couldn't live up to my ideas if I spent too much time with him. I knew I'd abandon them for mere sex. Ken seemed to sense what I was thinking and after that one time had never put the moves on me again. I was afraid that he would however if I spent too much time with him alone. I must admit, that there was a part of me that wanted to be seduced.

When I started talking about Marty and the distinct possibility that he hadn't killed himself, Ken was all ears. I had no need to fear seduction just then, Ken smelled a mystery that was right up his alley. I told him all that had been going through my mind, all that I'd pondered about for so very long. He agreed that the pieces didn't fit.

"It's all just speculation however. I don't have any real proof that what I believe is true. I've got to find out however. I've got to know." I told him.

As I talked to him, I'd been edging the conversation toward the reason I'd come. There was a way I might be able to get some proof, and Ken was the one person who might be able to help me.

"If I could get a look at Marty's autopsy records, I might be able to figure out something." I looked at Ken. His dad was the coroner. Ken looked rather thoughtful.

"You think you could get your dad to show them to me?" I asked.

"No way. He's totally anal about stuff like that. No one touches his precious records unless they're wearing a badge or have a court order. However," he said grinning "I think I could 'appropriate' them for you."

I smiled back at Ken. I knew I'd come to the right place.

Chapter 5

The Truth Revealed

The next day after school I went straight home and finished my homework so I'd have some time to puzzle over what had happened to Marty. It wasn't a pleasant topic, but it wasn't something I could let rest either. I pulled off my shirt and watched the news while I lifted weights once more. I had taken to watching the local news about every evening, just in case it said something I didn't know about Marty's death.

There was no mention of Marty, well, not in the part of the news I was able to see anyway. The picture got all fuzzy and finally went out. I'd been watching my little television too much. The batteries were dead. I tapped the TV, but it was no use. I took out the batteries and tossed them in the trash. I was not happy about losing my television, it was my only link to the outside world in that dreary old place.

I turned my attention to my weights and watched myself in the mirror as I did barbell curls. I wasn't exactly built, but I liked to watch myself work out. Guys working out with weights kind of excited me, even if it was me. I liked to watch my muscles in action. I only wished there was more to watch. I wasn't all that content with my body. Sometimes I felt like every guy I saw at school was better built than me.

I halted with the barbell pressed to my chest and stared into the mirror. I wasn't staring at my body however. I closed my eyes for a second and opened them again. I could have sworn I saw someone standing behind me for a moment, someone dressed in clothes that were way out of date. There was nothing there however, so I wrote it off to my overactive imagination. The old house made me think I saw lots of things.

My mom knocked on the door and poked her head in. I wished she'd stop doing that. She always knocked, but she always opened the door half a second later. I needed more privacy. I'd only been lifting weights, but I still didn't like her sticking her head in my room with so little warning. What if I'd been doing something I didn't want her to see? I was always afraid she'd walk in when I was relieving a little tension, if you know what I mean.

"Honey, your friend is here."

She opened the door further and Ken came in. Before I had a chance to forget, I asked my mom to pick up some batteries for me.

"Sure honey."

She left me alone with Ken. He was holding a big manila envelope. I didn't have to ask what was in it.

"So you decided to come and visit the haunted house huh?" I asked.

"Uh, yeah." said Ken. His eyes darted around fearfully. That didn't surprise me. Walking into Graymoor was like entering another world, a creepy, spooky world.

I was a little self conscious standing there half naked so I wiped the sweat off my chest with my shirt, then slipped it back on.

"Here," said Ken, "I found this laying around my dad's office." He had a bit of a smirk on his face. I could just imagine how he'd 'found' it.

I pulled a thick stack of papers out of the envelope and began looking through them. I was surprised at how thorough it was and how much of it was useless detail.

"Man, your dad records every little detail doesn't he?"

"Yeah, I told you he was anal. That's also why I have to get these back. If they are gone for more than a few hours he'll notice for sure."

As Ken and I looked through the report, I realized that not all the details were useless. Some of them were quite revealing and made it possible to draw some conclusions. I was no detective, but I understood a few things. I'd read about every Sherlock Holmes novel ever written. One of the first things I checked for was powder burns. Sure enough, the report detailed them. According to it there were powder burns on Marty's head consistent with what one would expect from a shot with a .45 at close range. That did seem to support the suicide theory. I still wasn't convinced about that, but I did have an open mind. If the report proved to me that Marty had killed himself, then I would accept it. I was looking to find answers, whether or not they were the answers I wanted.

"You might not want to look at those," said Ken as I moved to open the folder that contained the autopsy photos. "They are pretty gruesome, and since Marty was your friend...."

I swallowed hard and opened the folder. I wasn't looking forward to seeing what was inside, but I had to do it if I was going to get to the bottom of things. When I glanced at the first photo, it made me retch. I had to look away because it was making me sick to my stomach. I could watch any type of gore in a movie, but this was different, this was real. What's more, it was Marty. Seeing what had actually happened to Marty's skull was just about more than I could take. It was more than I could handle for a few moments. I had to walk away and look out the window. It didn't help much however, the image was burned into my mind. I had the feeling that I'd never be able to get it out. I took a deep breath and returned to the photos, my hands were shaking. Knowing that it was Marty in those photos was overwhelming. I had to do it however. I had to find out what had happened to Marty.

I couldn't really tell much from the photos, but they gave me an idea.

"Come on." I said.

I led Ken into dad's room and took out my father's revolver. It was a .45, just like the one Marty allegedly committed suicide with.

"You know it's not too smart to be messing with that," said Ken.

"Give me some credit will you?" I said. "I'm not going to play with it."

I was never supposed to touch dad's revolver and I never did, except that once. I made sure the safety was on because I knew it was loaded. I carefully measured it and wrote down its dimensions. I put it back in its place so that dad would never know I'd taken it out. If he found out, there'd be hell to pay. He sure had no reason to worry, I wasn't stupid enough to play with a gun. After seeing the autopsy photos, I sure wasn't going to take any chances.

Ken and I went back into my room and I dug into one of the boxes that I still hadn't unpacked. I dug out a couple of my old toy pistols. One of them looked just like dad's. More importantly, it had the same dimensions.

"What you are doing?" asked Ken.

"You'll see." I said.

The report and drawings showed the entry point at the back of the head. I took the pistol in my hand and tried to point it to the exact spot on my own head. I couldn't do it. I tried with one hand, then the other, even with both hands at once. I tried from every possible angle. I didn't give up. I kept trying over and over, using every method I could devise to line up the barrel with the entry point. I just couldn't do it. If I couldn't do it, Marty could not have either. We were almost exactly the same size. There was no way he could have pointed a pistol at his own head from that angle.

Ken quickly caught on to what I was doing and watched with great interest. He even tried it for himself, with no better luck. We put the toy pistol aside and sat down on the bed looking at each other. I didn't know whether I was more disturbed or relieved.

"Marty didn't kill himself did he?" I asked Ken. It wasn't really a question, as I already knew the answer.

"No," said Ken, "Marty was murdered."

The Truth Revealed

We just both sat there looking at each other as what we'd discovered sank in. I was glad that my friend had not killed himself, but knowing that someone had killed him was disturbing to say the least.

"We've got to tell someone about this." I said.

"Who are you going to tell Sean?" asked Ken. "You think the police are going to listen to you? You're just a kid. Besides, how are you going to explain how you got a hold of this huh?" he said, indicating the report. "If my dad ever found out I took something like this out of his office, he'd ground me for the rest of my life."

I was sure Ken was exaggerating about his potential punishment, but he'd taken quite a risk getting that report for me and I wasn't going to pay him back for it by narking on him. I was sure he was right about the authorities too. They'd just brush me off as a kid. As far as they were concerned, it was a suicide and that was that. If I wanted to find out who had killed Marty, I'd have to do it myself.

"Okay, so I handle things myself." I said. I was talking both to Ken and myself. As I said the words out loud my resolve grew. Yeah, I would take care of things myself. I'd figure out who had killed my best friend. I looked at Ken, I was certain that he could read the determination on my face. I didn't know how I was going to do it, but I was going to get to the bottom of it.

We looked through the rest of the report and I made some notes. When we were done, I handed the report back to Ken.

"Thanks," I said, "I won't forget this."

"No problem, but I think I'll get this back where it belongs before my dad finds out it's missing."

I showed Ken to the front door so he wouldn't get lost in Graymoor. Anyone who wasn't accustomed to its winding hallways could lose their way pretty easily. I didn't want Ken to be wandering Graymoor forever searching for the exit.

* * *

I knew the truth at last, or at least part of it, but there wasn't much I could do about it. To be honest, I felt pretty overwhelmed. I didn't really even know where to start. I was determined however, one could even say obsessed. Just knowing that whoever had killed my friend was still out there gnawed at me. Marty was such a kind boy, he didn't deserve to die. No one had the right to do that to him. I'd find out who had done it, no matter what I had to do, or how long it took. No one killed my best friend and got away with it.

The first thing I had to consider was motive. Who would want to kill Marty? I thought about that for a long time, but I couldn't think of a single person. The only motive I could think of was Marty's homosexuality. That was the only thing that could have made someone want to kill him.

Killing someone just because they were gay seemed a very weak motive to me, but I knew there were those who would find it quite a strong reason to take someone's life. I wasn't naïve. I knew the kind of unreasonable hatred that existed in the world. It made me shudder to think that it existed even in my little town.

I thought back to the morning of the day Marty was killed, when we walked into the school together. There had been a lot of stares, even some hateful glares, but no one stood out. There just wasn't anyone who I thought could be a killer. I thought too about the dance, where Marty had kissed me, but not one suspect came to mind. We'd been called "faggots". We'd been on the receiving end of some pretty nasty looks. None of that added up to murder however. There was a great difference between calling someone a faggot and killing him.

I thought and thought about it and still came up with not a single suspect. I kept thinking about it during the following days. The days passed, but I came no closer to an answer. Whoever had killed my friend was well hidden. Discovering his identity was going to be even harder than I thought.

Chapter 6

A Bizarre Idea

As soon as school let out for the day, I walked to the site of the murder before going home. An eerie feeling crept up my spine. There was nothing to see really, but I thought being there might make me better understand. The site was not too far into the woods, just a couple of dozen feet off the forest path. It was just out of site of the path, and the soccer fields. It was a good enough place for a murder. No one would have been able to see unless they were right there. The leaves provided an effective cover from anyone who would have been walking by.

I thought about the sound of the shot. Anyone very near would have heard it. It had happened well after school was out however. Soccer season was over, so no one would have been very close by. It wasn't likely that anyone was near enough to have realized someone had been shot. If I had been in the general area, I would probably have thought it was just a truck backfiring or something. Things like murder just didn't happen in Verona. The last thing anyone would have thought if they had heard the gun shot, was that it was a gun shot. No one ever got shot in Verona.

Whoever had killed Marty had picked the right time and place to do it. I wondered about that. What was Marty doing in the woods? Had he just been walking there? Had he been lured there, dragged there, forced there at gunpoint? There were too many questions and no answers. I wasn't getting anywhere.

*   *   *

That very night I saw something on television that caught my eye. I had a habit of watching TV while I lifted weights, pretty much every evening. I got a late start that evening however because I had a ton of homework. My trip into the woods cost me some time and pushed my whole schedule back about an hour. As a result, one of those "most wanted" shows was on when I flipped on the TV. I didn't usually like that sort of thing. In fact, I started to change the channel, but the narrator was talking about this psychic that helped solve a crime. It immediately caught my interest. He claimed to be in touch with the spirit world and to have access to information possessed by those who had died.

I was skeptical to say the least. I had never really believed in stuff like that. Some of the things the psychic came up with were pretty convincing however. He told the authorities where to find the murder weapon that had eluded them, and it was right where he said it would be. He also gave them a description of the murderer and his first name. That description matched a past boyfriend of the victim. When the police checked the gun for fingerprints, they found those of the guy the psychic had named and described. Not long after, the guy admitted to having killed his former girlfriend out of jealousy. It was a case that the authorities couldn't crack, but the psychic pretty much discovered all the details.

I turned off the television as a thought began to take shape in my mind. At first I dismissed it as just plain crazy, but then I thought that just maybe it was worth a try. After all, if it was just crazy, then I wouldn't be any worse off that I was already. If there was something to it, then I owed it to myself, and Marty, to try.

Mom walked past in the hall and I called out to her.

"Mom, hey thanks for getting me those batteries."

She looked at me in confusion.

"But I didn't honey. I'm sorry, but I didn't have time to pick them up yet. I'll get you some tomorrow."

"Oh," I said. "That's okay."

She departed and I stood there confused. I turned the television back on. Nothing happened, no picture, no sound. I kept hitting the button, but it didn't make any difference. I turned the television over and opened the battery compartment. I just looked at it stunned. It was empty.

I put the cover back in place, turned the television right side up, and turned it on. Nothing. I flipped it on and off several more times. Nothing happened. I just stood there looking at it like it was from another world.

*   *   *

Once again I had no idea where to start. Then again, maybe I did. There was one person who just might be able to help. If anyone knew something about what I had in mind, Marshall would.

I caught Marshall in between classes the next day and told him I wanted to talk to him after school. I told him it involved ghosts. I knew without a doubt he'd be waiting on me at my locker at the end of the day. I wasn't wrong. I tossed my books in my locker, slammed the door shut, and filled Marshall in on my investigation as we walked to Graymoor.

When we arrived, he stopped for a moment and just stared up at the great Victorian mansion. His eyes were wide with awe.

"You coming in?" I asked. I thought he would have been just itching to get inside, but he seemed a bit hesitant.

"Uh, yeah, sorry." he said. "I've always wanted to go in this place, but I could never work up the courage. I still can't believe you live here."

"Neither can I." I said sarcastically.

He followed me as I pushed back the heavy door and walked inside. He stopped again and stood there gawking at the front parlor.

"It's huge!" he said "And it looks like no one has been in this place for a hundred years."

"That's pretty much the way it was, until we moved in. Come on."

I led him upstairs and into my bedroom. He quickly walked over to the television and picked it up.

"Is this the one?" he said.

"Yeah."

He flipped the television on and off a few times. Nothing happened.

"You ever hear of a TV that works without power?" I asked him.

"Yes," he said, "as a matter of fact I have. Televisions, radios, all sorts of stuff. I've never seen it myself however." He looked at the television wistfully, as if wishing it would come on right then for him.

"Anything else happen out of the ordinary?" asked Marshall.

I told him about the footsteps I often heard at night and at other times when I was alone in the house. I told him about the lamps and candles that lit and went out by themselves, and about the way things disappeared only to reappear later. I also told him about the sounds that could have been distant, murmuring voices, and the figure I thought I'd seen walking down the hall, and the one I thought I'd seen behind me while I was lifting weights, and about the cat.

"It's all probably just the house settling or something, drafts, and reflections of light." I explained. I was fairly open minded, but it was hard for me to believe the house was really haunted.

"No," said Marshall, "it isn't that. There are ghosts here, I can feel them."

I peered at him closely. He had a weird look about him, almost as if he were in touch with a world that I could not see. I wondered if it was such a wise idea pursuing the course I'd chosen. Marshall was just a bit too bizarre for me. He looked me straight in the eye like he could read my thoughts.

"You think I'm crazy don't you?"

"Well, no, not really…"

"You can say it. I know everyone thinks I'm weird, but I know what I'm talking about. This house is haunted, without a doubt. Very haunted."

He looked at me closely again.

"Just what is it you have in mind Sean? You've told me all about Marty, but you still haven't told me what you want."

"I want to talk to him, Marty that is. Can you help me with that? I want to ask him who killed him." I felt more than a little crazy myself speaking those words. If there was anyone who wouldn't think I was crazy for suggesting such a thing, it would Marshall however.

"I'm sorry," he said, "I can't help you with that."

"Why not?" I asked, more than a little annoyed. I really expected him to jump at the chance to at least try.

"It's too soon. Marty has only been dead a few days. If he'd been killed a few months ago it would be different, but it's too soon." he said, as if that explained everything.

"What's that got to do with it?"

"He's in the transitional period, moving from the physical to the spiritual."

I looked at Marshall blankly. He looked back at me, and could see that I did not understand at all.

"It's kind of like when you have just been born," he explained. "You are alive, you can sense things, move around some, but not much more. It takes time to adjust, to be able to see and hear properly. It takes even longer to learn how to walk and speak. It's kind of like that when someone dies, not exactly, but that's as close as I can get to explaining it. I don't really understand it completely myself."

His words made sense, and yet it seemed pretty convenient. I almost felt like Marshall was trying to pull one over on me, but I knew that wasn't the case. My face fell in disappointment.

"I even thought I saw Marty the night after he was killed." I said. I told Marshall about the dream I had of Marty coming and sitting on the edge of my bed. I could tell he was very interested in what I was telling him.

"You sure it was a dream?" he asked.

"Well, yeah. Well, I guess so. I remember waking up after it happened. I think it was right after it happened. I'm not sure."

"What you've just described is something I've read about several times. Lots and lots of people have seen someone they were close to right after that person died. Sometimes it's at the very moment of death, but sometimes it's a few days later. I can't say for sure of course, but I have a feeling you really did see Marty."

"But you just said we couldn't try to reach him because he's in transition. How did he come to me if it's all like you said?"

"This is different. It's something the dead do before they leave, before they enter the transitional stage. Maybe Marty didn't even know he was dead when he came to see you. Sometimes the dead get a little lost, or confused."

"That's all the more reason for contacting him!" I said, almost shouting. "What if he is lost? What if he needs help?"

"Well, we still can't reach him, not yet."

"What if he appears to me again?"

"I hate to tell you this Sean, but it's not going to happen, not for a long time anyway."

"But what if?" I asked stubbornly. At just that moment I wasn't so sure that Marshall knew as much about all this as he let on. How did he know that Marty couldn't appear to me again? What made him so damned sure?"

"Okay," said Marshall, humoring me. "If he appears to you again, all you have to do is tell him he's dead and that he needs to go on. That's all it should take to help him if he's lost or confused." I could tell by the way that Marshall emphasized the "if" that he truly believed it wouldn't happen.

"And I could ask him who killed him." I said.

"Yes, you could—if he appeared to you again, but like I said, it isn't likely to happen. If he could contact you that easily, then we could contact him. I'm sorry all this isn't the way you'd like it to be, but I can't change the way things are."

I looked at Marshall. I'd grown a little cross with him, but I realized it was unfair to do so. He was trying to help me. I was angry because I was confused. It was just a bit too much to take in all at once.

Marshall didn't seem to notice my mood at all. He was far too busy thinking. He was clearly in his element.

"What we need," said Marshall, "is to contact someone who has been a ghost longer. If we can do that, then maybe he could help us reach Marty. Maybe he could communicate with him even if he is in a transitional state. Mind you, I'm not sure about it, but it might work."

Just then an icy breeze blew through the room, although it was a warm, still day outside. Marshall looked at me, then around the room.

"There are definitely ghosts here," he said. It had grown cold enough that I could see Marshall's breath.

"Maybe we could contact the ghosts in this house." I suggested.

"No!" said Marshall, looking at me as if I was out of my mind. "It's very, very dangerous to just contact spirits at random. You never know what you might get. You couldn't pay me to do it in this house, not with all those murders. You really want to take the chance of summoning up old man Graymoor?"

It was clear he was familiar with the history of the house. He was right. The last thing I wanted to do was unleash an ax murderer's ghost in the house.

"No." I said.

I was a bit confused about the whole thing.

"But you said you could tell there were ghosts here. If he's already here, what difference would it make?"

"Well, let's just put it like this. There are some boys at school that are real bullies. They are more than happy to kick someone's ass just for fun. They are there without you doing anything. Would you want to start something up with them and draw attention to yourself?"

"No." I said.

"It's just like that here. If one of these ghosts is old man Graymoor, it sure wouldn't be too bright to get his attention focused on you. Of course he may not be here at all. This old house probably has plenty of ghosts. It's not worth the risk however. If nothing bad had ever happened here we might want to risk it, but as it is I'd say it's a last resort. Even then, I don't know if I'd be willing to take the chance. I've read about some pretty nasty shit happening when something goes wrong. This is not something to play around with."

Marshall was really scaring me. I knew my face had gone pale. He looked at me and could clearly read the fear in my eyes.

"Don't get the wrong idea Sean. Most ghosts aren't evil, just like most people aren't. Very, very few are malevolent. In fact, most are rather friendly, even helpful. It's just that people think they are dangerous because of the disembodied voices, footsteps, and all that. It's easy to be afraid of what one doesn't understand."

"Yeah, I guess you're right." I said. As a gay boy, I understood his point well. A lot of people seemed to be afraid of homosexuals simply because they didn't understand. Their ignorance created fear.

"The ones that are malevolent however can be very hard to handle, very dangerous. It just isn't wise to mess with them."

Chapter 7

Ghosts 101

I showed Marshall around the house while he told me about ghosts, séances and various means of raising the dead. I must admit that it spooked me more than a little. It also confused me as well. There was a lot more to the whole thing than I'd ever guessed.

"I thought all ghosts were spirits trapped somewhere by something terrible that happened." I said, when Marshall told me there were lots of different kinds of ghosts.

"No. A lot of ghosts are just that, spirits trapped by some terrible deed they performed in life, or something terrible that was done to them, but there are a lot of other kinds. Some ghosts are cursed and can't leave until the curse is lifted. Some stick around because they want to, they just don't want to leave. Some stay around someone they love. Some have unfinished business that they believe only they can complete. Some ghosts are spirits that just don't realize they are dead. It's easier to get confused about that than you'd imagine. Then there are elementals, thought forms, and a few other types. The ghosts in this house could be any one of these, or any combination of them. That's why it would be so dangerous to just summon all the ghosts in the house, or summon one at random. There's no way to know what we'd come up with. We could summon something that is very nasty and very hard to control."

"How about a poltergeist?" I asked. "Like in the movies?"

"Well, that's possible, but I don't think so. I can feel a definite presence here, several of them actually. There are ghosts in this house. A poltergeist isn't really a ghost at all however. There could be poltergeist activity in addition to the ghosts, but I don't think so."

"Not a ghost? What do you mean?"

"Well, poltergeist means 'noisy ghost', but it's not an accurate term. It was once thought that a poltergeist was a ghost, but it's been found that the disturbances associated with a poltergeist don't come from an outside force like a spirit. All kinds of things can happen with a poltergeist; lights turning off and on…"

"NOT a problem here." I said interrupting. I wasn't happy at all about not having electricity. Marshall continued.

"…Knocking and tapping sounds, things moving by themselves, noises, doors slamming, and even fires breaking out."

"Sounds like a ghost thing to me." I said.

"Yeah, but it's not. It's caused by someone in the house, usually a teenage girl, but it can be an adolescent boy or even someone older. It's almost always someone having some kind of emotional or sexual turmoil."

"In that case, if it was me, this whole house would be flying apart. I've got sexual turmoil to burn!"

"No doubt." said Marshall smiling. "Or should I say, 'welcome to my world'. Anyway, without even knowing it, that person causes the sounds and movements by psychokinesis."

"Hold it." I said. "Amateur in the house. What does that mean?"

"Oh sorry, psychokinesis is the ability to move things with energy that is generated in the mind."

"Now that sounds like a load of crap."

"No, even scientists say it exists. Like I said however, I don't think there is a poltergeist involved here. Despite your uh, sexual frustration shall we say, I'm feeling the presence of more than one spirit here. I'm kind of psychic myself. I'm not too powerful, but I can pick up on a few things. One thing I know for sure is that there are definitely ghosts here."

I'd always thought that those who were into the paranormal were a little odd. Marshall didn't sound weird to me however. The things he was saying sounded rather scientific to me.

I took Marshall up into the attic. It was huge, like a vast storage room on the top of the house. The roof was only about five feet from the floor in the corners, but it was more than twenty-five feet above our heads in the center. There were boxes and trunks stuffed with things everywhere. There were stacks of old picture frames. The whole place was crammed with junk from the past. My parents hadn't even touched it yet.

Marshall paused.

"Something happened here," he said.

"A murder?"

"No. I don't think it was something bad, but I'm getting a really strong feeling about this attic. Something intense went on up here."

He didn't seem to be able to add anymore to what he'd said, so we continued on with our tour. I showed him through a lot of the rooms on the upper floors, then we returned to the ground floor. Before we looked at the ground floor, we went into the basement.

"This you're going to like," I said, "but personally it gives me the creeps."

I lit two oil lamps and handed one to Marshall. We slowly stepped down the stone steps.

"Man, it's as dark as a tomb in here," said Marshall.

"Exactly." I walked across the floor so that the light from my lamp fell upon a huge granite sarcophagus.

"Wow." said Marshall as he gazed upon it, fascinated. "This is fantastic!"

"You might not think so if it was in your basement." I said.

I'd only been down there once before and I didn't like it. It was cold and as dark as darkness. There wasn't a single window to the outside. No daylight had come there since before the house was built. It looked like something out of a vampire movie. It was the perfect place for a vampire. I half expected one to rise from a coffin and bite my neck.

"This is so awesome!" said Marshall. He held his lamp up to the walls, reading the names carved in stone. In addition to five large sarcophagi in the middle of the crypt there were row after row of burials within the walls. "There must be fifty people buried down here!"

"Yeah. Kind of a Graymoor family reunion." I said without humor.

I didn't look around much myself. The crypt terrified me. I didn't really want to be there at all. I pulled my arms up against my chest, trying to keep myself warm. The cold in the crypt didn't seen natural. It was the kind of cold that crept into your bones. I felt as if the crypt were trying to claim me and add me to its collection of bodies. I endured the crypt for a couple of minutes more, then led Marshall upstairs.

I took him into the kitchen and put a tea kettle on the stove. Despite the warmth of the day, I was still cold. I could tell that Marshall was chilled too. He gratefully accepted my offer of peppermint tea. I showed Marshall around the front parlor while we waited on the tea. The parlor was a dreary place, but it must have been beautiful once. It was filled with sofas, love seats, and chairs. There was a big marble top table in the center and smaller tables along the walls. In one corner there was a big old organ, with foot pedals. Marshall gave it a try. It still worked and the music sounded as creepy as the house looked.

"It looks like there was a picture here," said Marshall, looking above the mantle.

"Yeah, it was some kind of family portrait I think. I never really got a good look at it. Mom sent it out to have it restored. I guess it was the Graymoor's."

"Oh I'd like to see that!"

"I'm sure it will be back in a few weeks."

"Cool."

Marshall looked around the room at the ladders, tools, and paint cans.

"It looks like your parents have been doing a lot of work here," he said.

"Yeah, they plan on restoring the entire house. They'll never get it all done."

"You may be seeing more ghosts than ever in the future." said Marshall.

"Why?" I asked.

"Ghosts don't like changes. Most of the time they start appearing when changes are being made to a house. It upsets them."

"Oh great! Just what I need."

"Man I'd like to live here." said Marshall. I was beginning to think he was bizarre again. I couldn't imagine anyone, other than my parents, wanting to live in Graymoor.

"Wanna trade?" I said.

"In a flash." He laughed.

"You know," I said, "the ghosts here shouldn't get upset. My parents aren't really changing anything, they are restoring. They plan to make this place just like it was a hundred or so years ago. Mom is even trying to track down the same wallpaper that was originally used. She's really into this stuff."

"True, they might not get upset over that. They may not like it when your parents put in electricity however."

"Well I hope we found out about that as soon as possible. I'm so tired of living in the dark and you have no idea what it's like to live without a CD player!"

"I'd trade that for ghosts any day."

We returned to the kitchen and I poured us both a cup of peppermint tea. I started to warm up again as we sat at the table and talked.

"So tell me," I said, "if we come up with a spirit to contact. How does this whole séance thing work? And just what is a séance anyway?"

"A séance is simply an attempt to contact the dead. It's an attempt to focus the energies of those who are performing it in such a way to penetrate the barrier that exists between this world and the next. The idea is to form a sort of doorway or portal so that it's possible for the spirits to come through. If it works, it's possible to talk to the dead just as if they were a living person. There are people called trace mediums who can do the same thing without a séance, but I have no idea how we'd find someone like that."

"I knew it was a way to talk to the dead, but I didn't know how it worked or what it did."

"In a séance, a group of people sit in a circle and join hands, while one of them calls upon the spirits. It can be very draining for the one calling the spirits. It takes a lot of energy and concentration. It's something that looks pretty simple, but isn't really."

Mom came in carrying bags of groceries and we halted our ghostly conversation for the time being. We helped her unload the car. As soon as Marshall mentioned he liked the house, mom took up with him immediately. There was nothing she liked more than talking about that house.

Mom started rattling off details about Graymoor. She was so proud of that dilapidated old mansion that you'd have thought it was Windsor Castle or something. I rolled my eyes. I was sure she'd bore Marshall senseless in just a few minutes. He seemed almost as enthused as my mom however and he wasn't faking. Apparently everything about Graymoor interested him. He seemed to fit in with my mom better than I did. I began to wonder if we'd been switched at birth.

"There's so much we can do with this kitchen," said my mother. "Just look at those built in cabinets. They're a hundred and fifty years old if they're a day."

I shook my head. When mom got going on the house, there was no stopping her. She did come to an abrupt halt however as a kitchen chair slid about eight feet across the floor all by itself.

I stared at it wide eyed and I thought mom was going to faint, but Marshall was thrilled.

"Of course you'll want to fix that!" he said pointing to the chair. He laughed. I couldn't believe he was making jokes. "This place is so cool!"

He walked over to the chair and examined it closely. Mom excused herself to go lay down upstairs. I guess that was one way to get her to stop talking. If only I could get the furniture to move by itself on cue.

To be honest, I was kind of freaked out. Marshall had such happy reaction to the whole thing that I found it difficult to be afraid however. If it had happened when I was alone in the room, I think I would have shit my pants, but with Marshall there, it was totally different.

"This ever happen before?" asked Marshall as he continued his investigation.

"Not that any of my family have observed." I said. I had a feeling stuff like this happened regularly in Graymoor. There was just no one there to see it.

"Yeah," said Marshall, very excited, "this place is definitely haunted!"

Chapter 8

Kindred Spirits

I did a lot of thinking about what Marshall had said about the danger of contacting ghosts. I didn't want to just give up on my idea of contacting Marty however. I knew it was a long shot, but my investigation was going absolutely nowhere. Maybe trying to reach Marty was a crazy idea, but as there seemed no other course, I pushed ahead. The problem was, I didn't know who I could contact. Marty was really the only person close to me that I'd lost. And, like Marshall said, we couldn't just start contacting the dead at random.

Near the end of school the next day, I remembered something that just might help. Sometime in the past, I'd heard a story about a couple of boys who had killed themselves right here in Verona, years and years before. I didn't know them of course, as they had died before I was even born, but I had the feeling they would help me if I could reach them. I couldn't remember much about them, but I did remember one very important thing, both of them were gay and had killed themselves because of the way everyone in town had treated them. Wouldn't a couple of gay ghosts be willing to help out one of their own? Okay, so it was another long shot, but it seemed the only course open to me so I took it.

* * *

I walked to the town library, passing the big strip of pavement that all the kids in town used for roller-blading. There were a couple of really cute high school boys there, looking so good in their knee and elbow pads. I had to fight to keep my mind on my task. I had a tendency to be distracted by cute guys and I was troubled by it more and more often as time passed. Sometimes guys were all I could think about. I knew there were things in life more important than sex, or having a boyfriend, but most of the time I didn't know what those things were. I did know one thing more important however, and that was finding out who had killed Marty.

I entered the basement level of the library and dug out the rolls of microfilm that had copies of all the old newspapers. The trouble was that I wasn't quite sure where to look. I knew the deaths had taken place about twenty years before, but that was about it. I spent over an hour looking through rolls of microfilm, but couldn't find anything. I was thankful that the town paper was a weekly instead of a daily. I had a feeling I'd be down in the library basement for days the way it was. If it was a daily, I might have been down there forever. My eyes began to hurt as the print kept spinning past. I felt faintly nauseated as I looked for the needle in the haystack.

"Is there something I can help you with young man?" asked the lady who took care of all the genealogical and reference materials. I guess my frustration was easy enough to read on my face.

"Yes, um, I was looking for an article on the two boys that killed themselves. I think it was about twenty years ago."

A wave of sadness that was quite easy to read passed over her kind features.

"Here," she said, taking out the roll of microfilm for 1982. "Look near the end, in October, you'll find what you want there."

I watched her as she walked away. I had a feeling that she was well acquainted with what had happened.

I ran the roll up to October and pretty soon I'd found it. Yes, the names were even vaguely familiar, a couple of boys named Mark and Taylor had taken their own lives. Taylor had killed himself, and Mark had soon followed.

I read everything I could about their deaths, which unfortunately wasn't much. Taylor had killed himself by taking a bunch of pills. His body had been found on the soccer field by the high school, not too far from where Marty had been murdered. Mark had shot himself at the very same spot just a day later. I could only imagine the emotional pain they'd experienced. It must have been horrible if it drove them to suicide. My heart went out to them as I read about their deaths.

There wasn't much in the article that I could use however. I needed to know more if I was to find them. I looked over to the library lady working at her desk. I walked over and stood there until she looked up at me.

"I was wondering," I said, "Do you remember when the suicides happened? Can you tell me anything about it?"

She pushed her work away.

"I can't tell you a great deal, but I went to school with Mark and Taylor, they were nice boys."

"I'd like to know anything you can tell me, no matter how insignificant."

"Well," the library lady smiled "I had kind of a crush on Taylor. To be honest, a very serious crush. He was so beautiful he made my heart ache. He was very cute, and very sweet. Of course, nothing could have come of that, Taylor wasn't interested in girls."

"Yeah, they were both gay. I've heard that much."

"Yes," she said, "I was surprised to find that out, shocked really. When everyone first started talking about it, I didn't believe it, but it was true. Of course I didn't want to believe it. It was rather…disappointing.

"Anyway, a lot of boys were really cruel to them. They called them horrible names. Some boys even beat Mark up really bad. I felt so sorry for both of them. And then Taylor killed himself, I'm not sure exactly why, although I think everyone being so cruel drove him to it. Some of the boys from school found him dead out on the soccer field. Mark killed himself the very next day, right at the same spot, because he loved Taylor. I don't think he could live without him. It was all very sad."

"Yeah, I read about some of that in the paper. I figured Mark killed himself because of Taylor. Do you know where they lived?"

"Yes, Mark lived on Akron Street, in that big two story house with blue shutters. You know the one?"

"Yeah." I said.

"Taylor lived over on Marmont Street, in the old white house with the massive front porch, the house with the wishing well in the yard."

"Hey, I've been there. My friend Ken lives in that house."

The librarian smiled.

"That's about all I know. I didn't really know either of them very well."

"Thanks," I said, "that's more than I knew."

"You know,' she said, "there is someone who could help you out. He was pretty close to both of those boys."

"That's exactly what I need." I said.

"His name is Ethan. He lives not far out of town on a big farm."

"Just to the west?"

"Yes, you know him?"

"Yeah," I said, "I work for him and Nathan in the summers and sometimes on the weekends. So he knew them huh?"

"They were friends. Talk to Ethan, he can probably tell you whatever you want to know. He can certainly tell you a lot more than I can."

"Thank you so much!" I said and quickly departed.

Chapter 9

Calling on the Dead

I went right to a pay phone and called out to the farm. There was no answer. I was disappointed. I seemed to be so close to finding out something really useful. I didn't want to wait even a day. It wasn't much use going out to the farm however if Ethan wasn't there, or was busy in the fields. I almost went anyway, just in case, but I called Marshall instead and asked him to meet me.

By the time I got home, Marshall was there waiting on me. He had a stack of books under his arm, all about ghosts, hauntings, and séances. I filled him in on what I'd learned about the two boys. I told him about my plan to contact them. Marshall was all for it. His eyes lit up with enthusiasm.

"Let's try it!"

"Now?" I asked. I wanted to move quickly myself, but I hadn't thought about doing anything that very evening.

"Sure, why not?" asked Marshall. I couldn't see any reason why not myself.

"Okay, let's do it." I said. I paused for several seconds. "How do we go about this?" Marshall had explained a lot of it to me, but I was still pretty lost. After all, it wasn't like making a telephone call.

"First we need to decide where to try and contact them. Location is very important. We've got to figure out where they are now."

"That doesn't sound so easy."

"Well, most ghosts stick around the place where they died, or where they lived, or around someone that is special to them. You said they died at the soccer field right?"

"Yeah."

"Then that's the best place to try. If they are still around, that's where they'll be most likely. There's a problem though."

"What?"

"There's only two of us, not enough energy. It would work a lot better if there were three of us, or even more."

"I might be able to come up with someone."

"Good. I'm going to run home and get some things we'll need. You meet me at the soccer fields in say, two hours."

"I'll be there." I said. Marshall ran off like the wind. I had the feeling he was having the time of his life.

I walked to Kyle's house and invited him along. Kyle and I weren't quite what I'd call friends, but we talked to each other quite frequently at school. To be honest, I had developed quite a crush on him, so I'd made an attempt to get to know him a little better. We'd even hung out a couple of times and both of us had a lot of fun when we did. That was very encouraging. Kyle seemed to be developing an interest in me too and that was even more encouraging. Just looking at Kyle made my heart beat a little faster. I was starting to have warm thoughts about kissing him and even wilder thoughts than that. Time would tell.

I told Kyle about what Marshall and I were going to do, although not the reason we were doing it.

"This I gotta see." was his answer.

I called up Zoë from Kyle's house. She wasn't so interested and didn't really want to hang around Marshall. After a lot of pleading, she agreed to meet us at the soccer fields however. I could usually get Zoë to do what I wanted. I did a lot of stuff with her that didn't really interest me too much, so it was kind of a trade off. I think she was a little intrigued by the whole thing too. After all, how many invitations did one get to a séance?

I told Kyle I'd meet him at the soccer field, then walked the few blocks to Ken's house. I was in luck, he was home. I could have easily phoned him from Kyle's house, but I wanted to let him know exactly what was going on and I didn't want to talk about it in front of Kyle. I was afraid that Kyle would think I was a total freak if he knew why we were having that séance. By keeping him in the dark, he'd just think it was Marshall behind it all. Marshall had a reputation as being an oddball and having a séance didn't seem out of character for him at all. I didn't want Kyle to think I was strange. His opinion of me was important.

I looked at Ken's house with new eyes as he led me to his room. It was the very house that Taylor had lived in. I wondered if maybe Ken's room had not been Taylor's at one time. I didn't really know much about Taylor, but I felt like I was developing some kind of kinship with him. It felt odd to be in his old house.

Ken gave me a rather strange look when I told him about the séance and what I had planned. That didn't surprise me. I rather expected it. I would have been surprised if he didn't think the whole thing was a little bizarre. If our situations had been reversed, I would probably have thought he was a loon.

"I'm glad you don't think I'm a total freak." I said.

"No. I'm kind of skeptical about the whole idea of a séance, but I'm rather intrigued by it too. I've always liked reading those ghost stories that are supposed to be true, although I've never been sure if I believe them or not. I don't think you're a freak at all. Now Marshall is a different story." Ken laughed. I couldn't help but laugh myself, although I felt a little guilty doing so.

"He's really pretty cool when you get to know him." I said.

"He seems nice enough," said Ken. "I guess we need interesting characters like him around to keep things from getting boring."

Ken's eyes met mine and we stood there gazing at each other for a few moments. There was a connection there, a memory of the past, a shared thought.

"I've been thinking about you," said Ken. "I was thinking of last summer."

My face grew a little flushed and I suddenly felt warm and a little aroused. It had only happened once, but Ken and I had fooled around a little not too long after I came out. There wasn't really all that much to it, but we'd had our hands in each other's pants. It was the first time, and so far the only time, that someone else had touched me there. We'd never repeated what we'd done and had never even spoken of it. At the time I was struggling to accept myself and it was a little hard to deal with what had happened. That had changed, but for some reason, Ken and I had never done anything else after that one time. It was clear that he was thinking about that now. So was I.

"Maybe sometime you could come over when you aren't busy," he said. I knew his words meant far more than they seemed to mean. I was getting excited. Ken was a rather attractive boy and my desire for more sexual experience was growing daily in power.

"I'd like that very much." I said. Ken knew that I meant a lot more than I was saying too. We both smiled.

"We'd better get going." he said.

"Huh?"

"The séance, remember? We'd better get going or we'll be late."

"Oh, yeah." I said, feeling a little foolish. Ken had temporarily pushed all other thoughts out of my mind.

It was growing dark by the time Ken and I arrived at the soccer field. Marshall and Kyle were there already. Kyle was wearing a white tank-top that made him look very sexy. Kyle had a nice build. His broad shoulders and the bulges of his arms and chest made me breath a little harder. I looked at Ken. He was pretty sexy too. Sometimes it seemed like I had a thing for every boy around me. Sometimes I was a real horn dog. Once again, I had to force my thoughts to the task at hand.

Marshall set up a ring of white candles near one of the soccer goals. He'd brought a whole backpack full of stuff. I was willing to bet he was the only boy in town that had a séance kit.

"Over here." he called, motioning us toward the soccer goal. "This is where the energy is strongest. I can feel something here."

Kyle looked skeptical.

"Energy, freak boy?" said Kyle "Maybe you've just got a battery stuck up your…"

I smacked Kyle on the back of the head, but Marshall acted like he didn't even hear the last part. Maybe he didn't. He was pretty obsessed with what he was doing. Ken seemed mildly amused by Kyle. I could tell from the look in his eyes that he was interested in him as well. That didn't surprise me one bit. Kyle was pretty hot and Ken had no reservations about making his interest in another boy obvious. It touched off a spark of jealousy in my heart. I wanted Ken to stay away from Kyle. I wanted Kyle for myself. Marshall's voice snapped me out of my thoughts.

"There's a certain energy where something violent has happened in the past. It's as if space itself has a memory of past events. Some people can feel it."

"Some people can suck my…"

I punched Kyle in the shoulder.

"Would you stop it?" I said.

"I'm just kidding around. I'm a smart ass, I can't help it."

Kyle smiled at me evilly. He was such a punk. For some reason I found that very attractive. Ken looked at me. He hadn't missed what had passed between me and Kyle. It made me rather self-conscious.

Zoë showed up just in time to end the awkward situation. I needed to be rescued. Kyle was getting to me. With very little effort, he could have wrapped me around his little finger. I wondered if he knew that. I suspected that Ken knew it, just from what he'd observed. I wondered what he thought about that.

"Five of us, that should work!" said Marshall. He was clearly in his element.

"I don't know about this," said Zoë. "It looks satanic."

Marshall actually looked hurt.

"It is not!" he said. "This has nothing to do with that!"

"Calm down Marshall." I said.

He did, but eyed Zoë suspiciously.

"Okay, I'll light the candles, then everyone sit down and hold hands."

I made sure I was sitting next to Kyle. Getting to hold his hand was more than I'd ever got to do with him. As I took his hand in mine, it sent a shiver through my body. I looked at him. He was so cute and so built!

Ken sat on my other side and his touch reminded me of what had happened between us. I felt a surge of desire as I sat between those two boys. With a great effort, I forced my mind back to the task at hand. Everyone in the circle joined hands.

"Now," said Marshall, "I'm going to call upon the spirits. A lot of it is just mental force, so don't be surprised if I don't say anything for a while, then I'll say some things out loud. None of you need to say anything, just focus on calling to the spirits in your mind. Your job is to let them know we want them here."

Marshall gave me a significant look. I knew he was silently telling me to broadcast in my mind why I wanted them there.

"Okay, let's begin."

I closed my eyes and oddly enough, I felt as if some kind of energy were passing through me. It was as if it were traveling in a circle through our joined hands. All I could hear was a perfect stillness, there wasn't even any wind.

I opened my eyes and saw Marshall concentrating. His brow was wrinkled and his lips slowly moved. He looked quite eerie in the candle light. All was dark outside our little circle and I must admit I was afraid. Of course fear seemed a reasonable emotion when one was trying to raise the dead.

The stillness continued for a long time, broken only by the soft breathing of those of us around the circle. I drifted a bit into unconsciousness and jerked at the sound of Marshall's voice. I felt a little foolish, but no one seemed to notice.

"Mark, Taylor…" Marshall called quietly. "Are you here?"

There was no sound, not even a rustle of wind.

"Please come to us. Show yourselves, speak to us."

Nothing happened.

Marshall repeated their names over and over and kept calling to them, but with no result. After about fifteen minutes he stopped.

"You're such a fake!" said Kyle. "Ooohhh ghosts!"

"Shut up Kyle!" said Marshall.

"Oh, what are you going to do, haunt me?"

"Don't be a jerk Kyle." said Zoë.

"Yeah," said Ken "keep your opinion to yourself for once." The look on Ken's face didn't match his words. I knew what he was really on his mind. He was thinking about how he could get into Kyle's pants.

"Ah come on, I'm just kidding around." said Kyle.

"They just aren't here," said Marshall, looking at me.

"Are you sure? Maybe they just don't want to come." I suggested.

"Well, that's possible," he said, "but I don't feel any presence. I just don't think they are here."

"But if they're ghosts, why does it matter where they are? Can't they just come when you call?" asked Kyle. This time his question was sincere.

"No,' said Marshall. "It doesn't work like that. Look. Trying to raise a spirit is kind of like making a phone call."

"Oh geesh!" said Kyle.

Marshall ignored him and went on.

"If I called you and you were home, you'd probably answer. But if you weren't there, or were outside where you couldn't hear the phone, you couldn't answer. If your phone was ringing right now, you wouldn't know it because you are here. If the spirits we are trying to contact aren't here, they won't even know we are calling them."

"So how close do they have to be?" I asked. "Maybe we should try another part of the soccer field."

"No, if they were anywhere right around here they would come."

I was disappointed to say the least. Although perhaps I should have expected it. Making contact with ghosts wasn't exactly something that happened every day. I thanked Marshall for trying and walked Zoë home as the others went their separate ways.

Chapter 10

Uncovering the Past

The attempt to reach Taylor and Mark had failed, but I wasn't ready to give up just yet. Marshall had said they "just weren't there", which meant they were someplace else. If I could figure out just where that someplace might be then maybe we could contact them after all. I was wondering if maybe we shouldn't try a séance at Ken's house. Taylor had lived there after all and maybe his ghost still walked the halls. I hadn't told Ken yet that Taylor had lived in his house, but maybe I'd do that soon. A séance there would at least be worth a try.

I lay in bed that night wondering about those boys. I felt a sort of kinship with them. I had an idea of how horrible things must have been for them. I'd been called "faggot" and "fairy" plenty of times. I'd been on the receiving end of hateful stares. I had male cousins that wouldn't even talk to me and aunts and uncles that acted like I was some kind of freak. I'd been hurt by friends who used the word "gay" like it was a put down. I knew however that things were much better for gays in my time than they had been twenty years before. Things were far from perfect, but the world had come a long way.

As I lay thinking such thoughts, I heard the voices in the hallway again. I heard them often and felt like I could almost, but not quite, make out what they were saying. I was becoming more and more convinced that they were voices and not just some noise created by the house or the wind. I'd learned a lot about ghosts and hauntings from Marshall and I was beginning to be much less of a skeptic.

I arose from my bed and crept toward the door in my boxers. I opened it quietly and just caught a glimpse of what could best be described as a grayish fog entering one of the bedrooms down the hall. I followed it, my heart pounding in my chest.

I peered into the room and saw two figures standing there. The hair on the back of my neck rose and I felt cold, but oddly, not afraid. The figures faced each other, as if talking, but I couldn't hear anything just then. Both were quite distinct and I could easily make out their features. Both appeared to be very young men, or perhaps boys. Both were quite attractive and one of them had very long hair. At first I thought that the one with long hair might be a girl, but as I gazed at him, his face made it quite clear he was male. He was beautiful however, so beautiful that I felt like I was in the presence of an angel and not a ghost. The other figure had much shorter hair and was very handsome.

I wondered if maybe these were the Graymoor boys, but I didn't know enough about them to tell. All I really knew was that there were two Graymoor boys, about my age. The ghosts before me seemed like the best candidates. The clothing didn't look quite right however. Their clothing was the least distinct part of them, but it didn't look like anything from the nineteenth century. Of course, I was far from an expert on that, so who knew?

I was fascinated by the apparitions. I'd only seen such things in movies, or read about them in books. Being in the presence of real ghosts was rather overwhelming. I felt like I'd made contact with a whole other world. I realized as I stood there that I was shaking. That didn't surprise me one bit.

"Hello." I said quietly, but it seemed that they could not hear me. It was as if I was not even there.

I gazed at them for a few moments more until they just faded away before my eyes. I felt that they were still in the room, but I could neither see nor hear them. I walked back to my room, far more at ease than I would ever have guessed after seeing two real ghosts. There was no doubt about it, those apparitions were spirits of the dead. They weren't reflections or tricks of the light. They were real. Any doubts I had about the existence of ghosts were erased. I was more determined than ever to seek contact with Taylor and Mark.

*   *   *

The next afternoon, right after school, I rode my mountain bike out to the farm owned by Ethan and Nathan. I hadn't been out there for a few weeks, but I'd spent a couple of summers working there and several weekends, so I knew the place well. Ethan and Nathan were really cool guys, probably in their late thirties. One of the things I liked best about them was that they were gay. Ethan and Nathan were boyfriends and had been since they were my age.

I'd worked for them for almost a year before I came out. They were the very first ones that I told. I thought it would be safe telling them, they were gay after all. Everyone knew they were gay, they made no secret about it. I thought it was wonderful the way they acted like any other couple. The only difference was that they were both guys. Well, there was another difference; they seemed to care about each other a lot more than most couples did. I saw the way they looked at each other, with love in their eyes. I hoped I could find that someday.

Talking to them had helped me a lot. It was wonderful to have someone older and wiser who understood what being gay was all about. Ken had helped me out a lot too, but Ethan and Nathan were far more experienced. They'd been out for years and told me a lot of stuff that really helped. I'm not sure I could have made it without their help.

I left my bike out front and knocked on the door. Nathan answered and invited me in.

"I haven't seen you for quite a while." said Nathan, brushing his blonde hair out of his eyes. I'd forgotten what a good looking guy he was.

"No, been busy." I said. "I came to see if you guys would tell me about those boys who killed themselves years ago. I was told you guys knew them."

A look of sadness crossed Nathan's face, but it was gone as quickly as it had come.

"Yes, we knew them. Ethan knew them a lot better than I did however. He can tell you more than I can. He's out finishing up some repairs on a fence. If you can stay and have supper with us, I'm sure he'll be able to tell you all about them."

"I'd like that." I said. "Thanks."

I sat at the kitchen table while Nathan fried chicken and mashed some cooked potatoes.

"You heard from Dave recently?" I asked. Dave was Nathan's younger brother. I'd only met him a couple of times, but he was really nice.

"I sure have." said Nathan. "I'm an uncle again." Nathan wiped off his hands and pulled a photo off the wall. He handed it to me.

"Twins?" I said.

"Yeah, and their names are Ethan and Nathan."

I could tell Nathan was excited about having his nephews named for him and Ethan.

"Dave already has one boy right? Jeremy?"

"Yes, he's almost six now."

"That's a lot of kids. I bet your brother wasn't expecting twins."

"He sure wasn't."

Nathan went back to work on supper.

"So, you found a boyfriend yet?" asked Nathan with a smile.

"No." I said, turning a little red. My desire for a boyfriend was one of the things I'd talked to Nathan about before.

"Well, no need to be in a hurry. It will happen."

"I hope so!" I said. "I feel like I've waited forever already."

"Yeah," said Nathan, "I suspect you do. I felt the same way."

"Yeah, but you ended up with Ethan!"

"True enough, but I didn't think it was going to work out that way, not at all in fact. When you're my age you'll look back and see things a little differently. I understand however. I remember what it felt like when I was your age. I know telling you this won't really help right now, but you'll find someone, or he'll find you."

"You're right," I said laughing, "it doesn't help!"

Nathan smiled at me.

"Sometimes I think I just can't wait another second." I said. "Sometimes I think I'll die without someone to love. And, to be honest, most of the time I'm just so horny that I can't take it anymore. I want to get going with my life. There are things I can't wait to experience, things that I think about all the time."

"Yeah, I know about those things," said Nathan smiling. "When I was sixteen, I couldn't wait either. You might say I was obsessed. I had sex on my mind twenty-four hours a day."

"Exactly!"

"You'll get your chance Sean. Just wait."

"Ahhhhhhhhhh!" I yelled in frustration. "You keep saying that!"

Nathan laughed again.

My face darkened as I thought more about my lack of a boyfriend and my extremely limited sexual activity. So far all I'd done was kiss Marty and experience a little hand action with Ken. That didn't really amount to all the much.

"What's wrong?" asked Nathan. It was always hard to get anything past him.

"I just feel like I'm not attractive enough. I'm not very well built and I'm pudgy. What boy is going to be interested in me?"

Nathan wiped off his hands and sat down at the table with me.

"Listen Sean, there is nothing wrong with the way you look. You are a very attractive boy. Not every guy is out there looking for a jock. Take my word for it, there will be boys who are interested in you."

"Well, there is one." I said, talking about Kyle. "At least I think, I'm not sure. I'm probably just seeing what I want though. He's so cute. Why would he be interested in me? I'm fat."

As I sat there I sank lower and lower. Every time I thought about my body it happened. I just knew no one would ever love me.

"Listen to me Sean. Every boy your age has doubts about himself. At some point all of us think we aren't handsome, or built, or funny, or smart enough. Everyone Sean."

"I've seen some boys at school that sure don't look like they have doubts. They're cute and built and popular. They have it easy."

"I know it may look like it Sean, but that's not the way it is. Those boys probably have doubts too. They certainly have problems. It's very easy to think someone else has a perfect life because there is no way you can see it all. Looking at some hot boy like that is kind of like looking in the window of a house. The room you see may look all cozy and perfect, but you can't see the other rooms. You have no idea what kind of mess they are in. Those boys you think have it so well may have some serious problems, or serious doubts about themselves. No one has a perfect life."

I'd never thought of it that way. Nathan was right. I still wanted to drop a few pounds and get buff, but he sure made me feel better about myself.

Ethan came in just a few minutes later and we all sat down and ate while Ethan told me about Taylor and Mark.

"It was all very tragic. Mark and Taylor were secretly dating each other for a few weeks before anyone even suspected it. Even their best friends didn't have a clue. Mark's father found them out however. He walked in on them while they were making love. He threw a royal shit fit, went right through the roof. He forbid Mark to ever see Taylor again. He even called the school and told Mark's soccer coach. The coach exposed the boys in front of the whole team and basically all hell broke loose. They lost most of their friends and were marked as the school fags.

"They had to deal with all the usual stuff; name calling, threats, classmates giving them the cold shoulder, and finally physical abuse. Some guys worked Mark over so bad they put him in the hospital. Mark and Taylor kept meeting secretly and even openly spent time together at school, but it was extremely hard on them. I don't know how they even had the strength to come to school each day. Those boys had a very rough time of it, and that's putting it lightly. It all came to a head when Taylor's father threw him out of the house. He totally freaked, went off the deep end, and overdosed on drugs. The next night, Mark went to the soccer goal where Taylor had killed himself and blew his brains out."

There were tears in Ethan's eyes as he told me the story. After all those years it still hurt him to think about it. Nathan's eyes look more than a little moist too. Some pain never ends.

"Soccer goal? The one at the far end of the most distant field?"

"Yeah, that's the one," said Ethan. I could tell he wondered how I knew that. I didn't really know it, but that is where Marshall said he felt the most "energy". I was gaining more respect for Marshall with each passing day.

"Here," said Ethan, getting up. He pulled a big envelope out of a drawer and handed it to me. "If you'll promise to bring it back, you can borrow this. It's something Mark wrote right before he killed himself. It's sort of a suicide note. It explains a lot."

I looked into the envelope and there were pages and pages of typed text. Suicide note! It was more like a book!

"It's pretty much the whole story of what happened between Mark and Taylor, everything right up to just before Mark died. I was meaning to let you see it anyway, but I was waiting for the right time. I'll warn you, there is some very sad and very harsh stuff in there. Some of it is pretty hard to read. Some of it still makes me cry after all these years, so prepare yourself."

"I will, and thanks." I said, "I'll take good care of it." I'd come seeking information, but I never guessed I'd find what amounted to an autobiography. With all that information, surely I'd be able to figure out where Mark and Taylor could be found now.

I wanted to rush right home and start reading, but I didn't want to be rude. Besides, I loved talking to Ethan and Nathan, those guys had really helped me a lot. I don't know what I would have done when I first came out without them helping me through it. Just having someone who understood meant everything.

At first, my parents didn't want me working for Ethan and Nathan. They almost didn't let me answer the classified ad I found in the "help wanted" section. My parents seemed to think "the gay guys" were going to take advantage of me or something. At that time, my parents didn't even know I was gay, but they were still worried. They finally relented however.

My parents got all bent out of shape about me working for Ethan and Nathan once again when I told them I was gay. I guess they thought we'd be having a big three-way or something, which would have been downright hilarious if my parents hadn't been genuinely worried.

Ethan invited them out for a barbecue and spoke rather frankly about his relationship with Nathan. He was also very honest with my parents about how he and Nathan wanted to help me. Both of them had always been nice to me, but they looked out for me even more when they found out I was gay. They knew better than anyone that gay boys needed a lot of help.

Ethan set my parents fears at ease. He laid all the cards on the table. He told them they were free to come out anytime, unannounced. He told them he understood their fears, but they had nothing to worry about. I really appreciated that and I was very proud of my parents for agreeing to come, and for being so reasonable. By the time we left that day, my parents were more than happy to have me work for Ethan and Nathan, or just go see them any time I wanted. I think my parents were happy that I had someone to talk to about things that I just couldn't discuss with them. I think seeing Ethan and Nathan and the way they lived together set my parent's mind at ease about a lot of things. They learned pretty fast that those two guys weren't some kind of predators waiting to take advantage of me, but rather a couple not unlike themselves. They were kind of like a second set of parents.

The three of us sat around the kitchen table and talked of the coming summer and all the work to be done. Ethan told me I had a job waiting if I wanted it and I quickly accepted. Then we talked about things at school and eventually about Marty. I didn't mention how I thought he'd been murdered, but it was good to share how I felt with them. I could tell that Ethan and Nathan really felt for me, and for him. They understood.

I left pretty soon after that, thanking Ethan and Nathan for all they'd done for me. I raced home on my bike, rushed upstairs, and began reading. I'd been devouring the pages for over an hour when I came to something that took me completely by surprise. Taylor and Mark had been in my house. They had come to Graymoor to talk and be alone shortly after being exposed. They had come often after that, to talk, to be together, and to make love. They'd even mentioned how wonderful it would be if they could fix the place up and live there together. They'd never had the chance however, a few weeks later they were both dead.

As if on cue an old photo fell from its hiding place among the pages. It drifted to the floor and I kneeled down to pick it up. The back read "Taylor and Mark 1982". As I turned it over and looked at the image, my breath caught in my throat and my heart raced. It was a photo of two boys with their arms around each other's shoulders smiling, and they looked exactly like the ghosts I'd seen just down the hall the very night before!

As I had been reading the journal, I'd noted that the descriptions of Taylor and Mark closely matched the ghosts I'd seen. A suspicion had been growing in my mind. When Graymoor was mentioned, I became pretty sure just who it was I'd followed down the hall the previous night. The photo clinched it however. There was no doubt. Taylor and Mark were haunting Graymoor Mansion. I'd hoped to find where the spirits of the boys roamed, but never once did I guess it would be my own house!

I gazed at the photo in the golden light of the oil lamp. Both of the young men were handsome. Mark was very athletic looking and had short, dark hair. Taylor was so good looking he was beautiful, almost too pretty to be a boy. No wonder they were smiling so in the photo. I'd have been smiling too if I had a boyfriend that looked like either one of them.

I had to remind myself that there were far more important things than looks. I certainly hoped so as I was never quite happy with my own. I didn't think I was all that bad looking, but I definitely needed to put on some more muscle and drop a few pounds. I didn't linger long on thoughts of myself, especially after my talk with Nathan. He'd put me a little more at ease with myself. My mind quickly focused again on Taylor and Mark. Finding out they were right there in Graymoor changed everything.

I went back to reading again and had been doing so for about twenty minutes when I heard the murmuring voices as I had the night before. I got up quickly and went out into the hall. I turned my head one way, then the other, checking both ends of the hall, but there was nothing to see, nothing to hear. I found myself disappointed. I halfway expected to see the ghosts of the boys again, as if they had come to visit me.

I closed my door once more. I didn't feel quite as spooked by the house any more. I guess knowing the identity of the ghosts set me at ease a bit. Of course, I wasn't exactly sure that the ghosts were Taylor and Mark. I supposed a ghost could take any form it wanted. Even if they were, they might not be friendly. I had a feeling they would be, but who knew? They weren't necessarily the only ghosts roaming around either. Marshall seemed to think Graymoor was crawling with them and I had come to respect his opinion when it came to the supernatural. According to Marshall I was living in spook central. That didn't exactly set my mind at ease. Still, I felt like I had a couple of friends among the dead.

Chapter 11

The Second Loss

The next day I went to school all excited over my discovery. Less than forty-eight hours after I'd remembered the long ago suicide deaths of Taylor and Mark, I knew pretty much all there was to know about them. I sought out Marshall and was all set to tell him about it, but he had his own news.

"Did you hear about Ken?"

"No." I answered, "What did he do this time?" Ken was always making a scene. He was our school's gay rights activist.

"It's not what he did," said Marshall. "It's what someone did to him. He's dead."

"What?" I asked incredulously.

"Someone beat him up real, real bad, either killing him, or leaving him for dead. Either way, he's dead now. Some guys found his body out near Koontz Lake. I guess whoever did it really worked him over. I don't think you want to hear the details. No one could even tell who it was at first, they had to identify him through his dental records."

I felt sick to my stomach. No one deserved to die like that and certainly not Ken. I was so upset I had to lean up against the lockers. Marshall put his hand on my shoulder to steady me. My eyes filled with tears. Ken and I had been hanging out a lot in the past few days and we'd become closer friends than ever. First Marty, now Ken, I'd lost two friends in only a few days. It seemed that being my friend was fatal.

I immediately wondered if there was any connection between Marty's death and Ken's. They had been killed in very different ways, but one clear fact stood out in my mind, both of them were gay. As if to increase my suspicions, Marshall mentioned one thing more.

"They found a note card pinned to his shirt. It said 'God Hates Queers'".

That made it pretty obvious why he was killed. There was the possible alternative that someone had killed him for another reason, and just pinned the note on him to throw everyone off, but I didn't think it likely. I thought it was an intentional message that was quite clear in its meaning. I must admit, I was afraid. Being gay in Verona, Indiana had suddenly become a lot more dangerous.

Everyone was talking about Ken of course and would be for who knew how long. Our little town didn't have much to offer in the way of excitement and a murder really stirred things up. Little by little I got all the details, some of which I would rather not have heard. Ken had died a nasty death and most likely a slow and painful one too. Hearing about something like that always got to me, but this time it was far worse. I knew Ken. He hadn't been my best friend like Marty, but he was a friend and it hurt a lot to lose him. He'd done a lot to help me, and other gay boys too. It was a loss that would be felt by a lot of people. I couldn't believe he was dead.

Late in the day I did manage to talk to Marshall about what I had discovered. He was as excited as I was over the whole thing. Perhaps even more so if that were possible.

"And you really saw them, right there in your own house?"

"Yes." I told him for the third time.

"That is so incredible. I've always wanted to see a distinct, full torso apparition like that."

"You've never seen a ghost? I thought if anyone would have, it would be you."

"Well," he said, "not one like you did. Once I saw what I thought was a ghost. It was a misty, kind of foggy shape in the graveyard one night. I couldn't be sure, but it was moving around and not just floating around with the wind."

I considered asking Marshall what he was doing in the graveyard, but I thought better of it. I wasn't sure I wanted to know. Marshall could get pretty bizarre.

We made arrangements for a séance at Graymoor that very night. I considered holding off on it because of Ken's death, but I had a feeling it was more important than ever that I get to the bottom of things. Someone had killed two boys in our little town already and there could be more to come. I certainly hoped not, but my investigation had taken on a new urgency.

I tracked down Zoë and she agreed to be a part of it as well. I don't think she expected us to be successful, but was interested nonetheless. I also sought out Kyle and invited him.

"So you want to spend more time with that freak Marshall?" Kyle asked me.

"He's not a freak, just a bit odd. Anyway, he's the one that knows about all this stuff. We need him. Besides, he's a pretty cool guy when you get to know him."

"If you say so," said Kyle. "Count me in. It'll be fun to watch freak-boy fall on his ass again if nothing else."

"You're such a dick!" I said to him laughing.

"And you love it." He said smiling and flashing his eyes at me. I actually blushed a little. I did love it when he acted cocky. Something about his punk attitude excited me, in more ways than one. I had a feeling that Kyle knew I was hot for him.

I was glad Kyle was coming. As Marshall had said, the more people involved, the more likely we were to be successful. We "need the energy" as he put it. I must admit that my ulterior motive was as important as Kyle's usefulness to our séance. The truth was I was looking around for any excuse to spend time with him. At first I hadn't allowed myself to think about him much, because of the way there seemed to be something between Marty and Kyle the day after Marty came out. I felt a little guilty going after the very boy that seemed to have had an interest in Marty. I realized however that there was really nothing between them. Perhaps there would have been, but there hadn't been time.

My heart raced when I was near Kyle. My body reacted to him in ways that I found very enjoyable. Without a doubt, I had a serious crush on him. I'd long ago noted what an attractive boy he was, but it had gone way beyond that. I was always checking out cute boys, but this was different. Kyle's dreamy brown eyes made me weak in the knees. His feathery dark hair just made me want to reach out and caress it. To be honest, his sexy body made me want to caress it too. I yearned to take Kyle in my arms and press my lips to his. The very thought made my heart race. I wanted a lot more too, but I didn't want to even let myself think about that. I'd only get myself all worked up. I felt like I was in a perpetual state of arousal the way it was.

I was amazed that he paid any attention to me at all. He was way better looking than I was. He could have probably had any boy he wanted. There was something between us however. I wasn't sure what it was, but there was something. I just hoped that the something was what I wanted it to be.

I felt a little guilty thinking such thoughts about Kyle right after Ken had been so brutally murdered. Ken and I had fooled around a little, although it had just been that one time and had been no more involved than us giving each other a hand job. It wasn't like we were dating or anything. He certainly wasn't my boyfriend. What had passed between us had happened more than a year before. It did seem likely that something was about to happen again, but Ken was murdered before it could take place. No, I wasn't going to let myself feel guilty. If Ken had still been around he'd have slapped me for being so stupid. That thought brought a smile to my lips. It faded quickly however. I was going to miss him.

After school I went home and flipped on my little television, but I was a bit too late for the news. I left it on anyway. I liked something to watch while I was working out, it didn't really matter what was on. It was getting stormy outside and the reception was none too good. Most of the channels just wouldn't come in at all. I couldn't wait until my parents installed a satellite dish at Graymoor. It might be a long wait however. I was still trying to talk them into it. They weren't excited about the idea. If it wasn't from the past, they weren't interested in it. I'd talk them into eventually however. They could only resist the charms of their little boy for so long before they gave in.

There was only one channel that came through pretty well. Unfortunately it was one of those television evangelists, those guys that are always asking people to send money to keep their program on the air. It seemed like they spent most of their time asking for money, so they could stay on the air, to ask for money. It seemed a pretty useless cycle to me.

I never watched that kind of thing, but I recognized Reverend Devlin. He was the most outspoken and obnoxious of them all. "Reverend Devlin" had to be the most obvious oxymoron there ever was. There wasn't anything about that man to be revered. If ever there was an undeserved title, it was his. I reached out to turn it off, but something he was saying caught my attention.

"You see the homosexuals are so pervasive in the media that families are in danger. Hollywood has always glorified homosexuality and now gays are gaining a firm grip. Our children are being taught that homosexuality is okay and it's got to stop.

"Great Britain has even insisted that some Caribbean Islands recognize gays before they can receive aid. The Christians there have held out against this pressure, but the British government continues to attempt to shove homosexuality down their throat. The gays are gaining power and this is a real danger to family and basic Christian values. We've got to stand up and say 'no'. We can't allow the queers to gain the upper hand. If they do the American family is finished."

The first thing that ran through my mind was "What a load of crap." I don't think I'd ever seen anything so offensive before on television and it was a religious program! I also couldn't recall when I'd come across such ignorance. It completely blew me away that anyone would even suggest that gays were anti-family. I loved my family and I wanted to have my own someday. Sure, I wouldn't be getting married and having children, but I did intend to find one guy I could love, and spend my life with him. Maybe we'd even adopt kids that needed a home and raise them as if they were our own. I was sure a lot of gays wanted the same thing. We weren't anti-family at all. We were seeking to create families. It was too bad that some people couldn't get past the narrow definition of mother-father-children.

It was true that a lot of gays left their families, but it was not by choice. Many gay boys my age were forced out of their homes, kicked out onto the street by their parents. Their families rejected them for their sexual orientation, abandoned them to who knew what because they were different. Gays weren't against families, families were failing gays. Those traditional parents were the ones destroying the family. I knew better than anyone that what a gay boy craved most was acceptance, among family, and friends. I knew I was very lucky to have parents that loved me and accepted me just as I was.

I suddenly became very angry. How dare this person, this supposed man of God, spout such lies and present them as Christian values? He was the very worst kind of evil, the kind that cloaked itself in self-righteousness, the kind that pretended to be preaching love while he was really preaching hate. Such words could only break families apart. The person speaking them could have no desire to preserve the family. The person preaching such hate could only be willing to destroy families to hurt the group he hated. Surely no one was ignorant enough to fall for such a ploy?

I wondered about the motive of such people. What were they really after? The idea that gays were anti-family and anti-Christian was so ludicrous that there had to be another motive at work. Was it prejudice, hate, a lust for power, or some combination of them?

I couldn't believe someone who called themselves Christian could preach such lies and hate. Anyone who did so was not Christian at all. Anyone who did that was guilty of an offense against God.

I turned off the television. I refused to listen to more evil disguised as gospel. I started lifting weights again, without the company of the TV.

Chapter 12

A Perfect Night for a Séance

The rain pounded against the window pane as I watched the street below. I listened to the distant, and not so distant thunder, and watched as flashes of lightning lit up the sky. The wind was blowing, whipping the rain about in every direction, making it difficult to see for more than a few feet. I began to fear that my friends were not going make it. I was disappointed. I had looked forward to making an attempt to reach the ghosts of Graymoor.

I saw a figure coming through the heavy iron gate, in the dark and rain I couldn't even make out who it was. I walked downstairs carrying an oil lamp to greet whoever it was at the door. I pulled open the heavy wooden door before Kyle even had a chance to knock. The wind blew the lamp out, leaving us in nearly total darkness until I got it lit once more.

"You're the only person I ever knew that lived in a horror film," said Kyle looking around. "This place gives me the creeps."

"It's not so bad, once you grow accustomed to it." I said.

I led Kyle into the parlor, the main room at the front of the house. I lit the candles on the mantle and placed the lamp on a small stand. I had Kyle help me pull back the love seats and set up chairs around an oval marble top table in the center of the room.

I stole glances of Kyle as we worked. His face looked so handsome in the golden light of the candles and lamp. It was a warm night and Kyle was wearing shorts and a tank-top. He usually dressed like that and it sent me into fits of desire. It was even worse that night. The tank-top he was wearing was the fishnet kind. It was almost as if he wasn't wearing a shirt at all. I was drooling. He was aggravating my hormones to the point that I almost couldn't bear it. I looked again at Kyle's handsome face. His eyes caught mine and we gazed at each other for a few moments. I had an overpowering desire to pull him to me and kiss him. A knock at the door ended the moment.

Zoë was standing the on the step, looking a bit damp. I pulled her in and she wrung the water out of her hair. She looked at her surroundings with the curious, somewhat awed look I'd come to expect from visitors. No one was quite comfortable entering Graymoor. It had been Verona's most notorious haunted mansion for so many years that it had become a place of legend.

"Is Casper home?" she asked.

"Funny." I said.

Zoë's eyes gleamed as they lit upon Kyle. It was a look that made me uncomfortable. I knew that look. I felt it as I looked upon him. It disturbed me to think that Zoë was having the same thoughts about Kyle as I. That made me pause and think. I had been assuming, but I didn't really even know if Kyle was gay. The way he looked back at Zoë made me doubt it for the first time. Then again, I'd seen the look he gave Marty on that day not so very long ago, and the look he had given me.

Still, there was something in his glance as he looked at Zoë. Perhaps Kyle's interest wasn't limited to just girls, or just boys, maybe he went for both. That was an interesting prospect and one I had not considered before. It would sure be a first if Zoë and I were competing for the same guy! We often walked around together, checking out cute boys, but this was something totally new. I hoped I was wrong and that Kyle was just flirting, I didn't need or want the competition. Maybe that was it, maybe he was just flirting. I flirted with girls sometimes myself and I sure wasn't interested in them!

I was developing feelings for Kyle. It wasn't love, but it wasn't just lust either. I wasn't sure quite what it was. Perhaps he was the guy I could spend my life with. Perhaps he was the one for me. Perhaps not. Who knew?

"So, nice place huh?" said Zoë to Kyle.

"If you're the Addams Family," said Kyle. They both laughed at that. I smiled. It was kind of funny.

Marshall came rushing in just a few minutes later and we all took our places around the table. Marshall arranged a few candles around the room, in addition to the ones that were already there. He put an especially thick white candle in the center of the table. I wasn't sure if the candles really served some purpose, or if they were just for effect. They did give the whole room an eerie look however. Of course, it was pretty eerie to begin with. The sound of the rain outside, and the lightening and thunder added to the atmosphere too. It was the perfect night for a séance.

I was excited, but also nervous and a bit frightened. I kept thinking about all the spirits that Marshall said roamed about my home. What if we ended up contacting something nasty? An especially bright flash of lightning lit the room and thunder rent the air. I jumped.

"Marshall, I don't really get this," said Zoë, "What exactly is this séance supposed to do? I mean, I know it is to contact spirits, but just how does it work?"

"Well, by sitting in a circle and holding hands, we are concentrating our energies in one spot, forming a sort of doorway if you will. The idea is to make it easier for the spirits to pass through the barrier than exists between our world and theirs." Marshall had explained the process to me before, but I didn't mind the review.

"I thought we were just calling them," said Zoë. I thought that's what you were doing the other night on the soccer field."

"Well, kind of," said Marshall, "but it's more complicated than that. The focused energy will get their attention and attract them to his spot, hopefully. We are calling them and making it easier for them to communicate with us at the same time. You see, the spirit world and ours exist within the same space and time. Hmmm. This is hard to explain." He paused for a moment before continuing. "Okay, think of our world as a station on a radio, and theirs as another station. Two separate stations can come over the radio, but usually not at the same time, because they are on different frequencies. They are very similar, but not quite the same. Sometimes it's possible to bring in more than one station at once. That's what we are trying to do, set up the energy just right so that both worlds are in synch. When that happens, the spirits can come through."

"So when I saw the ghosts in the hall, that was what was happening?" I said. Both Kyle and Zoë turned their heads toward me and stared. They didn't know I'd been seeing ghosts.

"You've got to be kidding," said Kyle. We ignored him.

"Yes," said Marshall in answer to my question "but on a very weak level, kind of like a radio or television station that's out of range. It kind of comes through, but not well enough to really listen to or see it clearly. Our séance is kind of like putting up a big antenna so we can get a station that is normally beyond our reach. That's not exactly it, but it's as close as I can come to explaining it without taking hours."

"I think that ship has already sailed." said Kyle laughing.

"So if we establish this doorway, how long will it last?" I asked.

"That I don't know. There is a lot of argument about that. Some parapsychologists say the doorway is only open while the séance is taking place. Others say it remains open for a very long time, perhaps permanently."

"But only the ghosts we contact can come through it right?" I asked.

"Well, not exactly. Theoretically any spirit could make use of the doorway."

I didn't like the sound of that at all. I was beginning to doubt the wisdom of opening a doorway into the spirit world when there were so many spirits hanging around Graymoor. I could just image dozens of ghosts being loosed into the house. Then what were we going to do?

"I'm scared," said Zoë.

"It will be all right, really," said Marshall. "It's not likely that any spirits we don't call will come through. They don't tend to pay much attention to our world. For them it's 'been there, done that'. Other spirits probably won't even notice the doorway."

"So you've done this a lot of times before?" said Kyle.

"Not exactly."

"What do you mean, not exactly?" pressed Kyle.

"Actually this is only my second attempt." answered Marshall.

Oh great, just what I needed, someone who didn't know what he was doing. With my luck we'd open up some kind of doorway to hell. There was general doubt around the circle.

"I can do it! Really!" said Marshall. "I've read all about it, it's not that hard."

Everyone looked a bit uncomfortable, but determined to go ahead.

"Freak." said Kyle under his breath.

"Now, everyone join hands, just like the other night."

I took Marshall's hand on the left and Kyle's on the right. The contact with Kyle sent a surge of power through my body that had nothing to do with the séance. I had a feeling I was generating enough energy for at least two people.

Once again, Marshall remained silent for a good long time, but I could see by his wrinkled brow that he was concentrating very hard. His face looked downright terrifying in the candlelight. After several minutes, he began to speak in a voice that sounded more like a chant than anything else.

"Taylor, Mark, can you hear me? Come to us."

Nothing happened, although the occasional peal of thunder from outside made everyone at the table jump. Marshall repeated himself several times, so many in fact that I was getting sick of hearing it. I did get the sense that some kind of energy was flowing through and around us. It made the hair on the back of my neck stand on end.

All was silent, except for the storm outside. There was barely a breath to be heard in the room. The stillness was almost oppressive.

After a few minutes more the large, thick candle in the center of the table began to shake and its flame to flicker. I stared at it wide-eyed, absolutely terrified. I wanted to speak, but I could not find my voice. The energy that I felt intensified and I could feel my hair beginning to rise as if it had a bad case of static electricity. The candle vibrated more violently and then suddenly exploded, sending chunks of hot wax flying in all directions. Zoë screamed, Kyle yelled and I thought I might have just wet my pants. We jerked apart, breaking the circle. I pulled wax off my face.

"What the fuck was that?!" yelled Kyle.

I just sat there, my heart pounding in my chest like it was trying to break its way out.

"I must have done something wrong." said Marshall, looking quite bewildered. "That wasn't supposed to happen."

"No fucking shit! You're a lunatic!" said Kyle looking at him. Marshall didn't even seem to notice.

"I'm going home," said Zoë. "I think I've had enough excitement for one night."

"Me too." said Kyle. "The next time you have a séance Sean, count me out. This is just too fucked up."

They both made for the door in quite a hurry. I didn't blame them. I wished I had somewhere to go.

"It was an…interesting experience Sean," said Zoë. "See you at school tomorrow."

"Later Sean." said Kyle.

"Yeah, see ya."

That left just Marshall and I alone in the room. Marshall was deep in thought as if he were trying to figure out just what had gone wrong. He finally looked at me.

"I'm sorry it didn't work," he said. "I know what this meant to you."

"It's okay Marshall, you tried, and I wouldn't exactly say it didn't work. We sure blew the hell out of that candle. Or something did."

"Yeah, that was pretty cool!"

I smiled, his enthusiasm over the paranormal was unbounded. I wasn't sure I agreed with his definition of "cool" however. I think "frightening" would have better defined the event, or perhaps "terrifying" or "harrowing".

"Maybe we can try it again sometime." he said, "After I figure it all out."

"Maybe." I said. At that point, the last thing I wanted to experience was another séance. No telling what would happen the next time.

"Well, I better get going." said Marshall. I saw him out.

It was a little after ten. My parents weren't due back until past midnight. I wasn't looking forward to staying in that creepy old house all by myself until they returned. At the moment, I was more disappointed than afraid however. I had really gotten my hopes up that we could make it work, especially after finding out that Taylor and Mark had a connection to the house and after seeing them upstairs. It looked like I'd never figure out who had killed Marty, or Ken.

I stripped down to my boxers and lay on my bed staring at the ceiling. I knew that I shouldn't have got my hopes up, especially over something so far fetched as a séance. I knew most séances were just fakes, but I'd hoped ours would really work. I guess it had worked in a way, we'd sure blown the hell out of that candle. If Marshall had brought it, I might have suspected that it was some kind of trick candle or something, but it was one of mom's. I guess it could have been a coincidence, but I didn't think so. I'd sure never heard of a candle exploding before. And just before it happened, I felt a surge of power, far more intense than what I'd felt before. The more I thought about it, the more sure I was that we'd somehow caused it to happen. I just wondered what, or who, did it, and why. The possibilities made me uncomfortable.

I tried not to think about the possibilities and sought out other thoughts to put myself at ease. I wondered about Kyle. He seemed to be getting along a little too well with Zoë. I was jealous. I wondered if maybe I'd been assuming too much. Then again there were times when he flirted with me. And there were other times that there was a certain look in his eye, one that made me think he was experiencing the same wild desires that went through my mind when I was looking at attractive young men.

I found myself drawn to Kyle more and more. So much so that is was beginning to be a problem. I had enough on my mind already without wondering if he might be interested in me.

I tried not to think about Kyle and my thoughts went straight to Ken. I didn't seem to be able to escape from reality. I still couldn't believe he was dead and that someone had so brutally murdered him. That was the kind of thing one saw on television. It wasn't something that happened to a friend. It wasn't something that happened in Verona.

I put my hands behind my head and tried to just blank out my mind. I couldn't let myself think about anything, because everything in my life was so disturbing. There didn't seem to be any peace.

I partially succeeded, but random thoughts of the séance, Marty, Kyle, Zoë, and Ken slipped into my mind. I was growing a little more relaxed, although I could feel the tension in my muscles. Slowly my problems seemed to flow away from me, at least for the time being.

I sat up quickly when I heard the murmuring voices yet again. This time I was more certain they were voices than ever before. I could almost make out what they were saying. I could even catch a few individual words, but couldn't put them together to make anything out of them.

I stepped into the dark hall. I crept down the hall in my boxers, following the voices. This time they led me downstairs. I was hoping to see the ghosts of Taylor and Mark of course, but that's not what I found waiting for me in the front parlor. Instead I saw a young man of perhaps seventeen, arguing with an older man, that I somehow knew was his father. I couldn't quite make out what they were saying, or rather yelling, but it was clear they were very angry with each other.

Both figures were very distinct. They were a blue-gray in appearance, but I could make out every detail of their faces and clothing. It was obvious that these ghosts were from a far earlier time than the ones I'd seen before. Their clothing was clearly from another century. The man was wearing some kind of suit, and the boy was wearing a long nightshirt. I felt as if I'd stepped back in time.

I was terrified by the sight before me, but fascinated as well. I could not tear my eyes from the events that were unfolding. My heart clutched in terror as the older man grabbed the younger by the shirt. The young man pushed himself away and fell to the floor. The older man turned to the fireplace and picked up an ax. The young man scrambled to get up and disappeared into a mist.

His companion stayed as distinct as ever. His eyes looked toward the stairway. They locked upon me. I was stricken with sheer terror. My feet felt glued to the floor as the ax wielding figured advanced on me. I was so terrified I actually could not move for a few moments. I regained control of my body however and bolted up the stairs. I could feel that thing pursuing not far behind me. It was at my heels. What had we done? What horror had we released in Graymoor?

I ran into my room and threw the door shut, wishing that it had a working lock. I jumped in my bed and pulled up the sheets around me. Much to my horror the apparition passed through the door as if it wasn't even there. I huddled on my bed in fear. There was no place to go.

The ax wielding figure came at me in a rage. It raised its ax high and brought it hurtling down, straight toward my chest. I screamed at the top of my lungs, crying, consumed with terror. The ax came down and down, I heard the sickening sound of flesh and bone being cut and hacked. I heard the blood splatter on the headboard. I screamed hysterically, fighting to escape, and then it was all over.

I sat there gasping for breath, still crying and shaking. I ran my hands over my head and chest, as if expecting to find gaping wounds. There were none. I looked at the sheets. They were soaked in blood. I bolted from my bed, recoiling from the gruesome sight. The sheets, the headboard, and the wall were spattered with a massive amount of blood. I ran and looked at myself in the mirror. There wasn't a mark on me. There was no blood, no nothing.

I jumped as I heard a woman's scream in a distant room, then a sickening gurgle. Only moments later I heard what sounded like the scream of a little girl and I swear I could hear her crying "No father." Not long after that I heard the yells of a young man and the unmistakable sound of someone being hacked with an ax. I stood there shaking in terror, breathing so hard and fast I was hyperventilating. I covered my ears. I didn't want to hear any more.

There was nothing more to hear however. All was quiet. I looked at my bed and there was no sign of the blood at all. It was like it had never been there. I even wondered if I'd imagined it, but no, it had been quite real. I sat down in an old rocker and did not move or close my eyes until my parents returned. Only when my mom had stuck her head in my room to say "goodnight" did I get back into bed and close my eyes. Needless to say I didn't sleep well and had troubled dreams.

The next morning, in the full light of day, I walked through all the rooms of the third floor. There was not a sign that anything had happened there the night before. Just as in my own room, there was not one bit of evidence that anything out of the ordinary had occurred.

I knew without a doubt that I had witnessed the Graymoor murders, just as they'd happened more than a hundred years before. I had thought the man with the ax was coming after me, but I knew I'd simply been in the wrong place, at the wrong time. It made me uncomfortable to know that one of the Graymoor boys had been hacked to bits right in my own bed. I wasn't sure I wanted to sleep there any more.

*   *   *

At lunch the next day I told Marshall all about what I'd seen. He was all ears of course. I was more than a little annoyed when he laughed at me after I told him I had thought I was being hacked to bits.

"I don't think it's very damned funny!" I told him. "I almost died from the fright alone."

"I'm sorry," he said, still laughing despite himself, "it's just that it's so obvious what was going on. It's like being afraid that a chain saw murderer is going to jump off the screen at a movie and saw you up."

"Hey, guys in movies don't chase anyone up the stairs. That thing was after me! At least I thought it was."

"It was never after you. It didn't even know you were there. It couldn't. What you saw wasn't even real." said Marshall.

"So you're saying I just imagined everything last night." I was getting cross. I thought of all people, that Marshall would understand.

"No, that's not what I'm saying at all. What you saw wasn't a true ghost, not an actual spirit visible in our world."

"Then what was it?" I asked impatiently. "It looked pretty damned real to me."

"No doubt it did Sean, but what you saw was a reenactment of sorts."

"Huh?" I said.

"There are two theories about the type of phenomena you saw last night. Some parapsychologists believe that very violent or traumatic events affect the space in which they occur. If the conditions are right, or someone has enough psychic abilities to sense them, the events replay themselves. Kind of like a video tape of something that happened, only in three dimensions."

I didn't say anything. I just listened.

"The other theory is that the past sometimes intrudes upon the present. That it breaks through if you will. When this happens it's possible to witness what occurred in the past, just as you did last night. Either way, you were never in danger, although I'm sure it was terrifying. I sure wouldn't want to be in the middle of the Graymoor murders, not if I didn't know what was going on that is."

"Well, I think I was in danger. In danger of being scared to death. I almost had a heart attack!"

Marshall stifled another laugh.

"You know," said Marshall, "everything you witnessed last night fits in with the Graymoor murders. I've read everything there is to read about them."

"And?" I said.

"Well, no one knows exactly what happened that night because there were no living witnesses, but everything you saw fits. Mr. Graymoor was married at the time of the murders. He had two sons, one seventeen, one sixteen, and a daughter that was eight. The older son's body was found hacked to bits in his bed, your bed."

"You knew he'd been murdered in my bed and you didn't tell me?" I asked, almost yelled.

"Sean, would you really have wanted to know that?"

"I guess not." I said. Not knowing was probably the best thing. I sure wished I didn't know it.

"Mr. Graymoor's wife was killed in their bedroom, just down the hall from yours. At least her body was found there. The daughter's body was found in her bedroom, which was right next to her parent's bedroom. The younger son's body was found lying at the far end of the hall. From your description, it sounds to me like the screams you heard last night came from all the right places."

"Yeah," I said, "seems so."

"Well, maybe we can check it out if it happens again."

"What do you mean 'happens again'?" I asked, none too happy about the prospect.

"Well, often this kind of thing repeats itself, sometimes nightly."

"Oh no, I don't want to see that again!"

"Well, you may not have much of a choice Sean. It's not like some television program you can turn off and on at will."

"That's just great!" I said. "We couldn't get to Taylor and Mark and now I've got a murder being reenacted in my house every night."

"Maybe not." said Marshall. "Some times these things only occur for a few weeks or months then stop. Sometimes they take place just at a certain time of year, or on a certain date. Sometimes they happen just once. Each one is different."

I wasn't happy about the prospect one bit. Watching the Graymoor murders once was more than enough. I suspected that Marshall was hoping for a repeat performance. I guess I couldn't blame him for that. I was not looking forward to a mad ax man breaking into my room every night however, even if there was no real danger.

Chapter 13

History Repeats Itself

I paced up and down the sidewalk downtown. There was something I'd been thinking about doing since shortly after Ken's death and I'd determined that it was time to do it. Ken had been murdered only a few days before, but time was of the essence. While Ken was still alive, we couldn't tell his dad what we'd discovered about Marty's murder. If his dad knew what Ken had done, he would have been grounded for sure. Now that Ken was dead, that was no longer a problem. I'd promise not to breath a word about it, but I was sure Ken wouldn't mind. It couldn't hurt him now and it just might help with discovering Marty's murderer.

I'd stalled long enough. I pushed open the door to the Corner's Office and walked in. I was just getting ready to ask for Dr. Clark when he came in from the back. He smiled at me.

"What brings you here Sean?"

"I need to talk to you." I said. My tone was serious and Dr. Clark could tell something was up.

"Come on back." he said. "We can talk while I work."

I was a little apprehensive about talking to him while he worked, he was the coroner after all. I half expected to find some dead body laying out on a table or something. I was relieved to find he was only filing away some old reports.

"So what is it you need?"

"You may not like what I have to tell you." I said. "I've been doing a lot of thinking about my friend Marty's death and it just doesn't make sense. I asked Ken to get something for me that I needed to help figure it out. I needed to see Marty's autopsy records."

Dr. Clark stopped filing and looked at me. His face was serious, but not angry.

"Ken came in and took them for me, then brought them back later that night. I'm sorry for taking them without permission like that, but I didn't think you'd let me see them if I asked. Anyway, we found something when we looked over the records. I don't think Marty killed himself. Well, I'm sure he didn't. You can see it in the records yourself. He couldn't have shot himself in the head like that. Someone else had to do it."

I was afraid that Dr. Clark would start yelling at me or something, but he didn't. Instead he pulled out the records of Marty's autopsy and started scribbling a lot of calculations on a pad that I didn't understand. After a couple of minutes he looked up at me.

"I'll have to check this out more thoroughly, but I think you are right. It looks like what you said is true. You've found something everyone else overlooked."

"Well, me and Ken found it, and I guess everyone else overlooked it, because they weren't looking for it. I just knew Marty wouldn't have killed himself so that only left one alternative. Someone else had to have killed him."

"I'll let you know what I find out," said Dr. Clark.

"And you'll tell the police if I'm right?"

"Of course I will."

"I'm real sorry me and Ken did what we did, but you can understand it can't you?"

"Yes," he said. "I must admit I would have been furious if I'd found out Ken had done that, but now... Now I just wish he was here to do it again."

Dr. Clark looked like he was ready to cry. I knew he had to miss his son very, very much. I walked over to him and hugged him.

"I miss him too." I said. "He was a good friend."

Dr. Clark smiled through his tears and mussed my hair.

"I'm glad he had you for a friend Sean."

I smiled back at him.

"Now get out of here so I can check this out."

"Yes sir." I said and departed.

I felt good after it was over. Maybe now the authorities could make some progress. At least now they'd know there was a murder to investigate. Of course, Dr. Clark might discover that I was wrong, but that wasn't going to happen. I knew I wasn't wrong, someone had murdered my best friend.

* * *

I froze in my tracks. I was in the fourth floor hallway, just one floor above my room when I heard it. I couldn't quite be sure, but it sounded like someone calling my name. It was long and drawn out, almost like someone was singing it.

I swallowed hard as I heard it again. It sounded more than ever like my name. The voice was that of a young male, a boy perhaps, very clear and musical. It felt friendly, but it still made the hair on the back of my neck stand on end. I walked down the hall, holding my oil lamp out in front of me, toward the source of the noise. I wasn't sure where it was coming from, but it was in that direction.

I came to a cross hallway and looked left and right. I waited and soon the voice called out to me again. I turned right and passed by rooms I'd never even been in before. I heard the voice once more, coming from the very end of the hall. Along with my name I heard other words, but I couldn't make them out. It was as if they were just out of reach, just on the edge of being intelligible.

I came to the end of the hall and heard the voice call to me yet again. It was on the other side of a massive, heavily carved wooden door. I closed my eyes for a moment and licked my lips. I took a few breaths to calm myself and placed my hand on the doorknob. It turned with the sound of metal on rust. I knew no one had been in that room in ages.

A black cat bolted out the door with a great screech. I yelled and almost dropped the lamp. There were two particularly singular facts about that cat. First, we didn't have a cat and second, it disappeared into thin air as it ran down the hall. It didn't simply vanish into the shadows. It simply disappeared. It was there, then it wasn't. I wondered if it was the same cat I'd seen several nights before. It seemed that Graymoor even had ghost animals.

I stepped into the room. It was vast, like the parlor downstairs. The walls were lined with shelves loaded down with books, hundreds of them, thousands of them. The shelves ran up to the ceiling, so high that there was a ladder attached to a track on each wall, so someone could climb up and get at the books that were much too far above the floor for anyone to reach.

I stopped and listened, but heard no further sounds. I walked around the room, exploring. There were great overstuffed chairs and big tables with books on them. Everywhere there were books. I picked one up off a large desk and read the title "A Christmas Carol". I opened it up, there was writing on the inside cover "To Kenneth Graymoor, with compliments from the author, Charles Dickens". All I could think was "Wow".

I put the book back in its place and turned my attention to a large rolled up piece of paper. I unrolled it on the top of the desk and held it down with books. As I gazed at it, I realized it was a map of the house. There was a drawing of each floor indicating where all the rooms were located. I found the room I was standing in and, not surprisingly, it was labeled "Library". I peered at the map for a long time. It detailed some parts of Graymoor I'd never been in before. I was a little surprised that it didn't show any hidden passages, but perhaps the map maker left them out on purpose, or wasn't even aware of their existence.

I stayed in the library for some time. There was no further hint of the voice that had led me there, but at least I'd found something useful. I was forever getting lost in Graymoor. I rolled the map back up and stuck it under my arm. I explored a bit more, then went back to my room.

* * *

Marshall came over about ten that night and we walked around the house while he pointed out which room had belonged to which member of the Graymoor family. Marshall had been itching to come to Graymoor ever since I'd seen the ghastly murders reenacted. In the few days since I'd witnessed the event, it had not repeated itself. I hoped that it never would, but Marshall had other dreams.

He suggested that we try another séance, but I just wasn't up to it after what had happened. I was beginning to think that stuff like that was best left alone. I'd heard some pretty creepy stories about Ouija Boards and such and I was beginning to believe them.

Instead we spent a lot of time talking about Ken and the possibility that his murder was linked with Marty's. So far the authorities had failed to come up with a single suspect. About the only evidence was that they had found six different sets of footprints, all made by individuals wearing sneakers, at the site of the murder. Two sets had been matched up with the guys that discovered the body and reported it to the police. Another set was Ken's. That left three sets. Whoever killed him wasn't working alone.

The hour for the Graymoor murders was drawing near, so Marshall and I went down and stood in the parlor. I made sure that we were standing off to the side where we wouldn't be in the line of anything that might happen. Having that crazed man with an ax run toward me a few nights before was about more than I could take. I wasn't about to experience it again.

Marshall and I waited in silence for several minutes. I really didn't think anything was going to happen and that was fine by me. I would have been more than happy to have what I saw a one time event. I could tell Marshall was a bit disappointed however.

Just when I thought I was safe, I heard murmuring voices headed in our direction. They were upstairs in the hall. As the voices neared the top of the stairs, I could see the figures of Mr. Graymoor and his oldest son. Marshall grabbed my arm and turned as pale as chalk.

"It's Edward Graymoor," Marshall whispered, "the eldest son, he was seventeen, and his father, Kenneth."

The Graymoor's were in the middle of a heated argument. They stopped at the very same spot where I'd seen them a few nights before and yelled at one another. I had a weird sense of déjà vu. Everything was happening exactly as it had before. The only differences were the presence of Marshall and the fact that we were standing in a different place.

There was another minor difference. It was a little easier to make out what the two apparitions were saying. I could only make out a few words here and there, but I did hear Mr. Graymoor say "no son of mine…" and Edward say "but father, I love him" soon after. I don't know if the words were actually becoming more intelligible, or if I just understood more because it was my second time through the scene.

The father grabbed his son by the shirt and then Edward pushed himself away. Edward fell to the floor as his father turned and took the ax from near the fireplace. This time the ghost of Edward didn't disappear, but stayed as distinct as it had the whole time. He scrambled to his feet and bolted up the stairs, just as I had a few nights before.

Marshall and I followed as Mr. Graymoor pursued his son. We watched as he bore down upon the frightened boy as he sat upright in his bed. We heard Edward's screams and the sickening sound of a sharp ax on flesh and bone. Mixed in with the screams I could hear the words "sodomites die". Soon the room was all too quiet. Edward lay dead on my bed and it was one gruesome sight. The sheets were stained red and there was blood on the headboard.

I realized that a few nights before I had been the victim of spectacularly bad timing. I'd run to my room, Edward's room, just as he had more than a century before. I took refuge in the bed just as he had and cowered as the blows fell in the same way. No wonder I thought Mr. Graymoor was after me. It gave me a true appreciation for the things Edward experienced on that night long ago. My heart went out to him.

We followed Mr. Graymoor as he went to a bedroom down the hall. There we watched as he hacked up his wife in a rage. Everything was all gray, except the red blood, but the sight still made me sick to my stomach.

I could hardly bear to follow as the enraged Mr. Graymoor went into his daughter's room. I looked on in horror as the little girl begged her father not to hurt her. I heard the words "No Father!" screamed again, just before the little girl's pitiful and horrible scream. The father must have been insane to do such things.

Mr. Graymoor left his daughter lying dead on the floor and walked to another bedroom not far down the hall.

"He's going to William's room," said Marshall.

We entered behind the ghost to see William dressed in a nightshirt, keeping the bed between himself and his crazed father. They were exchanging heated words, but again I could not make much out. All I could make out was Mr. Graymoor saying "adopted," "still your brother...", "cannot suffer to live...", and "sodomy". I could catch even fewer of William's words but I could discern "we love one..." and "Edward..."

Mr. Graymoor swung at William, but the ax met only air. William vaulted straight over the bed without touching it. He must have been quite an athlete. He ran through Marshall and I, but I felt nothing as he passed through me. I stepped quickly aside as Mr. Graymoor passed through same space. We ran down the hall after Mr. Graymoor as he caught up with William and sank the ax head between his shoulder blades. The blood curdling screams made me want to cover my ears, as did the grotesque squishing, crackling, and gurgling sounds that followed.

Marshall and I stepped around the still form of William as we followed his father down the hall and down the back stairs. He led us outside and then disappeared into nothingness. I thought that was the end of things, but then I heard a loud murmuring. I turned to see a large group of ghostly figures gathered around the large tree just out back of the house. They were shouting. I couldn't make out a single word, but it was clear they were angry.

Marshall and I drew near and watched as a noose was placed around Mr. Graymoor's neck as he sat astride a horse. Pale, ghostly torches lit the scene as the rope was thrown over a branch the other end secured. The horse bolted and the rope went taut. The only sound was a wet crack as Kenneth Graymoor's neck snapped. We watched as he swung back and forth on the noose, eyes bulging, dead. Moments later he, and the angry crowd, were gone.

"And that's just how it happened." said Marshall. "Incredible."

When we went back inside, there was no sign of Edward, William, or the others. There were no blood stains, no evidence of the murders whatsoever. It was as if nothing had happened at all.

"You have the coolest house ever," said Marshall with adoration in his eyes. I thought that Marshall had to be out of his head.

I didn't find the reenacted murders the least bit cool. They were morbidly interesting, even fascinating, but I'd rather not have witnessed them. The recent murders of Marty and Ken brought it all far too close to home. I didn't want to be reminded of what had happened to them.

I sure didn't want to see grisly details that were all too similar to what had happened to boys I'd known.

Marshall didn't seem bothered by it at all. He was far too fascinated with ghosts to consider much else. He was having the time of his life, even if some of it frightened him. I guess it was kind of a dream come true for him. He'd been fascinated by the supernatural since he was a little boy and he was right in the middle of some clearly supernatural events.

*   *   *

My parents weren't quite as thrilled over the nightly supernatural show in our home as Marshall. I knew exactly when they discovered it because mom came screaming up the stairs one night. I just thought to myself, "I guess mom has met the Graymoor's".

I had already told my parents about it, but I don't think they quite believed me. I had no trouble with them believing my story after they'd seen the ghostly reenactment for themselves. Dad didn't really seem bothered by the whole thing. His reaction was more like Marshall's.

It was unsettling for us all, but we more or less grew accustomed to the horrible screams in the night. It was rather amazing how something so extraordinary became rather commonplace to us. I was still startled now and then, but after a few times the whole thing wasn't quite so scary. I did make it a point to be out of my room when the hour struck for Edward's murder. That's something I didn't want to see ever again.

I was glad my parents didn't just freak and want to move out. I had come to like Graymoor, despite the continued absence of electricity and other modern conveniences. Marshall was right, it was certainly an interesting place to live. There were times I wished that I was elsewhere, but the creepy old mansion was beginning to grow on me. I think knowing that Mark and Taylor were there had a lot to do with that. There was something comforting about having a couple of gay ghosts in the house. I sort of felt like I had friends there.

Chapter 14

First Contact

One afternoon, not long after I arrived home from school, I heard a heavy knock at the front door. I had just come downstairs to take a break from lifting weights and get something to drink in the kitchen. It was lucky I was in the kitchen and not my room, otherwise I'd never have heard the knock.

I opened the door and was surprised to see Jill standing there. I knew her well from school. I'd talked to her a lot and had even danced with her a few times. We were on friendly terms, but I sure didn't expect to see her standing on my doorstep. She was the first person ever to just show up at Graymoor. I just stood there for a second or two before I said anything.

"Is this a bad time?" she said.

"Uh no. I'm just surprised to see you. Come in."

As she stepped inside I realized I wasn't wearing a shirt. I never did when I worked out. I felt a little self conscious bare-chested in front of Jill. Sometimes I was a little shy.

"It's nice to see you." I said. "Was there something you wanted?"

"Actually yes," she said. "There's something I've been wanting for a long time."

The way she said that made me nervous. Jill was acting really strange.

"Interesting house." she said. "Are you home alone?"

"Uh yeah." I said.

"Why don't you show me your room?"

"Okay." I answered.

I led her upstairs. The whole thing was quite bizarre. I almost felt as if I were inside one of those dreams that don't seem to have a point and just don't make any sense. I wouldn't have been too surprised for Marshall to stop by, he loved spending time in our haunted house after all. I would have been very surprised if any of my other friends just dropped in. They all avoided Graymoor. I spent a lot of time with my friends, but always somewhere else. Jill coming to the house was completely unexpected.

We walked into my room and Jill looked around.

"This is nice. I've always wondered what your room looked like."

"Really?" I asked. "Why?"

"I'm interested in everything about you. That's why I'm here." She took a very deep breath. I could tell she had something big on her mind. I was clueless as to what that might be.

"You look very nice," she said, looking at my bare chest.

"Um, thanks. You look nice too." I was extremely uncomfortable with her looking at me like that.

"You really think so?"

"Of course, you are very pretty." She smiled at me.

Jill walked toward me, getting so close I was uncomfortable. I had to fight my natural instinct to step back.

"You know I've always liked the way you look." she said.

Jill took me completely by surprise by reaching out and running her index finger down my chest. She looked me in the eyes and licked her lips. I looked back at her wide-eyed.

"Uh, Jill…"

She placed her finger on my lips to silence me. I swallowed hard.

"Shhhhh" she said and brought her face closer to mine. She inched in ever closer. I pulled away quickly.

"Jill, what are you doing?"

She didn't say anything, just closed on me again. I found myself staring into her eyes. She leaned in, bringing her lips closer and closer to mine.

"Jill, stop!" I said, pushing her away. "What are you trying to do?"

"I want to kiss you Sean. I want you to kiss me. I want to do a lot of things with you."

Jill just being there seemed bizarre, but what was going on seemed unreal. I really did feel like I was inside some kind of weird dream, but I knew I was awake.

"Jill, you know I'm gay. Everyone knows it! I like guys!"

"I could do some things for you Sean. Things I know you'd like. So what if I'm a girl. It will still feel good." Her hands were beginning to wander over my torso, and lower still.

"No!" I said, pushing her hands away.

I grabbed my shirt and put it on.

"Why are you doing this?" I asked her. "I'm not interested in you. I'm not interested in girls. Of all the guys out there, why are you going after me?"

"Because you're the one I want. I'm not asking you to love me Sean. I just want to be with you. I'll do whatever you want."

I swallowed hard. My mind was reeling. I had no idea where all this was coming from. I'd never suspected Jill had such feelings for me. I'd never heard of a girl making a play for a guy she knew was gay. The whole thing was just too weird and fucked up.

Jill wasn't taking no for an answer. I couldn't keep her hands off my chest. She even groped me through my shorts before I had time to push her away.

"Get away from me!"

"Come on Sean. I'll make it feel so good."

"No! Go make some other guy feel good. Now get out!"

"Ah, you don't mean that Sean."

"Yes I do. Get away from me!" I was shouting. It seemed to be the only way to get her to understand.

Suddenly she looked very hurt. She turned and ran out of the room, down the stairs, and out the door. I was surprised she could find her own way out. I just stood there dumbfounded. The only thing I could think was "What the fuck?"

I just stood there for the longest time. The whole thing with Jill made no sense at all, at least not to me. The fact that she was attracted to me did make me feel good about myself however. I guessed Nathan was right. There was someone out there who found me attractive. Too bad it was a girl.

*   *   *

Ken's funeral was an unpleasant experience. It hadn't been that long since I was in that same funeral home. I couldn't stand the oppressive air in there; all the pain and suffering that was caused by his death. Whoever killed him harmed not only Ken, but all those around him too. His parents looked like they were visiting hell. Ken's dad looked like he was only seconds away from killing himself over his grief. Ken's mom couldn't stop crying. Who could be so cruel and twisted to cause so much grief?

Ken's casket was closed. Apparently no amount of work on the part of the mortician could make him look presentable. I tried not to think about what he looked like inside that coffin, but rather focused on the photo of him his parents had placed on the top of the casket. It wasn't fair that Ken die so young, that his life be stolen away from him. I'd get to the bottom of all this if it was the last thing I did. I'd find out who had killed my friends one way or another. I'd finish the task, or it would finish me.

I rode in the back seat as my parents drove out to the graveyard. It was the second time in only a few days that I'd been to the cemetery to say goodbye to someone I knew. I wasn't quite so close to Ken as I had been to Marty, but I don't know that losing him was any easier. The death of Ken brought all the grief and pain of Marty's death to the surface once more, not that it had sank very far beneath the surface.

As the funeral procession pulled up to the graveyard, anger was heaped on top of my grief. Those damned protesters were there again, holding their wicked signs. I could not comprehend how anyone could be so cold or cruel.

The sign that read "Ken And All Fags Burn In Hell" especially roused my anger. In my opinion, the protesters were not one bit better than the Nazi's who had murdered millions during the holocaust. They had the same mentality, the same willingness to wipe out an entire group because there was something they did not like about them. Those people wanted nothing less than genocide aimed against homosexuals.

I was angered even more when I read the sign that said, "God Punished Ken, He Got What He Deserved". How could anyone be ignorant enough to think that God would support such a heinous crime? I half expected lightening to strike the protesters for their evil.

My eyes did not fail to catch the sign that read "God Hates Queers". I'd seen it at Marty's burial. It was the very same words that were on the note that was pinned to Ken's body. I suddenly wished that I had a camera to get a shot of each of the protesters faces. I had a feeling Ken's murderer was among them, and perhaps Marty's too.

I noticed that someone was taking pictures of them. He was in plain clothes, but I recognized one of the town cops. I smiled inwardly. Maybe lightening was about to strike those bastards. I was glad to see the police were doing something at least. I had no doubt Ken's dad had something to do with that. I wondered if he'd confirmed my suspicions about

Marty's death. I wasn't about to ask him at the moment however. I already felt bad about approaching him so soon after his son's death.

A caught a recognizable face in the crowd of protesters. It wasn't someone I knew, but it was someone I'd seen before. For a few moments I couldn't place him, but then it dawned on me, it was that television evangelist that had angered me so when he'd uttered such lies on his program.

I just stood there and stared at him. There was no doubt. It was him. I knew then that the protesters were members of his church. They were known for being fanatics, not unlike one of those cults where all the members eventually commit suicide. It was almost unbelievable that members of a church could perform such evil. To me being a member of a church was all about helping others and doing good. These people had perverted that into something horrible. They were no less than evil masquerading as good. It was the most dangerous kind of evil and a true offense against God. I was so horrified by their blasphemy that I crossed myself, I felt soiled by their mere presence.

I wanted to march over and give those monsters a piece of my mind, but I knew they would be deaf to my words. People like that would not listen to reason. They would remain deaf to the truth until the day they died. All that mattered to them was their hatred. Instead I turned away from them and prayed that God would have mercy on their souls.

It started to rain as the graveside service began. The mourners stood there and let the rainfall down upon them like tears from the sky. I looked behind me and saw the ink running in streams on the signs of the protestors. It was as if God himself were erasing the hateful words and lies of the evil ones. I turned my back on them again.

* * *

I stirred in my sleep. In my dream I felt something tugging at the sheets on my bed, as if it was trying to pull them off. Then I heard my name quietly called to me. In that state between sleeping and waking I wondered if my mother was trying to rouse me from bed. I opened my eyes, but it was dark.

I'd been dreaming. At least I thought so until I heard my name called again. It was the same voice I'd heard on that day I found the library and the map of Graymoor. The voice was so beautiful that it sounded like an angel. I looked to the foot of my bed and there stood a beautiful boy with long golden hair. I knew in a moment that it was Taylor. Had I not known his identity, I think I would have mistook him for an angel. He was so beautiful and radiated such kindness and love that I felt he'd been sent by God. Perhaps he was.

He looked right at me and I had no doubt he could see me as well as I saw him. He was ghostly, blue-gray, and transparent. I could see right through him to the wall behind. He was quite distinct however and I could make out every feature. I wasn't the least bit afraid, even though I knew I was in the presence of a real ghost, and one that was quite aware of me. This wasn't some playback of a previous event. It was real. I should have been terrified, but I was without fear.

Taylor looked as if he were concentrating, focusing all his mental powers upon one task. He looked at me and simply said "be patient", then disappeared into nothingness. I could still feel his presence in the room, but I could neither see nor hear him.

I was not sure what his message meant, but it filled me with hope. All my recent failures disappeared. Taylor had made contact with me. I thought of trying another séance, but something told me I should not. Somehow I knew that "be patient" meant not to force things, that they would come. I closed my eyes once more and fell immediately asleep.

I awakened again some time later. I don't know how much time had passed, but it was still dark. I heard the sound of laughing and running in the hall. I climbed out of bed and stepped into the hall in time to catch a glimpse of two boys running down it. At first I thought someone had gotten into the house and was messing around.

The laughter and voices I heard were so very clear. As soon as I heard one of them say: "You can't catch me William." I knew the boys weren't intruders, but ghosts.

I quickly followed them down the hall and down the stairway. The boys were playing in the parlor. William was chasing Edward, while Edward ducked behind furniture and put every obstacle he could in his brother's path. They were laughing. I recognized them from when I'd seen them before, but they were a lot younger. Edward looked about ten or eleven and William a little younger than that. I smiled as I watched them. It must have been great to have a brother like that.

William tackled Edward and they fell laughing. They never hit the floor. They just disappeared into nothingness before they hit. I didn't know if I'd seen ghosts or some reenactment of a past event, but the sight set me even more at ease. I felt like I was getting to know the ghosts of Graymoor and, with the exception of Mr. Graymoor, I liked them.

Chapter 15

Hatred and Lies

The next day at school, I told Marshall about the visitation from Taylor and about seeing the young Graymoor boys. He devoured every detail. He asked me so many questions I thought my head would explode. I didn't mind however. I had a feeling none of what had occurred could have happened without Marshall. I owed him big.

Just after school I shoved my books in my locker. I noticed a booklet lying on the bottom. Someone must have shoved it in my locker during the day. I had no need to wonder what the booklet was about. The front read "God Hates Queers" and showed one guy kneeling down in front of another. I stuffed it in my pocket and went straight home.

I dumped my stuff on my desk and pulled out the booklet. What I read filled me with disgust. I'd never come across such an accumulation of misinformation in my entire life. I almost couldn't believe the words I was reading.

"The average queer has between twenty-four and one hundred partners per year. The average heterosexual has only six in a lifetime." That almost made me laugh. According to the booklet, I was at least two dozen sexual encounters behind in the current year alone, maybe as many as a hundred. Maybe I just wasn't average, the total of my sexual partners for my lifetime was exactly zero (or one if I counted what had happened with Ken, which hardly seemed worth counting). I thought about the few gay guys I knew. Including what I'd read about Taylor and Mark, the highest number of partners in an entire lifetime that I could come up with was one. That didn't seem too promiscuous to me. I think monogamous would have been a better term to describe it. I had no doubt that many gay guys had lots more sex than I did, but twenty-four to one hundred partners a year! That was at least two a month and up to almost two a week. Give me a break!

The next statistic was even more appalling. The booklet read, "50% of queers admit to five hundred or more partners in a lifetime, 40% admit to one thousand or more in a lifetime, 20% admit to two thousand or more."

Who were these people trying to con? Did they think anyone would be ignorant enough to buy this crap? I was far from naïve. I knew the score and I also knew that such high numbers were almost an impossibility. I doubted even a prostitute could rack up that high of a total.

The next part made me downright mad because I knew it was nothing less than total bullshit. "Queers prey on children continuously. Queers commit more than half of all reported child molestation's in the United States, which, assuming queers make up 1% of the population, means that at least 15% of queers are child molesters, while less that .25% of heterosexuals are child molesters."

I'd read the statistics on child molesters myself. Anyone who did any reading at all knew that the profile for the most likely child molester was a white, heterosexual male, in his 20's. Even if I wasn't familiar with the accurate information, the statistics listed in the booklet were ridiculous. The accepted percentage of gays was 10%, not 1%, and I personally believed it was probably in excess of 20%. After all, when asked about their sexual orientation, most homosexuals would not admit they were gay. The consequences for such an admission were too severe for most. If heterosexuals faced the same consequences for being known as heterosexuals, I was sure their reported percentage would plummet.

The idea that half of child molestation's were committed by gays was ludicrous. The number just didn't fit with the known statistics.

The next part actually made me laugh out loud. "Queers Recruit Children: Because queers can't reproduce naturally, they resort to recruiting children. They can be heard chanting "Ten percent is not enough, recruit, recruit, recruit!" in their immoral parades and un-American demonstrations. Some queers aren't as outspoken about this, but rather try to secretly infiltrate society and get into positions where they will have access to the naïve and innocent minds of young children (clergy, teachers, camp counselors, child psychologists, Boy Scout leaders, etc.)."

Whoever wrote that booklet didn't know shit about sexual orientation. It was no more a matter of choice than height or eye color. Homosexuals were born homosexuals, heterosexuals were born heterosexuals. There was no changing that. All the recruitment tactics in the world couldn't change the sexual orientation of a single individual anymore than they could transform an apple into an orange.

Even if such recruitment were possible, I couldn't imagine anyone wanting to become homosexual when gays were the constant targets of threats and abuse. We were beaten, spit on, called horrible names, denied jobs, discriminated against in all sorts of ways, looked down upon, and sometimes even murdered. That wouldn't exactly make for a successful ad campaign. What would the slogan be "Go gay, get treated like shit"? Or maybe "Join the Gay Club and Get Your Head Beaten In"?

There were lots of cool things about being gay, but the world made it very, very hard. I couldn't imagine anyone choosing homosexuality if they had a choice. I wouldn't change myself if I could, but I also knew that I would not have chosen to be gay. It was just too difficult. I'd had a fairly easy time of it myself, but I had been called "faggot", "fairy", and a lot of similar things more times than I could count. I'd been beaten up a couple of times and had experienced a lot of things I just didn't want to remember. The positive side of being gay outweighed the negative, but someone who was not gay couldn't possibly see that. I couldn't imagine anyone deciding that they'd like to be gay. It was a moot point however, there was no choice to be made. Changing from one to the other just wasn't possible. I knew I could just as easily transform myself into an eagle as I could change into a heterosexual.

By the time I'd finished the booklet I was so mad I couldn't see straight. Not since Nazi Germany had there been such a blatant dissemination of misinformation. The lengths some people would go to in their hatred and bigotry was without bounds.

What struck me most of all was that the booklet was put out by a church! It was Reverend Devlin's church however, so maybe I shouldn't have been quite so shocked. There were even several Bible quotes strewn throughout the booklet that were supposed evidence that "God Hates Queers". I'd never come across such a clear-cut case of blasphemy in my entire life. I noted too that all Biblical passages that demonstrated tolerance for homosexuality and God's love for all were suspiciously absent. It always angered me to see someone abuse the Bible to support their own views.

I finally had to just throw the booklet in the trash where it belonged. I halfway expected it to spontaneously combust like some tool of Satan. I wished that I had never read it, but perhaps it was best to know what the evil ones were up to. Like my grandfather always said, "If there's a snake in the grass, it's best to know where he is."

One thing I wondered about was who put the booklet in my locker. I hadn't noticed anyone else with one, so I assumed they weren't stuffed in every locker. It frightened me a little to be singled out. I was open about being gay of course, but I still wondered what had brought this on. I wondered if Marty and Ken had received one just before they were murdered.

I paused. The thought stuck in my mind. What if they had both received the same pamphlet before they were killed? I swallowed hard and became even more fearful.

Chapter 16

Marshall's Makeover

That night, I heard laughter in the hallway again, but this time it was a little girl. I followed the sound out into the hall. I seemed to roam the halls in my boxers pretty much every night. Maybe far into the future someone would see my nightly adventure reenacted. They would see the half naked ghost boy roaming the halls of Graymoor.

The little girl ran up and down the hall squealing. She seemed to be chasing a ball or something that I could not see. She was pretty distinct however. She was quite beautiful, with long curly hair and a very fancy dress. She looked about six years old. My guess was that she was Edward and William's little sister.

I was almost sorry I'd seen her. I still had the vision of her murder in my mind. Hearing her little voice cry out "No father!" would be even harder to take the next time I heard it. I'd heard that cry several times. Mr. Graymoor murdered his family all over again every few nights.

The little girl was certainly happy playing in the hall however. She giggled and laughed and the sound echoed through the house. William came out of his bedroom and his little sister ran to him and jumped in his arms. I heard him say "How's my girl today?" He stepped down the hall carrying her, then they both faded away.

I turned to go back to my room, but I heard the organ playing downstairs. It was a pleasant enough melody, but it was rather spooky in the middle of the night. I walked down the stairs and could see light. As I drew closer, I could see the old pump organ in the golden glow of an oil lamp. The two candles on the organ were lit too. The organ kept playing, but no one was there. I could see the keys moving up and down, as if unseen fingers were playing a tune, but no one was visible, not even a ghost. I just stood there and listened for a while.

The melody eventually faded until there was only silence. I started to walk over to the organ to blow out the candles and lamp, but one by one they were each snuffed out as if someone had blown on them. I turned on my heel and went back to my room. It was quite a sight, but it didn't really frighten me. I'd never have dreamed just a few weeks before that I could witness such a thing without fear. If it had happened my first night in Graymoor I think I'd have dropped dead from fright.

*   *   *

The next day after school, I waited until no one was around, then worked the combination to Marty's locker. When I opened it, a wave of sadness flowed over me. I was with Marty the last time I'd seen that locker open. It made me miss him all the more.

There wasn't much in the locker. All this books and personal belongings had been removed. There were a few papers in the very bottom. I dug through them, but there was no pamphlet there.

I went next to Ken's locker. I didn't have his combination, but it wasn't too hard to break into it. Those lockers weren't all that secure. Ken's locker was pretty much the same as Marty's, only with more junk left behind. I sorted through the papers. My breath caught in my throat. It was there, a copy of the pamphlet. I felt like I'd just received the kiss of death.

*   *   *

That Saturday I took Marshall to the beach at Koontz Lake. I borrowed my parents' car and picked Marshall up at his house early in the afternoon. Marshall walked out to the car wearing a black swimsuit and a gray shirt. It was a good look for him, but still kind of strange. I liked Marshall, but he tended to dress a little odd.

"Hey, you look nice." I said as he got in.

"Thanks." he said.

I could tell my compliment made him uncomfortable. Most people seemed to be like that. They just couldn't handle anyone saying something nice about them. Marshall did look really good in those shorts however and his shirt suited him perfectly, even if it was gray. I sometimes wondered if that boy knew that colors other than black and gray existed. No matter, he still looked pretty good. Maybe he'd catch the eye of some girl at the beach. Marshall needed a girl. He didn't seem to have many friends and a girlfriend would be just the thing for him. That is, if he was into girls.

Once the thought crossed my mind, I began to wonder. I'd never seen Marshall with a girl, and he never talked about them. I wondered if he was just shy, or if he had a thing for guys. I'd never really thought about it before, mainly because it just didn't matter to me. Marshall was fairly good looking, but he didn't really do anything for me personally. I'd never had any sexual thoughts about him. I was sure Devlin and his crew would find that shocking; a gay boy who wasn't attracted to another boy.

We talked about ghosts on the way to the lake, that was our usual topic. I filled him in on my latest ghostly encounters and he told me more about the world of the supernatural. While we talked I stole a few glances at Marshall, wondering if he was straight or gay. I was getting some ideas in my head about hooking him up with someone, but I needed to know what kind of someone would interest him. I thought about just asking him straight out, but I was uncomfortable doing so, and Marshall probably would have been uncomfortable too.

Marshall was kind of backward and shy, so I figured that was why I'd never seen him with a girl. I wasn't quite sure however, so I didn't want to put him in a spot by introducing him to girls if he was into guys. I knew how uncomfortable that situation made me. It was something I no longer had to worry about, as everyone knew I was gay. No one tried to set me up with a girl, but it wasn't always that way. I understood only too well.

I gazed at Marshall, making some mental changes that would pull him into the twenty-first century. Yeah, I could get him fixed up without much trouble. It would just require a little alteration here and there.

I parked the car and we walked out onto the beach. I pulled my shirt off and tossed it on the sand. I loved to feel the hot sun beating down on my bare chest, even though being shirtless made me a little self-conscious. I liked watching all the other guys with their shirts off too. The beach was definitely my kind of place.

Marshall pulled off his shirt. I don't think I'd ever seen a boy who was so white before in my entire life. Taylor had a better tan than Marshall and he'd been dead for twenty years. I was a little pale myself because it was just then getting warm enough to get out into the sun, but Marshall looked like he had been bleached. His pasty white skin look particularly pale when compared to his jet black hair.

Marshall looked pretty good without a shirt regardless. He didn't have any muscle to speak of, but he had a nicely shaped, slim torso, with some pretty nice looking abs. A little work with some weights and he'd be looking fine. He already looked better than I did. Of course, that wasn't saying much in my opinion.

We swam for a while in the lake. The water was a little cool, but it would warm up soon enough. Summer hadn't even started. When the temperatures got up into the 80's and stayed there, the lake would be awesome. I was more than happy with it the way it was. I loved just being in the water. We stayed in for a good hour or more, swimming and just floating around.

My stomach was growling, so Marshall and I walked up to the little food stand and each ordered a hot dog and a soda. I liked mine with ketchup and just a little mustard and relish. Marshall put just about everything on his.

We sat at a picnic table and watched everyone while we ate. There was a pretty big crowd. I think everyone was just itching to get out since it was finally warm enough to do so. My eyes were roving all over the place. There were lots of good looking boys there, mostly high school guys. I especially liked checking out the wrestlers and the soccer players. Yeah I loved the beach!

Marshall looked like he was having a good time, which was the whole reason for us being there. Marshall definitely needed to get out more and get his nose out of all his books. I had nothing against reading, but the boy needed a life. He'd helped me out, so I was hoping to return the favor. Besides, I enjoyed his company and didn't mind getting away from my troubles for a while either.

We spent three hours at the beach; swimming, sunning, and just having a good time. Marshall didn't talk to anyone much, but he seemed to come out of his shell a little. I could tell he was enjoying himself, although he seemed rather tense at the same time. I think he just didn't quite know how to act around others. He was especially shy with girls. It was almost as if he was afraid of them or something. That was understandable, they were pretty mysterious at times. I was glad I didn't have to deal with them in the way most boys did. Being a gay boy did have a few advantages.

We tossed our stuff in the car and headed back to his house. We'd lingered at the beach most of the afternoon and it was time to find something else to do. I loved the beach, but I didn't want to stay there forever.

"Hey, after we change, you want to go get something to eat, then catch a movie?" I asked as I drove.

"Uh, yeah." said Marshall. He seemed more uncomfortable than ever. Something was clearly eating at him. He'd been a little edgy all afternoon.

I turned and looked at him.

"Marshall, what's wrong?"

He looked at me and I could read fear in his eyes.

"Look," he said. "I've had a lot of fun today and you're a really good friend, but I just…"

His words trailed off. I could tell he didn't want to finish the sentence. He didn't need to do so, I knew where he was headed. It also answered some of the questions I had about him.

"Marshall, you can relax. I'm not interested in you that way. I want us to be friends, that's all."

The tension flowed from his body right before my eyes. The look of relief on his face was almost amusing.

"It's not that I have anything against you being gay," he said. "It's just that I'm not. I like girls. I was afraid… Well, you've been looking at me a lot and I was just afraid you were getting some ideas in your head."

I smiled.

"No. No ideas. I promise."

"So you're not interested in me?"

"As a boyfriend, no."

"Why not?" he asked, almost as if it upset him. I actually laughed out loud. First he was worried that I had a thing for him, then it irritated him that I didn't.

"I'm sorry." I said, trying to stop laughing. I had no need to apologize, Marshall started laughing too. "Look, it's nothing against you. You are a good looking guy, you're just not quite my type. At least you aren't my type for a boyfriend. You are exactly my type for a friend however."

He smiled.

"But you were right. I was looking at you, but not for the reason you thought."

"Why then?" he asked.

"Interested in landing a girlfriend?" I said.

"Oh yeah! I sure am!" he said. "But I don't think I've got much of a chance. Girls don't give me a second look, or even a first one." The edge of depression in his voice saddened me, and made me more determined that ever to help him. After all, straight guys had problems too.

"I think we can change that." I said.

* * *

"I'm not so sure about this," said Marshall.

"Trust me." I told him as I pulled him into the Richard & Company Hair Salon.

Marshall was still hesitant, so Zoë and I pushed him from behind. I'd called Zoë from Marshall's house. I knew I'd need her help to transform him. We stuffed him into a seat and kept an eye on him so he couldn't escape. Zoë and I thumbed through some hairstyle magazines, determining Marshall's fate.

"Here," she said, pointing to a picture of a really cute guy with short hair, "how about this one?" It was the fifth time she'd said that.

"Yeah, that's it." I said, looking from the photo to Marshall and back again. Zoë's four previous suggestions didn't seem quite right for Marshall, but her last selection did.

The stylist came for Marshall, who looked like he was going to his execution instead of getting his hair cut. We showed the stylist the cut we thought would look good on Marshall and he agreed with our choice.

Zoë and I watched as Marshall's bushy hair fell victim to the clippers. Little by little, a whole new Marshall emerged. More than half an hour later, the stylist presented him for our inspection.

"Something's missing." said Zoë. Her eyes lit up and she looked at the stylist. "How about some highlights?"

Another forty-five minutes later and Marshall was done. His shorter, lighter hair gave him a whole new look. Zoë and I weren't finished with him yet however.

"Come on." said Zoë, as she grabbed Marshall by the hand and pulled him toward a clothing store.

Marshall stood there in a daze as Zoë and I picked out a new outfit for him. I was glad I'd asked Zoë to come. I knew what looked good, but I wasn't that much of a shopper. Zoë was a shopping prodigy. When we were done with Marshall, he was wearing a white lycra tank top and white mesh pants over white soccer shorts. We thought the all-white look would combat Marshall's former all-dark image. I was pleased with the result, Marshall looked good enough to date. I almost wished he was gay.

He wasn't quite done however. Zoë added a tan baseball cap and a gold chain that made Marshall look as sexy as could be. It was the first time that I'd ever thought that boy was sexy. We tried talking him into an earring, but he wouldn't go for it. We didn't press it, he'd changed enough for one day. Marshall was hot. He looked like he belonged on the pages of XY Magazine.

Chapter 17

Contact from Beyond the Grave

My eyes snapped open. I grabbed my watch from where I kept it at the side of the bed. It was 11:30 p.m., I'd been asleep for less than an hour. I had no idea what had awakened me, then I heard the whispering voices in the hall. I sat up, getting ready to leave my bed, but I had no need. The voices grew louder and more distinct. As I watched wide eyed, two ghostly figures passed through my door and came to stand at the foot of my bed. I wasn't afraid. It was Taylor and Mark.

"You have a lot of questions," said Mark. The clarity of his voice and the ease with which he spoke surprised me. He sounded just like any living person, except he wasn't, he'd been dead for twenty years. He'd be an eighteen year old for all eternity.

I just looked at them both for a moment, in a kind of shock. Even with all I'd already seen, it just didn't seem like what was happening could be real. It was just too wild and unbelievable. Had anyone else told me it had happened to them, I would not have believed it. I couldn't argue with my own senses however. It was too incredible to be true, but it was true. The boys standing before me were quite real, if bluish gray and somewhat transparent. I did note that they looked more solid than before.

"Yes." I said, finally finding my voice. "I need to talk to Marty."

"Marty?" asked Taylor. His questioning tone disturbed me. I guess I expected him to automatically know everything, and everyone who had ever died. It was clear that he did not.

"Yes, my friend, someone killed him. I need to know who. I need to talk to Marty. Please."

Mark looked as if he were concentrating for a moment, like he was searching with his mind, or communicating silently with someone I could not see.

"I'm afraid we can't help you with that." said Mark. "Marty has gone on."

"But I need to talk to him!" I said. "I've worked so hard to reach him, to reach you. There's no other way to find out who killed him!"

"I'm sorry," said Taylor. I could tell he genuinely regretted not being able to help me.

Tears formed in my eyes and I started to cry. I'd come so far, the impossible had happened, and then, just when I was on the verge of contacting Marty, it all collapsed.

"Can't you find him?" I asked, wiping the tears from my eyes.

"No." said Mark. "We cannot. He was here, but he has gone on."

"What does that mean? Gone on?"

"It means he has passed on to where he belongs. He has gone to his life."

"I don't understand. You are speaking in riddles."

"No." said Mark. "I'm merely stating it in the best way possible for you to understand. There aren't really words to describe it."

"Well, if he's gone on, can't you go and get him? Or take a message to him?"

"He hasn't gone to a place," said Taylor. "He's gone to his life. It's not a place as you know it. We cannot reach him."

"Why not? Are you trapped here? Are you doomed to walk the halls of this old mansion forever?"

"No." said Taylor. He smiled. "You've been reading too many of your friend's ghost books. We are not trapped, nor doomed, we are in our life, we are where we belong."

I could not quite comprehend what they meant, but it was clear I could not contact Marty through them.

"Can I reach Marty? Have another séance or something? There's got to be a way."

"There is only one way for you to reach him," said Mark. "But you must not follow that path."

"What way? Why not?"

"To reach him you must die. You must give up the rest of your life in your world. It is not something you should do."

"Well," I said, "I don't mean to be rude, but isn't it a little hypocritical of you to be saying that. I know both of you killed yourselves."

"We did," said Taylor, "and it was a mistake. By ending our lives we cheated ourselves of the lives we could have led. We threw away many years that we could have lived in your world together. Once done, suicide cannot be undone. We cannot go back."

"But you did escape from your problems that way." I said. "There is that."

"Not really," said Mark. "We escaped from our situation. The problems remained. What you must understand is that suicide in not an ending, it's not an escape. The soul is eternal and those who kill themselves will go on having the same problems they had in life."

"You're talking about hell? Being trapped forever in something horrible?"

"Not at all." said Mark. "Hell does not exist as you understand it. There is no place the evil go after death to be punished forever. Our lives, yours, everyone's is a product of our thoughts and actions. We are what we say and do. If we mistreat others, bring harm to them, we thereby harm ourselves. We create our own hell and suffer in it, until we cease to harm others and free ourselves. Those whom you would consider evil are in their own hell, not after death, but while they are still alive. Their actions create it and only by learning not to do harm can they escape."

"So both of you are experiencing the same pain you did in life. You didn't escape from it?"

"As I said, we escaped from our situation, we did not escape from our problems. Our problem was dealing with those around us, with living our lives as we knew they should be lived despite what others thought of us. Those problems came with us, but we have learned much since that time. Those problems no longer plague us, not because we escaped them with death, but because we have learned and have dealt with them. We have passed beyond them."

Their words were somewhat hard to understand. I felt like I was in some kind of advanced philosophy or theology class. I was able to grasp at least a part of it however.

"Life after what you call death is wondrous beyond your ability to imagine," said Taylor. "But do not be in a hurry to embrace it. It will come of its own. Everyone dies. By ending your life early you only cheat yourself of the life you could have had before death and harm everyone you leave behind. Everyone will experience death, and what comes after, so why hurry?"

I saw his point in that. Death was a sure thing. I felt myself growing a little at ease. I felt that Marty was safe. It did nothing to help me with my task however.

"Why can't I communicate with Marty when I can communicate with you? I mean, you're right here in my bedroom!"

"That's just it." said Taylor. "Your life and ours overlap the same space. We exist where you do, in this house, in this town. Our world is very similar to that we lived in during our 'lives'. For others, the difference may be very great. The séance you and your friends performed opened a doorway, so to speak, that broke down the barriers between our world and yours, but Marty's world is not the same. You cannot reach his world from yours because they do not overlap."

What he was saying didn't quite seem to make sense and yet I knew he was telling the truth.

"Then it was all for nothing." I said, downcast.

"Not for nothing." said Taylor. "Mark and I can't reach Marty, but we can watch, observe. We can be places you cannot and observe things without being seen. Perhaps we can learn something that will help you find out who killed your friend."

"When Marshall finds out about this, he'll want to do another séance for sure." I said.

"No!" said Mark. "Tell Marshall that he must not attempt another séance. Your friend does not know what he is doing. He is messing with something far more dangerous than he realizes. He has come very close to disaster already. If he attempts it again he may well unleash something that is far beyond his control."

His tone was such it put fear in my heart. I had a feeling I didn't want to know more. Instead of asking questions about it, I took Mark at his word.

I told Taylor and Mark all I knew about Marty and his death. I told them also about the death of Ken and how I suspected there might be a link between the two. I showed them my notes, and the file of newspaper clippings on Marty. As we worked I found myself forgetting how fantastic the whole situation was. I was working with two ghosts as if they were guys from my high school!

I laughed to myself. I guess they were from my high school. It was just that they had went to school there twenty years or so before. I looked at them, wondering what it was like to never age. Despite everything, I envied them.

When I was done, both boys looked thoughtful.

"We cannot promise anything," said Taylor, "but we will watch and see what we can see. We will return."

With that they faded into nothingness as if they had never been. I crawled into bed and fell fast asleep.

Chapter 18

Skater Boy

The next morning, I almost thought the whole thing had been a dream. I knew it wasn't however. Even if I had believed it a dream, the papers spread all over my desk were evidence that I'd shown the ghosts all my work. No one else, except Marshall of course, would ever believe it, but that didn't matter. All that mattered was finding out who had killed my friends.

As I showered and dressed, I thought about what Taylor and Mark had told me. It was quite a lot to absorb. I felt like I'd been exposed to something that was far beyond my comprehension. It was the same way I felt when I tried to comprehend God, or the nature of the universe, or infinity. It seemed like it was just beyond me. I guessed that I needed to just take what I could understand and work with that. That's the best anyone could do. That's what we all really did with life.

I knew I could ponder the conversation of the night before forever and never come any closer to comprehending it, so I quit thinking about it for the moment. I grabbed my things and walked to Marshall's house. I wanted to catch him before he left. I wanted to be with him when he walked into school. I was curious to see how others would react to him. I arrived just as he was coming out the door. He was dressed in the clothes that Zoë and I had picked out for him.

"I don't know about this," he said.

"You'll be fine." I said. "You look great. I'm starting to wish you weren't straight."

He laughed. I was glad he was comfortable around me and didn't get all uptight over what I said. Some guys would have freaked. I did find Marshall rather attractive with his new look, but he had nothing to worry about from me. My mission was to help him land a girl. Besides, I understood the number one gay rule—never fall in love with a straight boy.

I told Marshall about my visitation from Taylor and Mark. He instantly forgot all about his worries over his new look. He must have asked me a hundred questions before we made it to school.

Once there, I could read apprehension in his face. I looked at him and gave him a reassuring smile. He smiled back, but I knew he was not quite at ease.

"Hey guys!" Zoë greeted us almost before we got through the door. I knew she'd be hanging around, waiting to see what happened with Marshall. Both of us were rather curious.

Marshall was getting a lot of looks. Most of our classmates gazed at him as if seeing him for the first time. Others looked as if they couldn't believe that the cute guy before their eyes was Marshall. I saw a few girls give him the eye. Marshall saw it too and smiled shyly. He looked really cute when he did that and it earned him even more attention from the girls. I noticed Tony looking him over too. Tony was a freshman and gay. It seemed that everyone had taken notice of Marshall. Zoë and I had done our work well. I made a mental note to tell Tony he was wasting his time if he had any plans for Marshall.

I really knew Marshall would be okay when Becky and Kate approached and started talking to him. Kate was smiling sweetly and twirling her hair with one finger. Marshall looked like he'd just fallen in love. I had a feeling he'd be wrapped around Kate's little finger before the day was done. It was the curse of straight boys, being controlled by girls.

I silently withdrew, feeling very good about Marshall. Zoë departed as well, but she didn't seem so happy. I wasn't quite sure, but I think I detected a little jealousy in her eyes. I wondered if she was falling for her own creation. It was an interesting thought.

*   *   *

I had done my good deed with Marshall and, that very same day, I had some fun of my own. Kyle stopped me between classes and asked if I had time to go roller-blading with him after school. I was a bit hesitant because Kyle was a kick-ass roller-blader and my skills were far less advanced. I was a little concerned over letting him observe my ineptitude. I wasn't about to let that stop me however. I'd have went if I knew nothing about it at all. I'd have probably gone skydiving if it meant that I could be near Kyle.

I met Kyle in the parking lot after school and we jumped into his little red pickup truck. We dropped by his house, then mine, picking up our pads and roller-blades. Kyle came out wearing a pair of purple and gray soccer shorts and a black shirt that made him look like the hottest boy on the planet. I had to fight to keep myself from staring at him. It was a fight that I lost more often than not. While I was grabbing up my stuff, I changed into my black soccer shorts and red shirt that I knew looked really good on me. I wanted to look nice around Kyle.

We drove out to Koontz Lake because there was a great place to roller-blade there and it was much less crowded than it was in town. It was a Tuesday, so there wasn't a big crowd at the lake, only a few people swimming and no one at all roller-blading.

Kyle stopped the truck and we climbed out with our gear. He let down the tailgate and we sat on it while we put on our blades and pads. Before putting on his elbow pads Kyle removed his shirt. My eyes were glued to his chest until I realized what I was doing. He looked especially hot after he put his elbow pads on. I don't know what it was about it, but he looked so sexy wearing those pads and no shirt. Just looking at him made me weak in the knees.

I kept my shirt on. I didn't have the build Kyle did and I was more than a little hesitant to let him see me shirtless. I hated being pudgy. Kyle hopped up and took off like a flash. That boy was a roller-blading stud. I followed him soon after, but I was no match for him. There was nothing wrong with my abilities, but he was awesome!

Kyle didn't leave me behind however. We raced side by side and skated in circles around one another. We did a lot of jumps as well. That's something that I needed some practice with, but I did pretty well. Kyle could not only jump, but turn all the way around in the air while he was doing it. I was thoroughly impressed.

I spent a lot of my time checking out Kyle from every possible angle. I just couldn't tear my eyes away from his chest, his abs, his shoulders, or his arms. I did a lot of looking at his cute little butt as well. Kyle filled me with desire, fueling my already raging passions. So far my only sexual activity with anyone had been that kiss at the dance with Marty and what had happened with Ken before that. I wanted more, much more, and I was getting tired of waiting.

We skated for more than an hour, getting all hot and sweaty. Kyle looked real good with streams of sweat running down his torso and into his shorts. I wished I had a few hundred pictures of him looking like that! We finally stopped and took off our blades. We were both over-heated. Kyle ran for the lake and jumped in. I pulled my shirt off and joined him, hoping he wouldn't notice that I wasn't as trim and firm as him.

The place was practically deserted, so we could pretty much do what we wanted. We swam and wrestled in the water, having a great time. Being able to touch Kyle's firm, young body, however briefly, sent me to new heights of arousal.

After several minutes of fooling around in the lake, we stood facing each other, waist high in the cool, gentle waves. We were mere inches apart. Kyle's lips beckoned to me. He was so attractive that I just could not resist him a moment longer. I leaned in toward him closer and closer.

Kyle put his hand on my chest and stopped me. He looked around the beach. I did too then and wondered what I'd been thinking. There weren't too many people around, but we were not alone. Anyone who happened to look could have seen what we were doing. Had I kissed Kyle, everyone could have seen it. It was well known I was gay, but I didn't usually go around kissing guys in public. Kyle was not a known gay boy, so I could understand his hesitance completely.

We swam some more after that. I had a lot of energy to burn. To be honest, I was so aroused and hyped up that I think I could have pushed the truck home. Kyle seemed filled with energy as well. I smiled thinking that he might be just as aroused as me.

We left perhaps an hour later. I had a secret hope that Kyle would pull off the road somewhere and kiss me passionately. I had a little daydream about us making out right there in his truck. It didn't happen however and he let me out at my house just a few minutes later. It had been a wonderful afternoon however. My mind was filled with images of Kyle's sexy little body. I had a feeling I'd get a chance to do more than just look pretty soon and that made me happy enough to just about walk on air.

Despite my urgent need for sexual activity, I was very selective. There were very few guys that I'd be willing to do anything with. Kyle was one of the few however. I wanted him and I wanted him bad. All Kyle had to do was ask and I'd be his. I felt a little weak around him. I had a feeling he could control me if he wanted. I think I'd have been willing to do just about anything Kyle wanted. I hoped he'd try something with me soon. If he didn't, I planned on trying something with him. I'd make sure to pick a more appropriate location than a public beach however. That hadn't been such a bright idea. The next time I put the moves on Kyle, I'd do it when no one could see us.

Chapter 19

The Murderer Unmasked

After Kyle took me home, I showered and did my homework. After that I went over all the details of Marty's death again, but I just couldn't turn up anything new. I also reread everything that I had gathered concerning Ken's death, but I couldn't come up with anything new there either. I was learning first hand how most of the detective shows on television were not very realistic at all. Things just didn't work out in the real world like they did on TV. I had a feeling I'd never get anywhere. As it turned out however, I had nothing to worry about.

I turned on the television at the very beginning of the ten o'clock news. The story was one about another death, but this time the situation was entirely different. A reporter was standing outside the county jail speaking into a microphone. I turned up the sound to hear better.

"...Apparently committed suicide by hanging himself with a sheet earlier today in the county jail. Guards discovered the body less than an hour ago. Rev. Devlin was the leader of the controversial "God Hates Queers" group that pickets gay activities all over the country and has been active in recent weeks in Verona. He was arrested early this morning in a police raid on his motel room in Verona. Rev. Devlin was arrested as the primary suspect in the murder of sixteen-year-old Ken Clark. Police report that a list including Clark's name and those of other gay youth were found in Devlin's hotel room."

"Was there any other evidence found that linked Devlin to Clark's murder?" asked the news anchor.

"Police aren't commenting on that at this time, but they did perform a thorough search of Devlin's motel room and removed several items as evidence. At least some of the items have been sent for testing. The police are hoping to come up with DNA evidence that will conclusively link Devlin to the murder of Ken Clark."

The report went on for a bit more, but said nothing of importance. The details didn't matter. Ken's murderer had been discovered and I had little doubt that the same guy had killed Marty. I sat back on the edge of my bed in silence. I was glad that I knew at last who had killed Marty, but part of me felt a little disappointed that I hadn't been the one to figure it out. Of course, that was stupid, it didn't matter who solved the murders, as long as they were solved.

Of course, nothing had really been proven yet, but the suicide of the main suspect was pretty good proof in itself. Why would that guy kill himself if he wasn't guilty? I was glad he was dead. I hated that bastard. He deserved death. Too bad he hadn't died before he'd killed two innocent boys. Maybe he'd even killed more. Who knew? He could have been killing for years. A lot of people had trusted Devlin. A lot of people were fooled by him. They really believed he was what he pretended to be, a man of God. It was the perfect disguise for one so evil. What better way to wreck havoc than to fool others into believing they were performing the work of the Lord when they were really doing quite the opposite.

I wondered if Devlin had used his position to get at those boys. It would have made it easier for him to lure them to their deaths. Who would suspect such a thing of a religious leader? Who would suspect that the man they saw on television all the time preaching would be a murderer? There was implicit trust there, trust that Devlin had betrayed.

I was not a violent person, but I really think I could have killed that bastard myself. What kind of monster murdered people like that? The way he posed as a man of God made it that much worse. The hypocrisy of it was too much to bear.

I wasn't surprised at all that it was one of the "God Hates Queers" group that was the murderer. I'd suspected all along that it was those bastards that had done it. I didn't forget either that three sets of footprints were unaccounted for at the site of Ken's murder. Rev. Devlin was not working alone. Surely now however the police would be able to get to the bottom of it all. More arrests were sure to follow.

I was left with a lot of questions, but at least one of the murderers had been found. I didn't think it would be too long before the others were discovered. My task was done.

I walked downstairs to get something to drink. All was quiet. My parents were actually at home for once, but they had already gone to bed. The house was so big that I felt like I was all alone even when they were home.

I poured a glass of ice water and sipped it. Water was always a lot better when it was cold. I spied a plate of chocolate chip cookies sitting on the table, but I didn't take one. I was trying to get myself into shape and lose a little weight and a cookie would not help. I did want a cookie, but I wanted even more to look good. The better I looked, the better chance I had at guys like Kyle.

I walked back up the stairway, holding my oil lamp at my side. I'd grown quite accustomed to using oil lamps and candles for light. Sometimes I felt like I lived in the past.

As I reached the landing on the third floor, I caught sight of movement just above me. I looked up and saw Edward and William quietly creeping up to the fourth floor. I could tell they were taking great care not to make any noise. I knew I was probably seeing a replay of past events. I must have been seeing something they did long, long ago. Graymoor seemed to be some kind of library of moments from the past.

I followed them. I was intrigued by the whole situation between Edward and William. I wasn't about to miss out on anything I had the chance to see.

They led me to the attic stair. I was right behind them as they ascended. Edward was carrying an oil lamp. I got the strangest feeling when I looked at it closely. It looked exactly like the one I carried and I had no doubt it was the very same one. Nothing ever changed at Graymoor. Nothing was ever thrown out. Anything that had ever been there was there still.

Both boys were in their nightshirts. They seemed to be about sixteen years old, so I guessed what I was seeing hadn't happened too long before the murders, within the same year at least. I'd seen the boys several times in Graymoor, at all different ages. The first time they were sixteen or so, the next time about ten or eleven, then fourteen, then six. I kept seeing little bits and pieces of their lives being replayed. It was a little confusing, like a story all out of order. It was like someone had taken a film, cut it into little pieces, tossed most of it away, and then spliced the pieces back together in no certain order. All I saw was random bits of their lives. It was often hard to tell what had happened when.

I followed them into the attic. They stood just a few feet from me. I stepped closer to them. I spoke, but they showed no sign they could hear. I always spoke when I saw them and they never reacted. I had come to believe that all I had seen of them was some kind of replay of the past, or maybe past time intruding on the present like Marshall had explained to me. Either way, I could see them, but they couldn't see me. It made me feel faintly like a peeping Tom, but I couldn't stop myself. It was just too fascinating.

I moved in really close and got a real good look at the Graymoor boys. They were both quite attractive, but they didn't really look anything at all alike. They were both about the same height, but their features were vastly different. Edward had rather delicate features, while William had a strong, squared jaw. It was hard to tell with their bluish-gray appearance, but it looked like William's hair was quite a bit lighter than Edward's. I had no doubt they weren't true brothers. That brought up intriguing possibilities. I wondered what I would have done if a boy my age was living with me.

I had the feeling I'd have done just as they were doing. Edward pulled William to him and kissed him passionately, right on the lips. He leaned back and looked into William's eyes and I could read the love there. They kissed again. Suddenly it began to feel a lot warmer up in that attic.

I would have been shocked by seeing those two boys kiss, but I'd suspected for some time that there was something between them. The bits of conversation I'd picked up as I watched their murders replayed seemed to indicate that their father had caught them doing something sexual together. This was the first time I'd actually had my suspicions confirmed however.

My eyes were glued to the boys as they pulled off their nightshirts. Edward had a firm, smooth build. He was beautiful. William had a much more muscular build, as if he'd done a lot of manual labor. If he was from my time, I would have assumed he worked out with weights, but I didn't think they had weight machines in the nineteenth century. William was down right hot. I must admit I was completely aroused as I watch those two boys make out right before me. Their hands wandered over their bodies, making me breath faster.

Just as it was getting really interesting, they faded away before my eyes. To say I was disappointed would be quite an understatement. I stood there for a good long while, hoping they'd reappear, but they never did. The show was over.

I felt a little self-conscious getting turned on by ghosts. I remembered too that both Edward and William were over a hundred years older than I. Talk about having a thing for an older guy! I laughed to myself.

It was interesting to think that there were boys like me more than a hundred years before. Of course, I knew there had always been boys like me, even hundreds and hundreds of years in the past. Actually getting a glimpse of two of them was something else however. It made it all much more real.

Marshall had said something had gone on up in the attic, and that it wasn't something tragic, just intense. I wondered if he'd picked up Edward and William making love there. From the little I saw, I knew that things were pretty intense between them. If only I could have someone like that! I returned to my room and went to bed. That night I dreamed dreams of the Graymoor boys. I wished I could have dreams like that every night.

Chapter 20

Back to Square One

I awakened the next morning feeling very rested. For the first time in a long time I could think about something besides murder. The day was bright and hot and I found myself wishing I could escape to the beach instead of going to school. There would be plenty of time for that however. The entire summer was still ahead.

I even felt lighter as I walked to school, as if some great weight had been lifted from my shoulders. I felt as if I could just be a boy again, instead of some kind of detective. I was glad it was all over. I hadn't been that good of a detective anyway.

The first thing I saw when I walked into school was Kate hanging all over Marshall, or rather Kate and Marshall hanging all over each other. Zoë walked up to me and we watched as the pair passionately kissed.

"I'm beginning to think everyone has someone but us." I said. Thoughts of Kyle sprung into my mind.

"No kidding," said Zoë. "Now why can't we do for ourselves what we did for Marshall?"

"Ah, we'll find someone. Wanna walk around and check out cute guys after school?" I asked. "We'll share, you can have the straight ones and I'll take the gay ones."

Zoë punched me in the shoulder.

"You're terrible!"

"Yeah! So, you wanna?"

"Okay." she laughed. She stopped and looked at me for a moment.

"It's just too bad you don't like girls," she said. "Maybe it's true, maybe all the cute guys are gay."

"Me? Cute?" I said.

"Yeah you!"

"I don't believe you for a moment, but I'm going to pretend I do. Come on, I'll walk you to class and you can tell me more about how cute you think I am."

Zoë was a really good friend. She almost made me wish I did like girls. That would probably have only messed up our friendship however, so things were probably better as they were. Zoë knew I couldn't possibility be attracted to her, so there was no hidden agenda in my mind. I wasn't secretly lusting after her body. Everything between us was true and genuine. We walked away leaving Marshall and his new girl to paw each other. I took one last look at them, wishing I could get Kyle to touch me like that.

*   *   *

Zoë and I met up right after school. We headed for the park where most of the high school kids tended to hang out. It was a wonderfully warm afternoon. I loved warm days because a lot of guys took their shirts off then. A young shirtless male was one of the sights I truly enjoyed. It was one of the likes that Zoë and I shared.

We walked around the park and there was some pretty fine scenery, and I'm not talking about the trees and flowers. Yeah, it was my kind of day and my kind of place! After a while we sat on a sunny hillside overlooking the volleyball courts. There were plenty of hot guys to look at. I chose to sit there mainly because Jimmy Riester was close by. Jimmy was, unfortunately, a straight boy, but he was so fine. I could have gazed at his chest all day long. Zoë seemed to like looking at him too. I felt just a touch jealous, at least she had a chance with him. She didn't have to steal glances like I did either. She could look right at him if she wanted. Who knew? Maybe he'd even notice her looking and it would lead to something.

Zoë struck up a conversation with him and the others sitting there. She knew him a lot better than I did. If I was her, I'd have definitely been making a play for him. I wondered if that was what she had planned.

"Did you hear about that preacher guy?" said Austin, who was sitting on the other side of Jimmy.

"Yeah." said Jimmy. "They arrested him for killing Ken."

"Well yeah, but that's not it. Now they think he didn't do it."

That got my attention real fast.

"What have you heard?" I said.

"Ah man, it was all over the news. He was one sick bastard. They were looking for murder evidence and they found all this child pornography shit. There were all these pictures of naked kids, and I mean little kids, like seven or eight."

"Ewwww" said Zoë. "I'm gonna be sick."

"Yeah, well the guy was a total freak They found all these e-mails on his computer to kids all over the place. He was some kind of child molester or something."

"Man, they ought to just take someone like that out and shoot him," said Jimmy. "That is so fucking sick."

"Guess he saved them the trouble." said Austin, then mimicked someone hanging on a rope with his tongue hanging out. Everyone laughed.

"That's not even all," said Austin. "The F.B.I. is investigating that whole group of his. Apparently that Devlin guy wasn't the only one into that shit. They're like a cult or something. The news said that the police even found a bunch of Neo-Nazi shit in Devlin's hotel room. Apparently he was some kind of leader of the Neo-Nazi movement. It's all over the television."

My mind was reeling, with disgust to be sure, but also with the knowledge that Marty's murder wasn't solved at all. I was right back where I'd started less than a day after I thought the whole thing was over.

The Neo-Nazi link really didn't surprise me all that much. The whole "God Hates Queers" group seemed like a bunch of Nazis to me. It was pretty scary knowing that such a group was operating right in Verona. The Neo-Nazi movement was some pretty serious shit. It seemed almost impossible that a group so filled with hate could even exist. I was even more fearful of the "God Hates Queers" group than I had been before.

I left pretty soon after Austin had filled us in on all he'd heard. I didn't feel like checking out cute boys as much after that. Marty's murderer was still out there and the connection between the murders, the "God Hates Queers" group, and the Neo-Nazis made everything seem so much more sinister than it had been before. I couldn't believe all this was happening in Verona, the world's most boring little town.

I made sure I was home in time for the six o'clock news. It confirmed everything that Austin had said. Apparently the only link between Devlin and the murders was the list of known gay boys. No one really knew what that meant, but it didn't prove anything on its own. The authorities weren't coming up with any other connections between the murders and Devlin. As horrible a man as he was, it was beginning to look like he wasn't the murderer. I suspected that someone within his group was however.

Within a few days the reports came back from the crime lab and there was no DNA evidence to link Devlin to the murder of Ken; no blood, no DNA traces, no nothing. If Devlin had killed Ken, there would have had to have been some DNA evidence of it, some trace, but there was none. Apparently Devlin was one sick bastard, but he was innocent of the murders. It made my skin crawl to think that my name was probably on that list found in his hotel room. There was no telling what that sicko was up to. As more and more details came out it was clear he'd molested a lot of kids, both boys and girls. He hadn't murdered my friend, but I was sure glad he was dead.

Chapter 21

The Third Loss

After the whole Devlin story came out into the open, I got back to work trying to figure out who had killed Marty. About the only conclusion I could reach was that I sucked as a detective. I couldn't come up with shit. I racked my brains, went over and over the details, and still came up with nothing.

I'd been going over all my notes one afternoon for what seemed like hours. It couldn't have been nearly that long however since it was barely five. I pushed my notes to the side. I needed to escape from reality for a while, so I turned on my television. The batteries were getting weak again. I'd be thrilled when Graymoor was brought into the twenty-first century. I guess it didn't really matter too much. There wasn't much reason to watch the news any more, it rarely had anything to offer.

I did not find escape in the world of television however. Reality was there waiting on me, ready to pounce. The first thing I saw on the screen were police cars and an ambulance. A reporter was trying to get information from an officer, without much success. She turned back to the camera.

"Police aren't releasing the name of the victim until family members are contacted." she said. "But authorities have confirmed that the victim was a young male, approximately fifteen years old, and the case is being treated as a homicide. This is the second murder of a youth in the last three weeks and, although authorities won't comment on any possible connection, the similarities between the two cases indicate that Verona may be dealing with a serial killer. I'm Karen Hopkins for WMAR News."

"To recap," said the anchor, "a teen male has been found dead only a few hundred yards from Verona Park. Witnesses who discovered the body say the victim as severely beaten and left for dead. The victim was alive at the time of discovery but lost consciousness and died before paramedics could arrive. This is the second beating death of a young man in less than a month. Authorities are advising that anyone under the age of eighteen not go out alone and they have also announced that the town's 11 p.m. curfew for those aged eighteen and under will be strictly enforced."

I sat down on the bed, wondering who had been killed. A great fear arose in my heart and I ran downstairs and out of the house. I ran all the way to Marshall's house. I was so relieved when I saw him that I felt like hugging him. For some reason a feeling had entered my head that it was Marshall who was dead. I was glad to be wrong.

"Did you hear what happened?" I asked.

"No." said Marshall confused. I filled him in on everything. Together we wondered who had been killed this time. Chances were, we knew him. I had such an eerie feeling as I waited to found out the identity of the victim. Which one of my classmates was dead? Which one would I never see again?

A new fear entered my head. I grabbed the phone and called Kyle. He answered on the second ring. I was relieved to hear his voice. I had feared that maybe he was the one who had been killed. Not knowing was driving me crazy. He wasn't aware of what had happened either so

I gave him all the details I knew. I hung up the phone, glad that at least it wasn't Marshall or Kyle who had been beaten to death.

I had always thought Verona was the most boring place in the universe. I was beginning to wish that it was. The short string of deaths was certainly exciting, but it was excitement no one wanted. I wondered when it would all end.

The phone rang. I knew without asking that Marshall was talking to a girl. I could read the excitement in his features. He just kind of lit up when he answered the phone. The way he smiled and his laugh gave him away too.

"It's Kate," he mouthed to me. I figured as much. No surprise there.

"Um, I'd like to, but Sean's here." he said.

"Sean is leaving." I said out loud. "You go have fun."

"Kate says 'hi' Sean."

"Hey Kate." I said. "See ya later Marshall."

"Later dude, and thanks."

I winked at Marshall and left. At least something was going right.

*   *   *

I finished my homework, then lifted weights, waiting on the ten o'clock news to start. I'd been working out for weeks and finally it seemed to be making a difference. At least I had shoulders and biceps anyway. I was far from my goal, but at least I wasn't the slouch that I had been. I had a fairly decent build, but I wanted to look more like some of the guys I saw at school, I wanted to be built. I was still too pudgy.

I looked at my bare torso in the mirror, flexing my muscles. I'd definitely made some improvements, but I wasn't where I wanted to be. I wasn't even close. I looked at my abs. I still needed to drop a few more pounds. I certainly wasn't what I'd call fat, but I wasn't slim either. I felt kind of awkward where my body was concerned. I sometimes wondered if another guy would ever find me attractive. Then again, Kyle seemed interested. If a boy that cute was interested, then there was definitely hope.

I'd become more and more concerned about whether or not other guys would find me attractive as time went by. My body had become a mass of raging hormones and I felt sure that I'd just explode any day. It made me feel just a touch wicked, but I was eager to dispose of my virginity. The truth was that there were things I just couldn't wait to try. I was primed and ready for action. I was a sexual hurricane just waiting to engulf some cute boy.

Despite my desperate and overwhelming need, I wasn't going to waste my first time on just anyone. I wasn't just going to meet up with some guy for the sole purpose of getting it on. Sometimes I felt like it however. Sometimes I felt like just grabbing some cute boy, or not so cute boy, and ravishing his body.

Even more than that, I dreamed about some cute boy grabbing me and going crazy on my body. I wanted to be touched, groped, fondled. I wanted to be loved and to make love.

I forced myself to think of other things. I was just getting myself excited. I was getting myself all worked up. It was a kind of self torture I put myself through almost daily. I guess it was just part of being a gay boy in a small town. I had strong needs and few ways to satisfy them. Sometimes I really envied guys who lived in larger towns outside the Midwest. At least they wouldn't have to die virgins.

Finally the news came on and the murder was the lead story. I watched my little television closely as the anchorman told me what I already knew and I saw the same footage I had earlier in the day. It didn't take long to get to some new details however.

"The victim was fifteen year old Tony Paulik of Verona. He was found bound and gagged approximately ten yards into a wooded site near Verona Park. He died shortly after he was discovered. The cause of death was massive internal bleeding from a severe beating with a baseball bat that was found not far from the body. Police could find no fingerprints on the murder weapon and are still looking for further evidence at the crime scene. This is the second murder of a Verona youth in three weeks and authorities...."

The report wandered into areas I'd heard earlier in the day. I tuned it out as I thought about Tony. I knew him, although he was a little younger than me. I knew something important about him too. Something that made me sure his murder was connected to Ken's. Tony was gay.

I had worked Tony through the whole coming out process just a few months before, much as I had Marty more recently. Tony was a great kid, but had been very afraid of telling his parents about his homosexuality. He was both surprised and relieved to find that they were so accepting and supportive. Even his older brother Dan, who tended to pick on him, had shown the same acceptance and supportiveness as his parents. That had come as a surprise to me. Prior to his little brother's coming out, Dan had been rather an outspoken opponent of "fags" and used the term "gay" as a general put down in every possible situation. He'd even given me some trouble and referred to be as "the fairy boy". Both Tony and I had worried a great deal about his reaction, but he really came through for his little brother when he needed him the most.

Things had worked out so well for Tony. He probably came out with greater ease than just about anyone. His family, his friends, everyone had been very supportive. There were a few jerks at school that called him names of course, but overall, he'd come out with little trouble. Now he was dead. I wondered what kind of monster would do that to such a nice boy. It certainly wasn't Devlin, his own death eliminated him as a suspect in this murder at least.

I pulled myself out of my own thoughts as the news report came to some interesting details.

"Authorities strongly suspect a connection between this homicide and the murder of Ken Clark earlier this month. The method used was almost identical and a similar note was found pinned to the victim. In the earlier murder a note reading "God Hates Queers" was found. In today's murder, the same phrase was repeated along with the message "The righteous will not rest until all fags are exterminated."

"Fifteen year old Tony was a known homosexual, having admitted it openly to friends and family a few months prior to his death. This fact, along with the notes, gives authorities a clear cut motive for the murders. Someone is killing the gay boys of Verona.

"The prime suspects for the murders are members of a fanatical religious group from Colorado that have taken it upon themselves to preach against homosexuality. Their catch phrase 'God Hates Queers' was found on the notes attached to both murder victims and, as seen in this footage, several members of group have displayed signs with the same message while picketing the funerals of local gay youth. It has recently been discovered that members of this group are connected with the Neo-Nazi movement here in the United States. Five members of the group have also been arrested on charges of child pornography and child molestation.

"The leader of the group was arrested earlier this month as a suspect in the death of Ken Clark, but no conclusive evidence was discovered.

"The group has been observed picketing in many areas of the country and has twice appeared in Verona at the funerals of the previous murder victim and that of sixteen year old Marty Crawford."

The mention of Marty's name really got my attention. I listened attentively, praying that my batteries would hold out.

"In related news, authorities have begun to investigate the death of Marty Crawford as a homicide. Previously believed to have been a gun related suicide, the case was reopened due to the similarities between Marty and the other victims. Marty had admitted his homosexuality just one day before he was found dead near Verona High School. The local coroner has released a statement that, upon close examination of evidence gathered at the time of death, the gun wound that was thought to have been self inflicted was in fact inflicted by a second individual."

"It's about time!" I said out loud. At last things were beginning to move. I was sure glad I'd told Ken's dad about what me and Ken had discovered. Maybe now there was a chance to figure out who had killed Marty. The report went on to mention how Marty had not been beaten to death, but that the other similarities strongly indicated that he had been murdered by the same individual or individuals as Ken and Tony.

The link between the murders was good news as far as solving the case was concerned, but it added a new sense of urgency. Someone was killing the gay boys of Verona and if they weren't stopped soon someone else would die. Being open about being gay had become a dangerous thing in Verona. I must admit that I was more than a little afraid.

I worried not only about the deaths, but about the effect all this would have on those who had not yet come out. I know that if I was a gay boy still hiding what I was, that I'd think long and hard before admitting my homosexuality. On top of all the other reasons to fear coming out, it had just become a possible death sentence too.

Things had changed however. The authorities were aggressively going after the case and the town was in an uproar. I knew there were those that wouldn't care about the murders because the victims were gay, but from what I saw on the news, most people were appalled. It made me feel good that the people in Verona were supportive and not just willing to sweep the whole thing under the rug.

I was pulled away from my thoughts when I realized I wasn't alone in the room. I looked up to see Taylor standing before me. I smiled and Taylor smiled back at me. Never in a million years would I have thought I'd be so at ease around a ghost. Of course, never in a million years did I ever think I'd actually meet one.

"It's happened again." I said, indicating the television screen where the report continued.

"Yes. I know." I could tell by the look on Taylor's face that he was truly sorry.

"We've got to put an end to this." I said.

"You'll get no argument from me." said Taylor. "I wish Mark and I could be more help. We have been keeping an eye on things, but we can't be everywhere at once. Maybe if we'd been there, we could have done something."

I could tell Taylor was quite upset about the recent murder. It was almost as if he were blaming himself for it.

"And if I'd been there, maybe I could have done something" I said. "If some of Tony's friends had been there, maybe they could have stopped it. You can't beat yourself up for this. Like you said, you can't be everywhere at once."

"I know." said Taylor.

"So let's concentrate on what we can do. The two of us feeling sorry isn't going to help Tony, or whoever is next."

"You could be next," said Taylor.

"I've been thinking about that, believe me."

"Maybe it would be best if you went somewhere else, at least for a while. This isn't a good place for guys like you right now."

"No," I said, "I'm not running away. I may be able to make a difference. I may be able to stop this. I'm not going to let some boy die just because I'm afraid." I hadn't realized it, but I was practically shouting.

"Okay. Okay." said Taylor. "But be careful! You know you may well be a target. Stay away from anyone you don't already know and be wary of those you do. It would only take a few moments for someone to grab you and take you somewhere there is no help."

"I'll be careful." I said. "Now can we stop talking about it. I don't really need to be reminded about what could happen."

"Sorry," said Taylor, "I just don't want to see you get hurt."

"I don't want to see me get hurt either."

I thought about the possibility of my own death and that immediately brought me back to thoughts about Marty. It wasn't fair that he had to die so young. He'd been cheated out of nearly his entire life. He was my best friend and I missed him desperately. I'd have done anything to have him back.

"He's not really dead you know."

I looked up to see Taylor gazing at me. Somehow he had read my thoughts, or maybe he could just tell what I was thinking from my expression. He was truly a kind soul. I could read the sympathy in his features.

"Death isn't at all like you think," said Taylor. "It's not an ending. When Marty died, he didn't cease to exist, he didn't disappear, he just changed. I know it was hard on you to lose him. I know it's hard to be without him, but you shouldn't let yourself keeping mourning him. I don't know where Marty is, or what he's doing, but I'm sure he's happy. I'm sure he's happier than he ever was alive. He was cheated out of his life, but he has another even better one now. Some day, you can join him. So don't take it all so hard okay?"

I looked up at him and smiled sadly.

"I know what you are saying is true, but it's still difficult."

"I know." said Taylor. "You just need to know that all will be well in the end."

"Thanks." I said. I did feel better.

"I should go," said Taylor. "I can do more good out there watching than I can here. I just came to tell you that there is really nothing to tell, not yet anyway."

"Okay." I said. Almost before the word was out of my mouth, he was gone.

I sat there and pondered the whole situation. I'd talked about putting a stop to the murders, but the truth was, I didn't really know what to do. I didn't have a plan. I barely had a clue. I felt useless.

As I sat there, Edward came running into the room, followed moments later by his father. I witnessed Edward's murder yet again. I'd forgotten what time it was. I always tried to be somewhere else when the hour of Edward's death struck. Even so, I'd seen the grisly scene more times that I cared to think about. No matter how many times I saw it, it disturbed me. It was over in a few moments, then I heard the horrible cries from the other rooms. I went about my business. I'd learned not to let images of the past disrupt my life.

Chapter 22

A New Boy in My Life

Right after school the next day I checked out Tony's locker. It was just as he'd left it. No one had yet had time to clean it out. It didn't take me long to find what I was seeking. I found the "God Hates Queers" booklet stuffed in one of his folders. He'd received one too. That made me more uncomfortable than ever. I wondered if it was a pattern, or a coincidence. Was the murderer giving each victim a booklet in advance, like a calling card of death? Or was it just someone who was anti-gay and had no connection with the murders at all? The number of questions grew daily, but the answers never seemed to come.

I didn't have time to ponder the many questions running around in my head. I had to get out to Ethan and Nathan's farm. With the warmer weather, farm work was beginning in earnest and I'd been asked to start working. I was looking forward to it. I'd be working three afternoons a week and most of the day on Saturdays. I was paid very well and I liked being out on the farm. It was so peaceful there and such a change from Graymoor. I needed the escape.

I rushed home, changed into some old work clothes and rode my mountain bike out to the farm. I'd been able to purchase that bike because I'd worked for Ethan and Nathan the previous summer. It was metallic ice blue, had kick ass shocks for rough terrain, and had twenty-one gears.

I made sure to wear my helmet. I had always thought wearing a biking helmet was a big pain until the day I wiped out. My head hit the pavement so hard it gave me a headache. If I hadn't been wearing a helmet that day, my brains would have been splattered all over road. I almost hadn't worn it, but something told me I should. That experience kind of shook me up. I knew I'd have been dead if I hadn't worn it. From that day on I always wore my helmet. I guess my parents had been right about one thing at least!

It didn't take me long at all the reach the farm. It was a nice little ride. I left my bike by the farmhouse and walked out toward the barn. I could see Ethan in the distance on a tractor, plowing the dark earth. The fields seemed to stretch out practically forever, until they met the edges of the woods in the far distance. The farm was like a little world of its own. I loved seeing the horses, cattle, sheep, and chickens. It was such a peaceful place, and so beautiful. I think I'd have wanted a farm like that if it wasn't so much work.

When I arrived, I found Nathan gathering tools in the barn. He wasn't alone. There was a boy about my age helping him. I didn't recognize him. He was my age, but I'd never seen him before. I thought that odd. I mean, the boy did have to go to school.

"So, ready to start Sean?" asked Nathan.

"Sure." I said, "I'm always ready." I was eyeing the boy as I spoke to Nathan. I was wondering a lot about him.

"You may not be for what I need you to do for the next several days, but more about that later. I'd like to introduce you to someone very special. This is my son, Nick."

My eyes grew wide and my mouth dropped opened. I gaped at Nick and at Nathan. A son? How was that possible? I mean, Nathan was gay. I knew he was capable of fathering children, but a son? Why had he never mentioned him? Where had he been all this time?

Nathan smiled at me. It was a smile on the verge of a laugh. Soon enough it did turn into a laugh.

"Ethan and I adopted Nick," said Nathan in explanation.

"Oh!" I said. It was unexpected news, but it did explain everything. A look passed between Nathan and Nick. They looked at each other as father and son. It made me feel warm inside.

I turned to Nick. I'd been so taken back by the revelation that Nathan had a son that I'd all but ignored him.

"Hey Nick." I said, looking him over and wondering how all this had come about.

"Hey." Nick smiled at me. "Nathan and Ethan have told me a lot about you. It's nice to meet you."

"You too." I said, shaking his hand.

"We'll have Nick helping us out now and it's a good thing too" said Nathan. "There is more than ever to do. We just bought a lot of new acreage and it's going to take a lot of work to get it going."

"You sure you want a dad like this?" I asked Nick. "It sounds like you've been brought in as slave labor."

"Hey!" said Nick, with mock suspicion in his voice. He glared at Nathan with a smile in his eyes. Nathan laughed. I could tell Nick had a great sense of humor. I knew it would be fun to have him around. I loved working on the farm, but sometimes it could get a little lonely if Nathan or Ethan wasn't around.

"Your first task, or rather ours, is going to be to clear all the small trees out of the fence rows on the edges of the property. It hasn't been done in a long time and the trees are starting to get big enough to tear up the fence. So, we need to cut all of them."

"Whoa." I said.

"Yeah." said Nathan. "Told you. I'm going to be helping you today and whenever I have the time, but it will mainly be up to you two."

I looked off in the distance at the miles of fencing.

"I guess this is what you call job security." I said.

Nathan laughed. "Hey if you think this is a big job, you should try putting in a fence." He looked thoughtful for a moment, as if he were remembering something meaningful.

Nathan handed me and Nick brush saws and axes and grabbed some up for himself, as well as some trimmers. We all walked across the fields to the first section of fencing. There were a lot of saplings growing near and through it. I could see what Nathan meant. A lot of small branches and even tree trunks were growing through the wire fence itself and bending it out of shape. In time, the trees would mess it up pretty bad. If they weren't removed, they'd eventually rip it out of the ground completely and there would be cattle and sheep wandering through the woods.

"We just need to cut the trees out as low as we can to the ground," said Nathan. "Don't worry about leaving a few inches of stump, looks don't matter. Let's stack what we cut in a pile over there. We'll burn it sometime later. We can have a big marshmallow roast. Before the summer is over, we can probably have several of them."

We got to work. The saplings weren't too big, but it still took a little while to cut through each one. It was a lot harder work than it seemed. It didn't take me long at all to work up a sweat. It was rather hot anyway and the work made it that much warmer. Within a few minutes, Nathan had pulled off his shirt and tossed it on the fence. I stole a few glances at Nathan. He was twice my age but he had a very impressive build. His shoulders, chest, arms, everything was hard muscle. Farm work certainly had its advantages. Nathan had once told me that he was rather scrawny as a boy, very thin with no real muscle at all. That was hard to believe. I couldn't picture Nathan as a little weakling. Nathan was built. I did believe Nathan, but it was sure hard to picture him as a puny little boy.

To be honest, seeing Nathan without a shirt excited me quite a lot. I found myself attracted to him despite the age difference. If he wasn't already taken, I'd have been thinking about making a play for him. Of course, I wouldn't even consider that since he had a boyfriend. I respected commitment. I wasn't at all the kind of guy that would make a play for someone that was taken, and I was sure Nathan would not appreciate such a thing either.

My attraction to him made me feel just a touch wicked, but I guess there wasn't anything wrong with it. It was just a natural thing, one guy being aroused by another. I had a few fantasies about Nathan, and about Ethan, but that's all they were or would ever be, fantasies. I had a lot of fantasies that I had no intention of trying to make real, and those about Nathan and Ethan were definitely among them. I guess my fantasies didn't hurt anything. My lust filled thoughts sure couldn't go anywhere. Nathan and Ethan had eyes only for each other. I thought what they had together was such a wonderful thing. I hoped I could find that someday.

I pulled off my own shirt. I was so sweaty it was sticking to me. I was eager to work on a tan anyway. One of the great things about working on the farm was that I had one sweet tan by the beginning of the summer. I also kind of liked going shirtless. There was just something sexy about it that made me feel good. I loved feeling the hot sun beat down on my naked torso. It made me feel so alive and vital. I was a little self-conscious since I was a bit pudgy around the middle, but I was around friends. Nathan was a friend anyway, and I was pretty sure Nick and I would be good friends soon enough.

I looked at Nick as I sawed through saplings and dragged them off to the pile that was slowly beginning to form. Nick was a good looking boy. He was my age, about sixteen, and had short hair so light brown that it was almost blonde. I liked his face. He wasn't what I'd call cute, but I found him attractive. He'd certainly never be on a magazine cover, but who cared? No one looked that good in real life anyway.

Nick's most attractive feature was his body, not that I'd seen much of it. At the moment he was wearing old jeans and a red tee-shirt. I could tell he was well built from the way his chest and shoulders pushed against his shirt. He sure had nice biceps. What we were doing certainly wasn't a strain, but I could still see his biceps in action. They were hard and about the size of baseballs. I loved the way they pressed against his shirt sleeves. I also liked the way Nick looked in his jeans. I just knew he had a cute little butt.

Nick was like a fringe benefit to working on the farm. I was sure going to enjoy looking at him every day I was there! He made for some nice scenery. I found him very attractive and arousing. I kept hoping he'd pull off his shirt, but the minutes passed and it didn't happen. I was just itching for a chance to see his bare chest.

Nathan noticed me looking at Nick. He didn't say anything of course, but he noticed. It made me feel uncomfortable. Nick was adopted, but he was Nathan's son and I was checking him out. Nathan knew a lot about me and I'm sure he knew what I was thinking. I wondered what he thought about that. I tried not to look at Nick quite so much.

The foremost thought on my mind of course was "Is Nick into guys?". I knew that the answer to that was probably "no", but I still wished I knew for sure. If I was right and about 20% of guys were gay, or at least bisexual, then that gave me a 20% chance that he was. The odds weren't in my favor. Girls who were after guys had it so easy! They had about an 80% chance that any guy they liked was into girls. It almost didn't seem fair.

Nick most likely knew that I was gay. Everyone knew it. Even though he was new, he'd probably found out already. Nathan or Ethan might even have told him. It sure wasn't a secret. It was kind of an advantage for me really. If Nick was interested in guys, even just a little, the fact that he knew I was gay would make it easier for him. I know things would have been easier for me if I knew if he was gay or not. I'd always wished I had the ability to tell. I wished that I could turn on some kind of gay radar and spot the guys who had a thing for other guys. That would have made life so much easier!

I had no such way of knowing however, so I had to wonder. The mere possibility was rather intriguing however. Just the thought that Nick might be gay, and that something might happen between us, was very exciting. That excitement was a little like torture too. I seemed to go around most of the time with quite a bulge in my shorts and such thoughts only made that bulge bigger. There was also a constant ache in my nuts that just would not go away. I relieved the pressure daily, but it never took long to build back up again. Thinking about Nick made my problem that much worse. It was a kind of sexual torment, both pleasurable and painful at the same time.

Nathan, Nick, and I joked around a lot as we worked and had a lot of fun. That made the time pass more quickly and the manual labor seem much less like work. I was taking a real liking to Nick, one that was quite independent of my attraction to his body. I was very happy I'd have him to work with all summer. I could tell he was going to be a real kick to have around.

We stopped working at 8:00, but I hung around just a little talking to the guys. I would have stayed even longer, but I'd promised to meet Marshall and Zoë at my house about 9:00. I was reluctant to leave. I really like being around Nick, and of course I always enjoyed Nathan's company. I got a chance to talk to Ethan a little too. I could tell he was really proud of Nick. I think he'd always wanted a son and now he had one. I was happy for him, and Nathan. I was happy for Nick too.

Chapter 23

Ghostly Encounters

Marshall was hot to see some supernatural activity and even Zoë had taken an interest in all the sightings I'd been telling her about. Graymoor was sure the place to see such things. Hardly a day went by without something out of the ordinary happening. Of course, nothing would probably happen at all since Marshall and Zoë were stopping by. That kind of thing didn't usually seem to cooperate very well. It didn't occur on demand. As it turned out I had no need to worry. Soon after I arrived at Graymoor it became obvious that my friends would not be disappointed.

Zoë was sitting on the steps waiting for me as I rode my bike through the gates.

"You been here long?" I asked. I hated it when anyone was late and I didn't like to keep anyone else waiting either.

"Just a couple of minutes." said Zoë. "I knocked, but no one answered. Are your parents having a party or something?"

"Huh?"

"It sounds like there are lots of people in there, and music."

I wondered what was up. My parents weren't even home. I walked up the steps and I could hear the music too. It sounded like some kind of old fashioned music, like a waltz or something.

I opened the door and my mouth gaped open.

"Holy shit!" I said. I could hear Zoë gasp over my shoulder. She grabbed my arm and pulled it around her waist so that I was holding her close.

I just gazed at the scene before me. There were candles everywhere and a big candle chandelier was hanging overhead. There were dozens of people dancing and laughing and eating. A small orchestra played in the far corner. It was all beautiful, except none of it was really there. Everyone and everything was transparent, even the candles and chandelier. I could see right through the big banquet table that was stacked with food. Couples were dancing right through furniture that sat in the room like it wasn't there at all.

Marshall walked up in the middle of it all.

"I thought you were into guys Sean," he laughed, getting ready to joke about the way I was holding Zoë. He fell dead silent as he stepped close enough to see the party going on in the parlor.

"Wow! This is incredible!" Marshall's eyes were glued to the ghostly spectacle before him.

As we watched, I caught site of Edward, and his brother. They looked very handsome dressed in their fine clothes. William was dancing with some very pretty girl, but he didn't look in the least interested. Edward was busy eating a big piece of chocolate cake.

All three of us just stood there and watched. It was beautiful. The music was enchanting and I could even smell the big bouquets of roses that decorated the room. Then, all of a sudden, it was all gone as if it had never been.

"Wow!" said Marshall. "That was really something!"

"I've never seen that before." I said.

We just stood there for a moment in a sort of awe. Even Zoë seemed pretty excited by it and she wasn't entirely enthused about ghosts.

"Come on, let's go to my room."

Both Marshall and Zoë were looking around everywhere, like they expected to see ghosts in every corner. At Graymoor, one never knew. I'd seen so many things since moving it that such events hardly surprised me at all. They were usually little things however and of short duration. I'd never seen more than two ghosts at once before. Of course, I didn't think the party we'd just witnessed was actually a ghost party. I was almost certain it was a replay of past events. Everything I'd seen connected with the Graymoor family themselves seemed to be like that. I had a feeling their ghosts weren't even in their old home.

Marshall plopped down on my bed and I speared him with a stare.

"Now what were you saying about me when you walked up?"

"Well, you were holding Zoë pretty close." He smiled.

"Are you accusing me of liking girls?" I yelled in mock anger. "Huh?"

"Girl lover!" he yelled at me.

I pounced on him and tickled him until he took it back. Zoë was laughing.

"You guys are so weird," she said.

"So what's your point?" I asked her and started laughing. She just rolled her eyes.

We all sat and talked for a while, then we looked around the house. Marshall took Zoë on what he called the "Graymoor Murder Tour", showing her all the spots the bodies were found. That part started right in my own room of course.

"There is no way I'd sleep in that bed," said Zoë. "It's the very same one Edward was murdered in isn't it?"

"Yeah, and knowing this house, it's probably the same sheets." I answered.

"Ewwwww." said Zoë.

I took a small amount of pleasure from grossing Zoë out.

"Why don't you change rooms?" asked Zoë. "I mean, this place surely has a few extra bedrooms."

"At least a dozen," I said, "but I've grown accustomed to this one. I kind of feel close to Edward. I like it here, even knowing what happened."

"I'd sure move," said Zoë.

"I bet this place has secret passages," said Marshall looking around at the walls.

"I don't know about that," I said "but it wouldn't surprise me one bit. I'm not even sure I've been in all the rooms yet. I've been exploring with this map I found, but it's still hard keeping track of where I've been. I can't imagine anyone building a house this big. Who could possibly need all this space?"

"Yeah, it's sure big all right." said Marshall.

"It's confusing too. Whoever built this place was odd. I've never seen anything designed like this house. It is kind of like that one built by the heir to the Winchester fortune."

"Oh yeah," said Marshall, "I've read about that place."

"What about it?" asked Zoë.

"Well," said Marshall, "It was built by this lady that was the heir to the Winchester Rifle Company fortune. She had this weird idea that everyone ever killed by a Winchester rifle was out to get her. What was even stranger was that she thought that the only way she could keep them from getting her was to keep building onto her house. She kept building onto it all her life, for more than thirty years. There are all these hallways and stairs that don't even go anywhere. There was room after room. The place was so big it had ten thousand windows and I'm not exaggerating. It was like she wanted her house so confusing that the spirits couldn't find her."

"Weird." said Zoë.

Marshall was dying to get back up into the attic, so we each grabbed an oil lamp and climbed the stair to the very top part of the house. The attic was an interesting place. I had not had much time to look through it myself. The last time I was up there, I was much too busy watching Edward and his brother making out to do any looking around.

Zoë opened an old trunk and took out a little sailor's suit. It was about the size for a six year old.

"Oh how cute." she said.

"Oh my gosh." I said looking at it.

"What is it?" asked Zoë.

"It's just that I've seen that before. I saw a little boy playing on the stairs a couple of weeks ago and he was wearing that very suit." It was so odd seeing the actual clothing that little boy had worn so long ago. I should have known it would be somewhere in the house. The Graymoor's never threw anything away.

"Here's something interesting." said Marshall, digging through a stack of old framed photos. "Tell me who this is Sean."

I took the frame from Marshall and dusted it off a bit.

"It's Edward and William." I said. It was a rather formal portrait and both the boys looked quite serious. I could detect just the hint of a smile however. Edward looked about fifteen in it. I guessed it dated to maybe a year before the boys were murdered. I cleaned the glass off a bit better. They really were good looking boys.

I turned the frame over and saw a date written on the back.

"June 22, 1871." I read out loud. I put the framed photo to the side. I'd take it to my room later and hang it on the wall.

We looked at several more things, but nothing interested me quite as much as that photo. While we were digging through trunks and boxes, the music started up again downstairs. We rushed down the attic stair, then through the halls and down the main stairs until we reached the second floor. We crept quietly up to the banisters and looked down below at much the same scene we'd witnessed before. It was sure a lot more pleasant that watching the Graymoor murders over and over again. I wondered what Zoë would have thought if she'd seen that!

I was mesmerized by the scene being played out below. It had a certain eerie beauty that I found irresistible. It was odd knowing that all those people were long since dead. I thought about that. In a hundred years or so, me and everyone I knew would be gone. It kind of put things in perspective a bit. It kind of made the way people felt about things less important. I knew there were those who hated me because I was gay, but did it really matter? In a hundred years we'd all be dead. What others thought of me didn't matter. It wouldn't change anything in the end.

Marshall grabbed my elbow and pointed to Edward below. All three of us moved down the stairs to get a better look. We stood not far from the boys watching them. They were strikingly handsome and I found myself wishing they were real, live boys. Of course, I might not have cared for them if they were. I knew some very cute boys that were real jerks. That made me think of Andy. He was very cute and he was gay. He was also a major dick. Being gay didn't necessarily make one a great guy. Gay guys could be jerks too.

As we looked on, William disappeared into the study and Edward followed him a few moments later. I could tell something was up from the way Edward looked cautiously around the room before following his brother into the study. Marshall, Zoë, and I walked through the dancers and tagged along. The study was lit with a few candles too, ghost candles that is. I could see clearly in any case. Ghost candles seemed to give off as much light as the real kind.

William closed the study door. At least to him and Edward it was closed. I could see him go through the actions of closing it, but the actual door didn't move. I gave that little heed however, I was too intent on watching the boys. Marshall and Zoë seemed just as interested. The brothers drew close to one another. Zoë gasped as they leaned in still closer, pressed their lips together, and kissed. I'd told her they were gay, but I don't think she was quite ready to see two ghost boys making out.

The sight both excited and amazed me. Seeing two boys kissing would have been exciting enough, but knowing the time they were from made it all the more interesting. It wasn't just a simple kiss either, they were practically devouring each other. Those boys were really taking a chance. I found myself fearful that they'd get caught making out, then I remembered I was seeing things that had already happened over a hundred years before. Whatever had happened was over and done with long ago.

Edward and William went at it for quite a little while. All three of us watched in amazement. Marshall and Zoë found the ghostly scene fascinating of course. I did too, but there was an added attraction for me. Finally, the boys stopped kissing, straightened their clothing, and returned to the dance.

I remembered bits and pieces of the heated argument between Edward and his father. Apparently Edward and William had been doing a lot more that just kissing and apparently they'd either been caught at it, or their father strongly suspected it. I imagined that they had been caught getting it on. I wondered just how that had happened. It was clear what the argument between Edward and his father was about however. Since I'd first seen the grisly murders acted out, I'd developed a pretty clear picture of just what had been going on, and just why Mr. Graymoor had killed his sons.

I still wasn't sure why he'd killed his daughter and wife though. I could come up with all kinds of theories, but I'd probably never know for sure. I guessed it didn't matter. After all, it had happened more than a hundred years before and the murderer himself had been hung by a mob.

I did wonder a lot about Edward and William. What must their lives have been like? If I was right about William being adopted, I wondered when he'd been adopted. What was it like to suddenly have a brother? What was it like to discover that he was attracted to boys too? I could hardly imagine what it must have been like to be gay more than a century in the past. It must have been almost impossible to bear. I was glad that Edward and William had each other, even if it did end up so very badly. That wasn't their fault of course, they didn't choose to be brutally murdered. That thought brought me back to the present. I thought about Marty, Ken, and Tony. They didn't deserve to die either.

Marshall, Zoë and I left the study and walked through the dancers. We watched them until they slowly faded away several minutes later. Marshall and Zoë left pretty soon after that. They'd sure picked the night for ghost watching!

I headed to my bedroom. I undressed and crawled into bed, wondering if my life would ever be normal again. I wondered if I'd ever find out who had killed my best friend. I drifted off with visions of Edward, William, Kyle, and Nick dancing in my mind.

Chapter 24

Going Nowhere Fast

The authorities didn't seem to be getting anywhere with their investigation and I was going nowhere with mine. I might as well have not been investigating at all. The truth was that I didn't know where to go with it. The common link with all three murders was that the victims were gay. That much was obvious and the motive was clear. With the "God Hates Queers" group in town, there were a wealth of suspects. Even without that group there were plenty of people in Verona that were down on gays. I doubted that most of them would go so far as murder, but perhaps a few would. I couldn't figure out a way to discover which of the many suspects was willing to kill. I didn't even know all the suspects. Some people were pretty outspoken against gays, but I knew well the murderers might not be nearly so open in their opposition.

I tried to think it through logically. If I were planning to kill one gay boy after another, how would I remain hidden? The members of the "God Hates Queers" group seemed the most likely candidates, so much so that I'd assumed Rev. Devlin was the murderer when he'd killed himself. The group was openly happy about the death of gays. Then again, they were just a little too obvious. If I were the murderer, I don't think I'd draw attention to myself like that. I wouldn't be associated with a group that would automatically make me a suspect. I think I would have been careful to never utter an anti-gay sentiment at all.

Then again, maybe the murderers were using a reverse psychology. No one would be stupid enough to commit murders of homosexuals and be involved in such a group as "God Hates Queers". Being a member of such a group might be the perfect hiding place. Everyone would suspect members of the group at first, but at the same time, no one would think the murderers would be stupid enough to expose themselves by being members, therefore being a member made one less of a suspect.

All I was doing was going round and round in circles, never getting any closer to an answer. It was a little like trying to figure out the truth when someone had said, "Everything I say is a lie. I'm lying." If everything that person says is a lie, then they were lying when they said they were lying. That of course means they were telling the truth, but they couldn't be because everything they say is a lie. And if everything they say is a lie then weren't they lying when they said, "Everything I say is a lie?" And if they were lying then, then sometimes they had to tell the truth, so then…Well, you get the point. Trying to even come up with a reliable list of suspects was nearly impossible.

I wondered if I should even be applying logic to the situation. The "God Hates Queers" group was not logical. Its members were fanatics. As more and more was revealed about the group in the press, it became obvious that it wasn't just a group, it was a cult. People like that probably wouldn't act logically, or even rationally. In fact, many of their actions were quite irrational. They seemed to live in their own little world, creating their own truths.

I was glad that they were being exposed for what they were. The "God Hates Queers" group had spread a lot of hate and created a lot of pain. Everyone was beginning to see through their lies however. Everyone was beginning to understand what they really were. There had been some arrests on charges of child pornography and even molestation, so their reputation was broken. It seemed ironic that the "God Hates Queers" group was guilty of the very charges it made against homosexuals. I was glad those monsters were revealed for what they were at last. Maybe they wouldn't be able to hurt others so easily any more.

As much as I despised them, I had no idea if the "God Hates Queers" group was responsible for the murders. They didn't have a monopoly on irrational behavior. It was all so confusing. Sometimes I felt like my head was going to explode when I tried to figure out who had committed the murders.

As I had to do so often, I forced my thoughts in other directions. I flooded my mind with images of Kyle. Yes, if anything could make me forget about the murders for a little while, it was him. I thought about Kyle a lot when I wasn't even trying to do so. He just kept coming into my mind unbidden. I'd always thought he was cute, but that had long ago developed into quite a crush. I was falling for him in a big way. The time we'd spent together made me that much more attracted to him. I wondered what would happen between us. The possibilities were both exciting and arousing.

I couldn't quite figure Kyle out. Sometimes I thought he might be interested in me, but at other times he seemed distant. Some times I got the feeling he didn't like me at all, but then just a few minutes later he'd be more friendly than ever. I didn't know how to proceed with him at all. He was sending me mixed signals that were so confusing that I didn't know which way was up. Sometimes he gave me looks that made me think he wanted me, but then at other times the look on his face made me think anything but that.

I hated to admit it to myself, but my crush on Kyle was mostly physical. I liked him to be sure, but it was mostly his face and body that captured my thoughts. I didn't really like that. I didn't want to be a shallow person. I didn't want all my thoughts to be centered around sex. Then again, most boys my age were like that. Most boys that had a thing for a girl had sex on their minds too. There wasn't really anything wrong with it. It was just the way things were.

I guess the problem was that reality didn't match up with my dream. I wanted what Taylor and Mark had together, or Ethan and Nathan. I wanted to fall in love. I wanted to care deeply for someone. I wanted sex to be sure, but I wanted it to just be a part of the relationship, not the basis for it. I had a feeling that I'd never experience love with Kyle. I'm not sure why, but I just had a feeling that he'd never be the kind of boyfriend that I really wanted. Despite that fact, I could not get him out of my mind. Whenever I looked at him, I just went weak in the knees.

I thought of Kyle's handsome face, his short dark hair, and those dreamy brown eyes. I imagined myself pressing my lips to his and kissing him deeply, passionately. I imagined pulling his shirt off and running my hands all over his smooth, beautiful chest. I imaged myself pressing up against him, feeling his hard body press against my own.

I had to stop myself. I was getting too excited. Already my jeans were under quite a strain. I was so worked up I thought I was going to explode. That seemed to be my natural state however. I felt like I was doomed to be forever in desperate need. I felt just a touch wicked, but I wanted nothing more than to rip away all of Kyle's clothing and just go crazy on his firm, young body.

Chapter 25

A Real Date?

The very next day Kyle invited me to go out with him for pizza and a movie. Was it a date, or was it just guys hanging out? I never knew where I stood with Kyle. It was one of the difficulties of being gay. If a guy asked a girl out like that, it was almost certainly a date, but if a guy asked another guy, it could be a date, and then again, it could be something quite different.

I didn't have to work that evening so I accepted. There was no doubt at all I'd accept. Kyle might as well have had me on a leash. I was so taken by him that I'd have done about anything just to be near him.

Kyle picked me up at Graymoor. He was wearing a white polo-like shirt and light blue jeans. He looked so fine. He was so cute he just made me melt. Once again I felt a little guilty because my attraction to him was so based on looks, but I just couldn't help it.

Kyle drove us to this great little pizza place and we ordered a large pizza with just about everything on it except those little fishies. We talked while we ate, but I don't really remember what we said. I was much too busy stealing glances of Kyle's hot little body. My eyes were drawn to his unbuttoned shirt. It provided a tantalizing glimpse of his firm, muscular chest. I could just see the middle part of his upper chest, but what I saw made my pants dance. The smooth skin and firm muscle made me yearn to pull off Kyle's shirt and run my hands all over his torso.

I was getting warm. The little candle at our table seemed to be putting out enough heat for a bonfire. I knew it wasn't the candle heating me up, it was Kyle. A little fantasy flashed through my mind where I jumped over the table and started ripping his clothes off. I took a big sip of diet cola. I had to cool down!

We drove to the theater and watched one of those horror films where teenagers get knifed by a psychopathic killer, usually while making out in the back seat of a car or getting it on in a bedroom. This one was better than most and actually had a story. It was hard for me to pay attention however with Kyle at my side.

I was keenly aware of his presence. I could catch the scent of his cologne and hear his soft breathing. I glanced at him from time to time and he took my breath away. How could another boy create within me such strong feelings of desire? How could anyone make someone else feel like that? I felt like something very basic and instinctual was at work, as if I were driven by primeval need. That only served to make my attraction all the more intense.

My mind was running away with thoughts of sex and Kyle. Nothing seemed to matter but that. I wanted to put my arm around him, but I still didn't know how he'd react. Even if our feelings were mutual he might very well want to keep them private. I nearly took his hand and held it where no one could see, but I couldn't seem to summon the courage to do even that. No matter how bad I might want Kyle, I couldn't make the moves to get him. I felt like such a coward.

Kyle drove me home. I wanted to move closer to him and put my hand on his knee. I thought about doing it over and over again, but my body wasn't willing to carry out my desires. To be honest I was terrified, mainly of rejection and just making myself look stupid. The whole process was intimidating however. Did straight boys have so much trouble putting the moves on a girl?

We pulled up in front of Graymoor and sat there for a moment.

"I had a really great time Kyle."

He didn't answer. He just looked at me. I stepped out of the truck, all confused. At the last moment Kyle slid over to the passenger side of the truck and grabbed my arm. He pulled me to him and kissed me on the lips. My entire body was suddenly a mass of raging fire. With a single kiss Kyle set me aflame with lust. He didn't prolong the kiss however. He pulled his lips from mine, slid back to the driver's seat and drove away without so much as a word. I stood there watching his taillights, wondering where all this was headed.

I turned and walked inside, still tasting Kyle's kiss on my lips. I'd never been kissed before, except by Marty that one time, and it was more wonderful that I'd ever imagined. I lit an oil lamp and walked up to my room. Graymoor was oddly silent. There seemed to be no ghosts prowling the halls that night, or perhaps I was just too wrapped up in what had happened to hear them. I felt as if I were floating instead of walking.

I pulled off my clothes and climbed into bed. I lay there staring at the ceiling with my hands behind my head. I closed my eyes for a moment and licked my lips, thinking once again of Kyle's kiss. My body was still on fire with lust. My hand trailed down over my chest until it found its way to the bulge in my boxers. I relieved myself of the sexual tension that had built up, moaning with the pleasure of it.

I lay there thinking about Kyle for the longest time. I couldn't seem to fall asleep. Every time I was on the verge of passing into unconsciousness, a new thought entered my head and kept me from resting. Finally, after what seemed like hours, I fell asleep, but my dreams were troubled. I kept dreaming about Marty's funeral. Over and over I walked up to his casket and looked down to see my best friend lying there dead. I was crying. It was all too much to bear. My own sobs thrummed in my ears.

I awakened. I felt like I hadn't slept at all. I had no idea how long my eyes had been closed. I still heard the sobbing, but it wasn't coming from me. It was distant, but distinct, as if someone were crying in a different room. I got up and lit the lamp. I opened my door and walked out into the hall in my bare feet. I followed the sobbing down the hall and down the stairs. It grew louder as I approached.

The old grandfather clock on the stair struck midnight just as I passed. The sudden sound startled me and made me jump. It wasn't the first time that had happened. It seemed to me that I should grow accustomed to it after a while. It was only a clock after all.

I looked down and saw figures in the parlor, ghostly figures. The scene before me wasn't like the ghostly party I'd seen before, there were only a few ghosts and all was quiet. They stood around hardly moving. I could catch whispers here and there, but nothing more. It was as if there was a silence that they did not wish to break. The only clear sound was the sobbing. More than one of those there were crying.

My eyes were drawn to a line of coffins. There were four of them, one of them very small. They were closed. I drew nearer. I reached out to touch one of the coffins, but my hand went through it as if it wasn't there. It didn't surprise me. I knew it wasn't really there at all. I was seeing what had been, rather than what was.

A man all dressed in black walked to one of the coffins. I crossed the space between us as he lifted the lid. I peered in and saw Edward lying there. The sight was beautiful and grotesque. Edward looked very handsome, as if he were sleeping instead of dead. He was covered up to his neck with heavy white blankets, but a large dark spot stained them. I knew it was blood from his horrible wounds. It sickened me and made me pity that boy all the more. He'd been killed a hundred years before I was even born, but I felt as if I knew him. Seeing him like that made me feel his loss as strongly as I felt Marty's. I turned my face from the sight. It was too painful, too close to home. When would boys no longer have to die for being gay?

* * *

Kyle had kissed me. One would think that everything would have been so easy after that. I was gay, everyone knew it. Kyle and I had gone out; first roller-blading, then for pizza and a movie. He'd kissed me. There was nothing to keep me from making a move. There was no need for further indecision. I still couldn't bring myself to do it however. I was such a coward that I just couldn't do it.

I couldn't get Kyle out of my mind. My long-time yearning for other young men had become a desperate desire for Kyle, an obsession. The mere sight of him was enough to set me on fire with lust. I felt like my body was taking control of my mind. Whenever I was around Kyle, I felt out of control, reckless. More than anything I just wanted to jump on him. It left me confused, I felt like I wasn't being me. The thoughts running through my head bore little resemblance to the dreams I'd always had of a boyfriend.

I was in a tormented state. It was pure sexual agony. I felt like I'd been waiting forever and I just couldn't wait a moment longer. All I had to do was reach out and grab him and he'd be mine. I wanted him desperately, but, at the same time, I was fighting to resist my impulses. Should I allow myself to be ruled by animal desire? I wasn't in love with Kyle. He wasn't my boyfriend. My attraction to him was purely physical. All my thoughts about him centered around his beautiful body. There was a war being waged within me. A war complicated by my own cowardice. I started to avoid Kyle. Being around him was just too difficult.

Chapter 26

A Message from Beyond

I arrived at the farm early, hoping to catch Ethan or Nathan alone without Nick around. I found Nathan working in the vegetable garden behind the house. It was hot as could be and Nathan wasn't wearing a shirt. The sight of him caused my heart to beat a little faster. What was wrong with me? Couldn't I look at another guy without getting a hard-on for him?

We talked about nothing in particular while I summoned the courage to talk to Nathan about my problem. I couldn't seem to get started however. I was beginning to think I was a coward in all things.

"What's on your mind Sean?" asked Nathan. He could tell something was bothering me. His piercing eyes studied me.

I looked at the ground shyly, then back up at him.

"There's this boy, and well, I, I think there's something wrong with me. I mean, things are going like I wanted, but I'm not sure. I feel like I'm doing the wrong thing. I feel like…Hell, I don't know what I feel like."

Nathan smiled wanly.

"Could you be a little more clear?" he asked. "Just take it slow and tell me what's bothering you."

I described Kyle and how he made me feel. I told Nathan about the times we'd gone out, about the mixed signals, and about the kiss. I also told him about my intense lust for Kyle's body.

"I wanted to fall in love and having something like you and Ethan, but I don't love Kyle. I think about him all the time, but it's always physical. If he wasn't so damned hot I don't think I'd like him all that much. I probably wouldn't give him a second thought. I feel so shallow."

"Maybe you are being too hard on yourself," said Nathan. "All of us are attracted to beauty and repelled by ugliness. That may well be the strongest prejudice of all. It's only natural to be attracted to a boy like that, even if you don't have feelings for him. You shouldn't be down on yourself for that. Everyone experiences such attractions. It's what one does or does not do about them that is important."

"I know what I want to do." I said. "I just want to jump on him and go wild!"

"That's probably what I'd want to do in your case too."

"Really?"

"Sure. Listen, I can still remember the first time I saw Ethan. I had just started working here on the farm for his uncle. I was straining my guts out trying to dig out a ditch when up walked the most gorgeous boy I'd ever seen in my life. He was shirtless and he was so built I just wanted to die for him. I got so hard I had to keep turned partially away from him so he couldn't see it. Not too much later on, I fell in love with Ethan, and I've loved him ever since, but in the beginning it was simply lust. I felt just like you do with this Kyle of yours. I just wanted to grab Ethan and do wild things with him."

"Wow!" I said. "That helps, but I feel that way about a lot of guys. I mean I even…"

I fell abruptly silent as I realized what I'd almost said. I jerked my head up and looked at Nathan with fear in my eyes. I could tell from the way he looked at me that he knew what I meant without me even finishing the sentence. I took a deep breath and said it.

"I even feel that way when I look at you."

"I'm flattered," said Nathan. "Just don't let Ethan ever hear you say that."

All the color drained from my face and I'm sure I had a look of pure terror on my features. Nathan burst out laughing.

"I'm kidding," said Nathan. "That wouldn't bother him at all."

"It wouldn't?"

"No. Ethan and I love each other very much. We'd never so much as touch another guy and we both know it. When you really love someone, you also trust. Ethan and I have complete trust in each other."

"I wish I could have what you have." I said. "I want to love and trust someone like that. It makes this thing with Kyle that much harder. Since he's kissed me, I don't think it will be too hard to get in his pants. To be honest, I want that so much I can taste it. But, at the same time, I want to hold out for something special. I want to fall in love and experience my first time with the one I love. And yet, I don't know if I can wait for that. I feel like I've been waiting forever. Part of me just wants the sex right now!"

"I understand." said Nathan. "This is a decision you have to make. I can't make it for you. Just don't be hard on yourself if you decide not to wait. To be honest, I'm not sure what I'd do in your spot. The boy you seek could be just around the corner, or it might take you a long time to find him. If this Kyle is as hot as you say he is, I think I'd have a very hard time resisting him myself if I were in your shoes."

"You have it so easy!" I said.

"Yes, I do, but it wasn't always this way. There was a time when I thought I'd die for lack of love, and sex. It all worked out for me in the end, but I had no idea that it was going to do so. Don't worry Sean, it'll all work out for you too." Nathan mussed my hair and smiled at me. I found myself loving him. He was like the older brother I'd never had.

Nick showed up soon after that and the two of us departed to do battle with the saplings in the fence row. It didn't take long for sweat to start streaming down my bare chest and back. I loved the feel of sweat. I loved heat. It could never get too hot for me. The hotter it was, the better I liked it.

It wasn't long before Nick pulled off his shirt. It was a moment I'd been eagerly anticipating. Nick's torso was long, slim, and firm. He didn't have a lot of muscle, but he had a slender, sinewy look that I found very attractive. I chided myself for getting excited over yet another boy, but what did it hurt really? I was only looking. It wasn't like I was having sex with every guy I found attractive. So far I'd only had sex with Ken, if you could call it that. I don't think many people would consider a little hand action sex. In any case, I was hardly a boy-slut.

I thought back to Kyle's kiss and involuntarily licked my lips. I wanted more of that, and other things as well. I was swiftly making up my mind to do more with Kyle at the next opportunity that presented itself.

I looked Nick over as we worked. He was definitely my kind of boy. Once again, I wished I could tell just by looking whether or not someone was gay. Nick and I were getting along just fine. He was funny, kind, a little wild, and just plain fun to be with, not to mention hot. Now there was boyfriend material. If only he liked guys.

The thought actually crossed my mind to just come out and ask him. If I did so, and the answer was "no", he'd probably be uncomfortable from then on. He'd be wondering if I had the hots for him. He'd probably realize I did too. It was hard to keep from looking at him. Asking him that question could really mess up the friendship that was developing. No, I wouldn't ask him, not yet. I'd find out eventually and who knew, maybe Nick was that boyfriend waiting around the corner that Nathan had mentioned.

I thought about asking Nathan if Nick was gay, but something didn't seem right about that. Or maybe it was just that I was uncomfortable with the idea because of the relationship between Nathan and Nick. I knew Nick was adopted, but I still didn't feel comfortable about asking Nathan. He might not even know. There was no easy solution.

I felt like I must have sweat a gallon as we worked. Even when the sun went down it was too hot for comfort. A little later, a cool breeze stirred the still air, but even then, it was rather warm.

We stopped work a little after eight. Before I had a chance to leave, Nathan asked me to stay for supper. I was ravenously hungry, so I did. I had something on my mind too and it seemed a good time to bring it up.

As the four of us ate I looked at Ethan. He might be in his late thirties, but he was fine. I dreamed of being built like that. It would probably never happen, but I'd be happy if I could have a body half that nice. I could well see why Nathan had been so hot for him when they met. I could just image what Ethan must have looked like as a teenager. Wow.

My thoughts turned to my reason for being there. I'd been giving a certain something a lot of consideration and I'd decided to let Ethan and Nathan in on a few things, one thing especially. It seemed only fair as it involved them, in a way at least. I was a bit uncomfortable talking about the subject in front of Nick, but he was part of Nathan and Ethan's family now. Besides, we'd become pretty good friends.

I wasn't quite sure how to begin (no surprise there) so I started with telling them of my murder investigation. They might even have some ideas that would help me. Who knew? Ethan and Nathan seemed rather impressed with what I'd done, especially figuring out that Marty hadn't killed himself. I began to feel a little bit proud of myself too. Maybe I'd accomplished more than I thought, even if I hadn't solved the murders.

It was time to get into more difficult matters.

"You know how I was asking you about Mark and Taylor?" I said.

"Yeah." said Ethan.

"Well, you never asked me why I wanted to know, but it was part of my murder investigation."

Both Ethan and Nathan looked a bit confused. Who could blame them? Nick had no idea what I was talking about of course.

"I uh, wanted to reach Marty by having a séance or something, to ask him who had killed him. I don't know if you guys believe in that stuff, but I'd seen something like it on television and it worked. Anyway, I found out I couldn't do it, because it was too soon after Marty's death, and I needed someone else to contact. Someone who had been dead longer."

I watched Ethan and Nathan as I talked. I think they were kind of taken back by all the talk of séances and talking to the dead. I found myself speaking rather quickly. I was nervous and wanted to get it all out before I lost my nerve.

"No one I know has been dead for a long time, but I got to thinking about Mark and Taylor, how they were gay and all. I thought maybe they'd help me if I could contact them. And well, I did it."

I looked from one to the other, but neither of them said anything. I guess that wasn't surprising. Most people would have been shocked at what I was saying. After all, I was talking about the supernatural. Nick looked at me oddly, like I was a bit of a freak. He didn't say anything however.

"You don't believe me, do you? You don't believe I contacted Mark and Taylor?"

"I believe that you believe," said Ethan. Nathan nodded his agreement.

"Which is another way of saying you think I'm nuts."

"No," said Ethan, "I don't think that at all. I think sometimes however that it's easy to see and hear what you want to. When I was a boy, after my parents died, sometimes I thought my mother was in my room, tucking me in the way she did when she was alive. I wanted her to still be with me, so I felt like she was there, even though she wasn't."

I felt like telling Ethan that his mom probably really was there, but I needed to focus.

"No, this wasn't like that at all. I saw them both, talked to them, and it wasn't a dream. I've talked to them several times. It's real."

Ethan and Nathan looked uncomfortable. I guess I couldn't blame them. I wouldn't have believed it either a few short weeks before. Nick seemed uncomfortable too, like he was embarrassed for me.

"I can prove it." I said. "I knew you probably wouldn't believe me, but Mark told me something, something that I couldn't possibly know without having talked to him."

I thought hard trying to remember exactly what he'd said.

"Mark told me you visited his grave, and Taylor's."

"This isn't funny Sean. If this is some kind of joke…" Ethan was getting mad. I knew he thought I was just jerking him around.

"No, it's no joke!" I said. "Mark told me that the two of you visited the graves. It started raining. You stood there for a long time. Nathan said 'This shouldn't have happened.' Then you said 'I know, but it did. We can't change it.' or something rather like that. I can't remember what Mark told me exactly. Then Nathan said 'At least they can be together now and no one will ever bother them again.' Then you put some flowers on their graves and left.

Both of them looked pretty shocked.

"You didn't tell Sean about that did you?" Ethan asked Nathan.

"No, I've never told anyone."

There was a stillness in the air as the impossible became the believable. Despite my proof, I could read in their features that they were fighting against belief. What I was telling them was just too fantastic, too hard to accept.

"There's more." I said. "I don't understand what it means, but Mark said that you'd know. Mark said to tell you 'Thanks for the little bear.'"

Ethan looked at me in complete shock and his mouth dropped open. Tears were flowing from his eyes and he was sobbing.

"What is it?" asked Nathan confused.

"You really did talk to them, didn't you?" said Ethan to me. It was not a question. He believed. He knew. He looked back at Nathan.

"At Mark's and Taylor's funeral, I went back in, right before they were getting ready to move the caskets to the hearses. Everyone else had gone, and you were waiting for me outside." Ethan paused. Tears were still rolling down his cheeks and it was kind of hard for him to speak. "It's kind of silly, but I had these two little bears hidden in my jacket. Each of my parents had given me one for my birthday when I was about four. I slept with those little bears for years and then, when my parents died, I always kept them near because they reminded me of them. I didn't feel so alone with them there. I felt so bad for Taylor and Mark. I didn't want them to be alone in those caskets, so I put one of my little bears in there with each of them to keep them company."

Ethan's tears flowed freely. Remembering those events was hard on him. I knew he'd never really gotten over the loss of Mark and Taylor.

"I never told anyone that." he said. "Not even you Nathan. I was alone in that room when I did it. No one saw, no one could have. No one else could possibly know."

He looked at me and I nodded.

"Are they okay?" Ethan asked me. He seemed like a little child seeking the answer to something that had always preyed on his mind.

"They are better than okay." I said smiling.

Ethan and Nathan were full of questions about their friends and it was late before I left that night. I told them everything that I could. Nick seemed a little shocked by everything. I knew it would take a lot of explaining on Ethan and Nathan's part to bring him up to speed.

"Sometime soon, come to the house." I said. "You can talk to them for yourself."

"We will." said Ethan. He had the look of someone who'd just witnessed the impossible return of a loved one who'd come back against all hope. I could tell Ethan was very tired. It had been an exhausting experience for him. I left soon after, feeling better for having told them. Somehow I'd just known that it was important for them to know.

Chapter 27

Nick and Kyle

I was wondering a lot about Nick at the school dance on Friday night. I was still debating whether or not to ask him if he was gay. I didn't think there was any other way I'd find out. He was dancing with a few girls and looked like he was having a great time. That didn't mean much however. I was dancing with Zoë, and had been dancing with a few other girls too. Dancing with girls didn't make one straight. I knew that better than anyone.

Whenever our eyes met, Nick smiled at me. He was looking so fine. Was it my imagination, or was there something more in his smile than friendship? I was really beginning to think he was interested in me. I just felt this connection between us. And then there was something in his eyes that I recognized. There was a certain hope, a certain longing for companionship and love.

I made up my mind that I would ask Nick if he was attracted to guys. I'd decided against that very thing before, but the probability that his answer would be "yes" had increased considerably. Now all I had to do was work up the courage to ask him. I'd been lacking in the courage department in a lot of ways, but somehow I'd manage it.

"Can I steal Sean away from you for a little while?" Jill asked Zoë.

"Sure, take him," said Zoë as if she were discarding something unwanted. Zoë loved to tease me. She laughed and went to get something to drink.

Jill started dancing with me. She was smiling and seemed to be in really good spirits, quite unlike the last time I'd talked to her. I was still a little nervous to be near her. I was afraid she'd start pawing me or something.

"I'm sorry about what happened Sean. I don't know what came over me. I'm not usually like that really." She seemed genuinely sorry.

"It's okay," I said, "No harm done. I just don't understand why you were so interested in me. I mean, you know I'm gay."

"I know." she said. "But I was still hoping. It's hard to tell you this, but…"

Her voice trailed off and she looked like she was ready to cry. I led her off the dance floor to a quiet corner.

"Hey," I said, taking her chin in my hand so she'd look at me, "it's okay."

"It's just that I really, really like you," she said. "I know you're gay. I know I'm being stupid, but I can't help it. I can't make myself feel anything other than what I feel. I think about you all the time. I guess the other day I was just hoping for the impossible. I know you could never go for a girl like me."

I smiled at her.

"Jill, I'll tell you one thing, if I was attracted to girls, I'd be all over you. You're beautiful and I'm not just saying that to make you feel good. I mean it. I may not be attracted to girls, but I know a hot one when I see her."

She smiled at me and actually laughed.

"You are very nice too, and sweet. I can't be your boyfriend, but I'd sure like to be your friend."

She didn't respond. She started crying and buried her head in my shoulder. I just stood there holding her and stroking her hair. After a little while, she stopped crying and looked into my eyes.

"I'd really like to be friends." she said. "And if you ever change your mind about girls, you know who to call." She laughed.

I could tell from the way she looked at me that she was still quite taken with me. I was very flattered and it made me feel very good about myself. I knew things would probably be hard on her as far as I was concerned, but I'd do what I could to make things easier. I'd never thought that things could work out so well with Jill. I had a feeling I'd just gained a very good friend.

"Let's dance." I said. I pulled her out onto the dance floor without waiting for an answer. Jill didn't protest in the least.

Kyle was at the dance and my eyes were much upon him. There was something about him that made it impossible for me to resist looking at him. Kyle was looking at me too, but what I read in his eyes was quite different from the longing I read in Nick's. Kyle's eyes had a certain wicked gleam that I found quite arousing. While I thought of Nick as a potential boyfriend, Kyle was a bad boy that I found irresistible.

I'd been avoiding Kyle, but I couldn't keep it up forever. When I saw him walking toward me, a part of me wanted to turn and run. Another part of me wanted to rip his shirt off.

"Why haven't I seen you lately? Asked Kyle.

"I've been real busy; school, work, you know."

The look on his face told me he knew I was lying. When he looked at me I felt like he knew exactly why I'd been avoiding him. It probably wasn't too hard to figure out. I couldn't seem to control myself when I was around Kyle. I practically devoured his body with my eyes. I must have had the look of a hungry wolf. I'm sure he could also read the fear there too. I did fear Kyle, in so many ways. He was so hot, so sexy. I wanted him so bad. I was afraid I couldn't resist him if he made a move on me. I wasn't even sure I wanted to resist. Part of me wanted him to put the moves on me. Part of me wanted to put the moves on him. I'd decided to try something with him, but I was too chicken to do it. I was afraid to try anything with him. I was afraid that he'd reject me, and that he wouldn't. I had a feeling that he was trouble, that I should just stay away, but at the same time, I wanted him more than I'd ever wanted anything. I felt myself pulled toward him and pushed away at the same time. It was torture.

"Hey, can you meet me after the dance?" asked Kyle. "I think we need to uh, talk."

"Um, yeah." I said nervously. I wondered why he didn't want to talk right then, neither of us was really doing anything and nothing would have kept us from slipping outside. I was apprehensive about the whole thing however, so I didn't mind the delay.

"Great!", said Kyle, "I've been thinking about this a lot and I think there's something…Well, we can get into that later." He smiled wickedly, causing my jeans to grow tighter in the front. "I'll meet you in the parking lot after the dance."

He disappeared into the crowd almost before he was done speaking. I didn't mind, I needed to think. Boy did I need to think! My head was spinning. Kyle's eyes had been on me the whole time we spoke and they told me more than his words. I could read the desire in his eyes that I felt in my own. There was something basic, instinctual, primitive, even predatory in them. When he looked at me I felt raw emotion and I had little doubt what fueled it.

I was so nervous I was almost shaking. This was it. My time had come. Something was going to happen between Kyle and I, something big. I knew we weren't going to just be talking. Something was going to happen. Part of me couldn't wait. Part of me felt like running.

I thought about Nick. What about him? What if I was right? Nick was exactly the type I wanted for a boyfriend. Was it right to do something with Kyle when I was soon to be asking Nick that all important question? I knew that I really should wait, but I also knew that I wouldn't.

The truth was that my body was doing my thinking for me. It had needs and it was determined they be fulfilled as soon as possible. My body forced Nick right out of my mind.

My whole body felt weird. I was excited, aroused, and afraid all at once. The emotions roiled over one another, mixing, shifting. I was glad I had a few minutes to think, to get myself under control. I wanted Kyle, I wanted him bad, and I was going to have him. I didn't care if he wasn't my dream boy. I didn't care if there was nothing between us but sex. I couldn't wait any longer. Kyle was willing and I was going to go for it. Still, a little part of me resisted. Some little corner of my mind told me to just walk away.

The minutes grew long. I both embraced and hated the delay. Part of me was afraid to move forward, part of me couldn't wait a moment longer. The dance ended. Had I been standing there for seconds, or centuries? I noticed Nick leave. My heart was drawn toward him, but my heart wasn't in control. The crowd cleared out and I went outside. One by one the cars disappeared. I envied my classmates that had their own cars. Whenever I wanted to drive, I had to borrow my parents' car. Of course, I didn't need one on a night like this. I only lived a few blocks from the school. It didn't exactly kill me to walk.

Soon everyone was gone and still there was no Kyle. I began to wonder if he'd ditched me. Or maybe something had suddenly come up. Even if it had, surely he would have taken the time to tell me. Where was he?

Chapter 28

Terror in Graymoor

Even as I wondered if Kyle had ditched me, he appeared. He looked so sexy in the moonlight. He smiled at me. We stood there in awkward silence for a few moments; me leaning up against a lamp post in the parking lot, Kyle shifting his weight nervously from one foot to the other.

"Want to go for a walk?" asked Kyle. "Maybe where no one can see us?"

He licked his lips. His meaning was clear. We were alone, but there was nothing keeping anyone driving by from seeing us standing in the parking lot.

We walked slowly across the empty parking spaces, then onto the soccer fields. The moon cast just enough light for us to navigate by. My heart beat wildly in my chest. I don't think I'd ever been so excited in my entire life. Years of waiting were about to come to an end. I don't think I'd ever been so aroused before either. I was trembling with desire.

I took Kyle's hand and held it in mine. It was such a wonderful feeling. I'd never have guessed that so simple a touch could bring me so much pleasure. If merely holding hands was so intense, what would the rest be like? I closed my eyes for a moment and pictured myself pulling off Kyle's shirt. It filled me with desire. I looked at Kyle in the moonlight. He was every boy's dream.

I stopped and we looked at the stars for a moment. The whole world seemed beautiful to me. I turned to Kyle and leaned in toward him. I brought my lips closer and closer to his. He smiled at me seductively, but placed his finger on my lips.

"Not here Sean. Come with me."

I followed him as we neared the edge of the forest, my head light, my heart racing. Tonight was the night. I was trembling with thoughts of what was about to happen. I knew that in mere moments I'd be all over that boy, I'd pull off his clothes and devour his beautiful body. I'd never been so aroused in all my life. My tortured virginity was about to come to an end.

I felt something racing toward me, like the wind, but making no sound. It wasn't even really something that could be felt physically and yet I could feel it. Kyle seemed completely unaware of it. I wasn't even sure it was real, but at the same time, I knew it was.

"Do not follow."

"What?" I said out loud.

"Huh?" said Kyle, looking at me confused.

"Why did you say that?" I asked him.

"I didn't say anything. Come on."

"No! Don't follow him. You are in danger."

I heard the voice more clearly and I recognized it as it became nearer and clearer. It was Taylor. I looked around, but couldn't see him. I could only hear him. Kyle stopped and looked at me in confusion. It was clear he couldn't hear anything at all.

"He's the one," said Taylor. "It's him. There is evil in his soul. I can feel it. You must leave. Now!"

I drew away from Kyle, looking at him in fear. I could not believe Taylor's words, and yet I trusted him. But Kyle?

"What's wrong with you?" asked Kyle.

I backed away further.

"Come on Sean, just a little further. Let's just go into the woods. You want it don't you?"

"No." I said, my heart full of suspicion and doubt.

"Come on." said Kyle almost desperately. "I know what you want. I want it too. Let's do it."

"No." I said.

Kyle's hand grasped my wrist and clamped down on it like a vise. He pulled me forward.

"You're just a little nervous. You know you want this. Come on."

"Run!" said Taylor. "What are you waiting for? Run!"

There was such a sense of urgency in his voice that I broke from Kyle's grasp and bolted. He was almost on my heels, racing after me.

"Come on Sean, I want you!" he called to me. I slowed at the siren call of his voice until Taylor screamed at me to run for my life. I ran faster than ever. As Kyle fell behind, his voice became cruel and full of hate.

"Come back here you faggot!" he yelled as he pursued me. "Get him!" he screamed out loud.

To my horror a figure jumped from the edge of the woods and rushed to intercept me. I shifted my course to avoid him. I could hear another pursuer join Kyle behind me. They were hot on my heels. I increased speed, tearing up the grass. I knew I was running for my life.

"We'll catch you faggot! You can't get away. It will just be worse for you if you run!"

I kept on running, as fast as I could manage. I ran for help and home. My pursuers fell back just a bit, but they were far, far too close. My breath came in gasps. My side began to hurt, but I didn't dare stop, or even slow. I ran for what seemed forever. The pain in my side intensified, became unbearable, but I did bear it, I had no choice. Graymoor loomed before me. That creepy old house was a welcome sight. I bolted up the front steps and across the porch. I slammed and bolted the door behind me.

"Mom! Dad!" I screamed. There was no answer. I realized to my horror they weren't home.

I knew I had to get out of there, go somewhere there was help. I opened the front door to make a run for it, but Kyle slammed himself against it. I smashed my shoulder into the door and forced it shut. I bolted it once more. I was trapped. I raced for the phone, praying it had been connected at last. I knew even as I picked it up however that it was as dead as always.

I heard a window break near the back of the house and someone trying to get in the front door. My instinct was to bolt, but there was nowhere to go, no way to get out. I calmed myself and crept quietly down the hall. Graymoor was dark, there were lots of places to hide. I'd have to be very quiet, very careful, and wait my chance.

I slipped into the massive dining room, just down the hall from the parlor on the first floor. I could hear murmuring voices in the front of the house. How I wished they were only the voices of ghosts, the living were far more dangerous. I crept forward, as silent as a mouse. I knew I couldn't take on the three of them, my only chance was to quietly escape.

I stiffened as a figure entered the room, in the dim light I couldn't make out who it was. I backed away, careful to make not even the slightest noise.

"Come on you little queer." said Kyle quietly. "You wanted me so bad, now I'm here. Come and get me." He paused often, listening.

He was drawing nearer. I felt like a fool. I'd trapped myself. The only way out was past him. I remained perfectly still, hoping he just wouldn't see me as he drew near. At the same time I tensed, ready to strike. If he noticed me, I planned to knock him on his ass and make a break for it before the others could arrive.

He drew closer. In the dim light I saw a glint of moonlight on something shiny as it flew through the air, then heard a crash as something shattered on the far wall. As my eyes adjusted to the dark, I saw a wine glass hurtle through the air, just missing Kyle's head as he ducked. Kyle rushed forward, falling over a chair that moved itself in his path.

"That's it faggot. You've had it," he yelled, scrambling to his feet and making for the far corner of the room. I watched as another wine glass sailed at Kyle's head, this time catching him square on the jaw. He snarled in anger.

I quietly slipped along the opposite wall as Kyle groped in the darkness for me. I knew he couldn't find me. I wasn't there. It wasn't me who had thrown the glasses and moved the chair. I had help, and I knew who it was.

I edged out of the room, fearful that Kyle's companions would come rushing into the room when they heard the racket. I'd barely made it out and a little down the hall when one of them did. He stepped into the dining room. I was nearly in the clear, but I backed into a plant stand and sent a potted fern crashing to the floor. My pursuer turned and spotted me. He rushed forward, but the dining room door slammed in his face. I heard him curse in pain.

It was my chance to break for the front door, but I heard someone coming from that direction. I couldn't get out. I turned and ran as I heard my pursuers beating on the door. They were pissed.

"Open it!" screamed Kyle.

"I can't, he's holding it!" said another voice.

I could hear them throwing their weight against the door as I moved farther down the hall. I stood still as they burst from the dining room.

"Get him!"

They looked around confused. I know they expected me to be right there. I had to be if I was holding the door. I wasn't however, it wasn't me. Either Taylor or Mark or both were helping me evade my pursuers. They had held that door shut, not me.

I looked around, there was really only one way to go. I set my foot on the stairs and stepped down. There was only pitch dark below me, but I felt my way down the worn stone stairway. I shook with terror. In any other house, downstairs would have meant the basement. In Graymoor, it meant the family crypt. I'd only been there a couple of times before. The place gave me the creeps. In total darkness, it was terrifying beyond belief. I found however that when murderers were just behind, that I feared the living more than the dead. Still, I had to fight sheer panic as I stepped down into total darkness.

I went down and down until my foot fell hard against the floor. There were no more steps. I extended my hands and walked into the crypt. I counted my paces and twenty steps later my hand touched hard, cold stone. I felt the edge of a sarcophagus and used it to guide myself to its far edge. I crept down behind it, hiding myself behind Edward's final resting place.

I heard voices at the top of the stairs, then saw faint flickers of light. They were coming. I fought to quiet my breath. I was breathing so hard I was nearly hyperventilating. I managed to bring it under control. I knew I was dead if I didn't.

The crypt was deathly still. The light of the candles seemed dazzlingly bright compared to the total darkness before. I could see Kyle and one of his murdering friends. They split up and searched around the room.

"You think he's down here? I hate this place."

"He could be anywhere, but we'll get him."

"Damn it!" yelled Kyle as his candle went out. He quickly re-lit it and continued his search. "When we get hold of that fucker, I'd make him beg me to kill him."

The hair on the back of my neck stood on end. It took all my concentration to keep my breath even and quiet. If they found me, I was worse than dead.

I could see the crypt illuminated in the candlelight. The sarcophagus of William stood next to that of Edward with that of their parents and little sister just beyond. Each was heavily carved and morbidly beautiful in the dim light. Within the walls more of the Graymoor's rested, going back to time out of mind. It was a place of the dead.

They were getting closer. I shook with fear. The crypt was the one place in Graymoor that still held terror for me. Even that paled next to the fear I had of the boys that were looking for me. I thought of how Ken and Tony had died and I was sure Kyle would give it to me worse. I wondered how long he'd be able to draw it out. I wondered what torment he'd put me through before I died. Maybe I could enrage him, make him mad enough to kill me quickly.

"Damn it!" yelled Kyle again. His companion uttered the same phrase moments later. Both their candles had gone out.

"I swear I think something is blowing this damn thing out," said Kyle.

"Maybe it's the wind."

"Do you feel any wind in here?" asked Kyle sarcastically. His companion remained silent. I watched as they both went through several matches trying to re-light the candles. Each one was snuffed out almost as soon as it was lit.

"God Damn it! Son of a fucking bitch!" screamed Kyle as the last of his matches blew out. His companion was out of matches too.

They groped about in the darkness. It was a horrible game of blind man's bluff. Suddenly, Kyle stopped.

"I know you're here Sean, I can hear you." said Kyle.

I swallowed hard. I was so terrified I nearly screamed.

"You know what I'm going to do when I find you Sean? I'm going to beat you until you beg me to kill you. Then I'm going to cut you open. Yeah, I'm going to carve you up, pull out your guts, and make you look at them while you die. But I'll do a lot of things before that Sean and you won't like any of them. You'll be begging me to stop. You'll offer me anything to quit, but I won't. You're going to get what you deserve. You'll pay for being a fag."

I had to fight to keep my teeth from chattering. I was so afraid, it was all I could do to keep from crying out.

"He's not here," said Kyle's companion.

"Come on," said Kyle, "let's look upstairs."

He'd been bluffing. He had no clue as to whether or not I was down there. He'd tried to frighten me into giving myself away. He had nearly succeeded. I really thought that he'd heard me.

I did not dare to breath a sigh of relief, but I knew I'd been given a reprieve from a death sentence. I remained completely still for several minutes until I was sure they were gone.

I felt my way across the crypt once more. I couldn't stay down there, they would return sooner or later to look for me. As much as I hated the thought, I had to go back upstairs and try to get out.

The moonlight coming through the windows seemed brilliant after the darkness of the crypt. I moved slowly, fearing discovery each moment. I was so terrified I felt like I could barely move.

There was a crash in a different part of the house and angry voices. I had a feeling Taylor and Mark were up to some mischief. It had to be them hurling things through the air and blowing out candles, unless some other ghosts had decided to come to my aid. It was too bad they couldn't become flesh and blood. I needed more help than ghosts could give. I was thankful for whatever help I got however.

I felt like I inched my way down the hall for an eternity. It was like a nightmare playing out in slow motion. I reached the foot of the stairs in the parlor at last. If I could only make it across the parlor to the door.

"Hello dead boy!" said Kyle as he shined a flashlight in my face from across the room. I turned and bolted up the stairs. Kyle dashed after me, but a loveseat slid across the floor and he fell over it. I didn't look back.

As I hit the landing on the third floor, someone grabbed for me. I kicked at him, felt my foot contact flesh, and heard a grunt. I didn't stop for a second, but ran on up the stairs. I reached the fourth floor and bolted down the hall. My instinct was to just keep running and that's what I did. I ran, turned a corner, and ran again all the way to the far end of the hall. I opened the door before me and rushed into the library. I closed the door and heard pursuing footfalls even as I did so. I was so stupid. I'd trapped myself again. There was only one way out of that room. I dove under a huge library table as the door opened and someone searched the room with his light.

"I know you're here." said a voice that I couldn't quite place. "You've no place to go. Just give it up and maybe we'll go easy on you."

I didn't believe that for a moment. I was terrified. I was crying and shaking. They were going to find me and kill me. Worse than that, they were going to do some really nasty things to me. It didn't seem like what was happening could be real. It was just too horrible. I knew it was real however. It had happened before. Now it was happening to me. I was on the verge of becoming hysterical.

A flashlight shined in my eyes and two figures rushed toward me. I backed up, but there was nowhere to go. Strong hands grabbed me and pulled me from under the table. I fought so fiercely that I broke free. I had no idea I could fight like that. I had no idea I had it in me. It wouldn't save me however. There were two of them and the third one was undoubtedly coming. I couldn't make out who they were. I was still seeing spots from the light that had been shined in my eyes.

They came for me. I dodged and parried, but there was really nowhere to go. One of my attackers cried out in pain, for what reason I did not know. Soon he cried out again. I saw it that second time. I saw the book sail through the air and smack him upside the head. Suddenly books flew off the shelves in scores, seemingly hurtling themselves at my attackers of their own volition. The air was filled with them, all aimed at my attackers. It was like standing in the middle of a tornado. I stood there dumbfounded.

Something pushed me, pushed me hard, right into a huge bookcase. I felt it give, felt it open up. The next thing I knew I was on the other side of the wall, with the sounds of the library faint behind me. It was so dark I could see nothing, but I knew I was safe for the moment. I didn't know how long it would last, but at least I had a chance. I felt along the walls until I came to something cold and metal. It was a candleholder. I felt up farther. There was a candle still there. I took it from the holder and pulled a book of matches from my pocket. I always had matches with me. I constantly needed them at Graymoor. I struck one and the light seemed brilliant. I lit the candle and looked around at my surroundings.

I was in a narrow passage that twisted and turned. I knew I was within the walls of Graymoor. I'd always suspected there were secret passages, and even secret rooms, in that colossal old house, but it was the first time I'd found one. I guessed that I still hadn't found one. Something had clearly pushed me into the bookcase. I had no doubt the ghosts of Graymoor had shoved me into the passage to save my life.

I couldn't stop to think about it. I had to escape. Sooner or later, my pursuers would find their way into the passage. They weren't stupid. They'd know I didn't go out by the door. I stepped down the dusty, cobwebbed corridor. The dust on the floor was undisturbed. I knew no one had been in there in over a century. The passage twisted and turned, following the contours of walls and hallways. Every few feet there was a candleholder fixed to the wall, all with candles still in them. Like the rest of Graymoor, the passage was as it had always been.

I nearly cried out when I disturbed a bat and it flew off squeaking. I had to be careful. If I made a sound at the wrong time it could cost me my life. I wandered on, pondering how I'd get out of the passage. There had to be an exit, at least one, probably more. I came to a narrow stair and followed it down. It dipped sharply. It was almost more a ladder than a stair. It went down and down and still there was no end in sight.

The walls became rough stone and I almost felt as if I were in a cave, although I knew well that I was still within the walls of Graymoor.

    The stair ended at last. I just stood there shaking with terror at what was before me. I closed my eyes and tried to calm my ragged breath and trembling limbs. I was so terrified of going forward that I actually turned and put my foot on the stair. That's when I heard them. My pursuers had found their way into the passage above. I turned around, only the fear of torture and death made my feet move forward. My hands trembled so that my candle almost went out. Hot wax dripped on my fingers, burning me, but I heeded it not at all.

    I forced my feet to move forward, bringing myself ever closer to that which I feared. The candlelight shined on the coffins, dozens of them. I knew where I was without doubt. I was behind the walls of the crypt. I'd assumed that the coffins in the walls were housed in niches carved out of solid stone, but instead they were arranged on thick slabs of stone, one above the other. What was before me looked like massive shelves, stacked six high with coffins. There was row after row of them, one after the other, all just behind the wall of the crypt. I followed the narrow path between the morbid shelves and the far wall, passing so close to the coffins that I could have reached out and touched them if I dared.

    The air was putrid with the smell of rotting flesh. No one had been lain to rest there in over a century and still the foul stench was everywhere. It made me retch. I couldn't imagine a more horrible place. I had to fight myself to keep moving forward. There were coffins before and after me, there was nothing to do but go on. The caskets were of all shapes and sizes, most of them simple pine boxes, but many of them very ornate and expensive looking. Some of them were very small, the coffins of children, even babies. All the Graymoors were there, generations of them.

    I tried to quiet my fears. Why was I so terrified of corpses in coffins when I counted ghosts among my friends? What lie in those caskets were mere bodies, the mortal remains of those who had passed on. Even if their spirits lingered on they were not here. They were just bodies, long dead. They couldn't hurt me. They weren't going to jump out and grab me, or drag me screaming back into their coffin with them. I had no need to fear the dead. It was the living that were dangerous. I quieted my fears with such thoughts and my hands no longer trembled. My fear did not leave me, but it was much subdued.

I heard the sounds of my pursuers. I had true reason to fear those that followed me. They would grab me if they got the chance, and do unspeakable things to me. If I did not escape them, I'd be as dead as those that lay in their coffins.

I passed the final grim shelf at last. The passage came to an end. There was a solid wall of rock before me. I was trapped, there was no way out!

"Calm down Sean." I told myself. "There has to be a way out of here."

I felt along the walls, searching for a hidden passage. There were none that I could discover. My eyes fell on the coffins. There was a way out, but it wasn't a pleasant one. The sounds of my pursuers drew nearer. I had to move quickly.

I grabbed the end of a coffin and pulled it as far from the inner wall as I could. I climbed into the shelf and pushed against the sealed opening. It wouldn't give. I could hear my attackers clearly, they were nearly upon me. I squirmed around until my feet were against the sealed opening, and my shoulders were to the end of the coffin. The handle dug into my back as I pushed with both feet. I felt something give, then crack. I'd broken the seal.

I pushed harder, using all my might. With a loud crash the sealing stone came loose and fell to the floor of the crypt. My pursuers were on top of me. I squirmed out the narrow opening even as strong hands grabbed for me. I threw myself into the crypt, jumped to my feet and bolted up the stone stairs. It was a wonder I didn't break my neck, running at top speed in total darkness. Somehow I knew where I was going however. Something guided me, or perhaps I should say someone.

I ran into the hall. I ran right into Kyle. He went sprawling onto the floor, but it didn't take him long to recover. He was on my heels in a flash. I made for the front door, but he blocked me. I couldn't get out. I couldn't escape. It was a nightmare.

I turned and bolted up the stairs. I ran to my room and closed the door, but there was no lock. There was nowhere to go in Graymoor that would allow me to escape from my horrible fate.

I shoved a table up against the door, but I knew it would only buy me a little time. My eyes darted around the room.

"F-a-g-g-o-t" I heard Kyle calling slowly. He drew the word out until it sounded like some kind of chant. His voice almost sounded pleasant, like someone playing a game with a child, but I knew the hatred that was behind it.

"Come out little faggot. It's time to die. It's time to get what you deserve." Kyle's voice filled me with terror like nothing ever had before. The way he chanted the words made it more horrible still. There was no escape.

Kyle pushed hard against the door. I grabbed up a baseball bat.

"You're just making it harder faggot. Don't make me any madder than I already am. I'll just hurt you that much more."

A few more tries and he was in. Kyle stepped through the door, followed by Justin, a boy I knew from school. They both had flashlights and I could see them well for the first time. My eyes looked from one to the other in terror. I could take out either one of them with the bat, but I had to do it fast when I swung. I knew the other would be on me in a flash. Justin was by far the strongest. He'd be my target. If I could take him out, I might have a chance to knock out Kyle before the third guy was on me. I wondered where the third one was, and if there were any more.

"You know, you're really pissing me off Sean." said Kyle, his voice dripping with malice. "We were going to kill you pretty quick, just a fast slash across the throat, but not now. Now you're going to suffer. We'll give you a little preview of hell fucker."

"I'm not going to hell." I told him, watching and waiting for my chance. My voice shook with fear. The boys were keeping their distance, playing the waiting game.

"Of course you are." said Kyle. "All fags go to hell. Didn't you read that booklet I left for you?"

"That's fucking bull shit!" I yelled.

"God Hates Queers!" yelled Kyle. "You're doomed. You'll all be gone soon. We'll get all you fuckers, one by one!"

Kyle seemed almost out of his mind. He was transformed by hate and rage.

"So you killed them didn't you? Marty, Ken, and Tony?"

"Duh!" said Kyle. "You are so fucking stupid! Of course I killed them. I took your little fuck buddy Marty out all by myself. He was easy. Wanna hear how I did it?"

"No!" I said.

"I'm gonna tell you anyway faggot. Marty wanted in my pants bad. Just like you. He wanted to blow me like all you faggots. All I had to do was lead him into the woods. He thought he was going to get what all fags want. Instead he got what they all deserve. I blew his fucking brains out right when he kneeled down in front of me."

Kyle laughed. I wanted to kill him.

"And Ken and Tony," said Kyle. "They were just as easy. I decided they needed to suffer more than Marty had however. Just getting their brains blown out didn't seem to be quite enough. Justin here was glad to help me and Dusty too."

Kyle turned his head to the door and yelled. "Come on Dusty, we don't have all night." Pretty soon, Dusty was in the room too. He was another boy from school, one I'd never have suspected. Hell, I'd never suspected a one of those guys.

"You should have seen those little faggots beg for mercy," said Kyle smiling. "Ken was the worst. He whimpered and cried like a girl. It was a pleasure to crack his skull."

"Stop it!" I yelled.

"What's wrong?" said Kyle. "Am I scaring you little fairy? You might as well put that bat down. You don't have a chance. God is on our side. God hates little queers you know."

"No!" I yelled. "That's a lie."

Kyle just laughed at me. He pulled a large knife from a pack he carried. He smiled at it in glee and then at me. I swallowed hard.

"I can't wait to cut you faggot. Maybe we won't beat you like the others. I think it's time for something different."

Dusty grabbed for the bat and I swung at his head. He lurched back and I caught him in the ribs. I could feel the bones break. Dusty fell to the floor screaming but Kyle and Justin were on me in a flash. I kicked and punched in terror. I was wild, like a cornered beast. Still, they managed to get hold of my arms. I twisted and turned, using every ounce of muscle I had. Kyle and Justin were all over me. Kyle punched me hard in the face. Justin jabbed me in the abdomen. I doubled over, but somehow managed to kick Justin square in the nuts at the same time. I nailed him full force. That brought him to his knees. I broke from Kyle's grasp, slammed into him with my shoulder, and fought my way out the door.

I ran for the stairs, but Kyle was right behind me. He dove for my ankles and sent me crashing to the floor. He was on me in a second, fists flying, but in my terror I fought him off. I wanted to make a break for it, but Kyle was standing at the top of the stairs. I couldn't get past him. I actually thought of jumping over the railing, but I knew the fall would kill me. I jerked back as Kyle lunged at me. I ran to the end of the hall. Kyle closed on me. Justin wasn't far behind. That kick in the nuts had only disabled him for a short while. I was trapped. I didn't even have the bat anymore.

Kyle smiled evilly. He drew his knife back out, ready to go to work on me. Justin limped forward, his eyes filled with hate.

"You are gonna die so slow faggot!" said Justin.

I tensed, ready to fight. Even as they closed on me I knew it was all over. I'd never make it past them. I'd never be able to fight my way through them both. I wasn't going to give up without a fight however. They'd kill me just the same anyway. There was no one more free than he who has nothing to lose. I sure didn't have anything to lose, I was dead already.

Between us a mist formed and took shape. I knew that my attackers could see it too. They stopped dead in their tracks.

"What the fuck!" said Kyle.

The forms became more distinct until they looked more solid than ever before. It was Taylor and Mark.

Kyle and Justin were frightened, but determined nonetheless. They hesitated, afraid to move forward, but I knew they'd get over their fear in a few moments. I just wished there was something Taylor and Mark could do, but I knew they had no physical existence. They couldn't stop what was going to happen.

I caught movement behind Kyle and Justin. Dusty had come to be a part of the kill. He was carrying the baseball bat I'd dropped. It was all over. I'd found the killers, but instead of stopping them, I was their next victim.

Taylor and Mark surged forward, uttering the most horrible moaning sound I'd ever heard in my life. I could read the terror in Kyle and Justin's eyes. They involuntarily jerked back. Dusty swung the bat and cracked Justin in the head, but it wasn't Dusty, it was Marshall. Only when he had drawn close could I tell it was him. I was never so glad to see anyone in my entire life. Without thinking I kicked the knife from

Kyle's hand. Marshall pounced on him, as did I. We wrestled him down and had his arm twisted behind his back in no time at all.

"Get some rope!" said Marshall.

He held Kyle as I went for rope, twisting his arm to keep him subdued. I was back in moments and soon Kyle was bound tight. We checked Justin, but he lay dead on the floor, no breath, no pulse, no heartbeat.

"Why did you come?" I asked Marshall. His arrival at just that moment seemed a bit much for coincidence.

"When a dead boy appears in your room and tells you to come running, you do as you're told." said Marshall. His face was animated with excitement and fear. "I really saw him. He really spoke to me. The real thing."

I was happy for Marshall, but I didn't really feel like discussing his night right then. I looked around for Taylor and Mark, but they were nowhere to be seen. I didn't have to ask who had summoned Marshall to my rescue.

I leaned back against the wall, my heart pounding in my chest, my breath racing. I started to cry. It had all been far too much. My nerves were frayed. I was shaking and I couldn't stop. I felt like I was going to pass out.

It wasn't over however. Even as I leaned against the wall I felt it. I felt something enter the hallway. I did not know from where it had come, but I could feel it as clearly as I'd felt Taylor when he came to me on the soccer field. This time however, I was afraid. Marshall could feel it too.

"Something's here." he said.

"What's here?" I asked.

"Your death." I looked at Marshall. It was he who spoke. He was laughing, a cruel and horrible laugh. His face was contorted. He didn't look like himself at all. He didn't seem like himself at all. Even his voice sounded like it belonged to someone else. I had no idea what was going on with Marshall. Even Kyle looked at him confused, and afraid.

Marshall grabbed up the fallen knife.

"Move!" he screamed as he stabbed at my chest. It was Marshall's usual voice this time. I threw myself to the floor just in time, the knife tearing through my shirt.

I jumped to my feet as Marshall stood, holding the knife in front of him. He swung it back in forth, kept it moving.

"What the fuck are you doing?" I cried.

Kyle sat there as astonished as I was. He had no more idea than I did why my friend had suddenly turned on me.

"I can't stop it!" said Marshall, even as he took another swipe at me. "Get out of here!"

I looked at him in terror. Marshall was screaming at me to get away, even as he tried to kill me.

"Run Sean! I can't stop it! Oh my God!" Marshall was screaming and crying as he slashed at me. I couldn't get past him. I couldn't escape. He was hysterical.

I grabbed up the bat and used it to fend off the blows. They were falling terrifyingly close.

"Knock me out!" he screamed at me. "Knock me out!"

"I can't!" I screamed back at him. "I can't hurt you. It could kill you!"

"You've got too! For God's sake hurry!"

I was confused, bewildered. I hadn't the slightest idea of what was happening.

"You lose fuckers," laughed Marshall, but not Marshall. The words were coming from his lips, but it wasn't him. "No way to win. One of you dies now, the other later. The only question is who goes first." There was unmasked delight in Marshall's eyes.

I fended Marshall off but he kept coming at me. He was relentless. I didn't have a moment to think. He slashed at me over and over. I just knew that at any second I'd feel the sharp knife slice through my flesh. I cringed at the very thought.

I took careful aim and swung the bat at the back of Marshall's head. I tried to hit him just hard enough to disable him without hurting him too much. I prayed I wouldn't kill him. I cried as the bat contacted with his skull. Marshall went down. He was out cold.

I kicked the knife away and checked Marshall. He was breathing and seemed to be okay. Tears were streaming from my eyes. Having to hurt one of my friends like that was about more than I could take. I tried to calm myself by remembering that if I hadn't done it, Marshall would have killed me. He would have had to live with my death on his conscience for the rest of his life.

"What did you do to him?!" I screamed at Kyle, grabbing him by the shirt and lifting him up off the floor. "What did you do?"

"Nothing!" he yelled, obviously terrified. "He's whacked out on drugs or something. I didn't do anything!"

I believed him. There was sincerity and fear in his voice. Besides, how could he have possibly done anything to make Marshall act like that?

I looked at Kyle. His eyes were wild with terror. As I looked at him, his eyes and features changed. It was as if he became another person. He suddenly went insane kicking and screaming, but the ropes held. I backed away from him, terrified of the sight before me.

"All of you will die horribly. Die! Die! Die! There is no escape. Die!" Kyle laughed hysterically. It was the most frightening sound I'd ever heard in my entire life. His voice was a weird mixture of his own and that of another. Something was inside him. I'd heard that frightening second voice as Marshall had spoken too, but I could hear it more clearly now. Before I'd thought I was imagining it. I had not been. The sound of it made my flesh crawl. I knew that I was dealing with something far more dangerous now than three murderous boys.

I grabbed Marshall by the shoulders and pulled him down the hall, getting him as far away from Kyle as I could. Kyle stared at us, as if he could kill us through sheer will. There was something so evil in his gaze that I could not bear to look him in the eyes. There was something more than Kyle there, something that had never been there before, something that did not belong. Kyle was a sadistic murdering bastard, but something told me that whatever was now in him was far, far more dangerous and evil. The situation had just taken a turn for the worse.

I wanted to get Marshall still further away from him, so I lifted him over my shoulders and carried him downstairs to the kitchen. It was no easy task lugging him down three flights of stairs. I had no idea how heavy a body could be. I sat Marshall down in a chair and stood there for a moment, gasping for breath. I wet a dish towel with cold water and put it on Marshall's face. In a few moments he stirred, then opened his eyes. My relief was considerable.

"How do you feel?"

"Like someone smacked me in the head with a baseball bat. How do you think I feel? Tell me what happened after you knocked me out."

I filled Marshall in on the few events that had taken place while he was unconscious. He looked more frightened that I'd ever seen him before.

"Oh fuck! Oh fuck!" he said. "I knew it! We are so fucked!"

"What is it?" I asked him.

"Possession."

"What?"

"You felt it come, that thing. It got inside me. I couldn't stop it. I wasn't strong enough. When you knocked me out it must have went in Kyle."

"Then let's get the fuck out of here while we can!" I said, practically screaming. I was so terrified that I was nearly irrational. I made for the door, but Marshall grabbed my arm.

"No. It's no good. You can't run from something like this. You can't hide. It doesn't matter where you go. It will find you. We've got to take care of it here, and now."

"And just how are we going to do that?" I practically screamed at him. I believed Marshall, but I still wanted nothing more than to just get the fuck out of there.

"Too late boys!" The door to the kitchen flew open and Dusty stood there glaring at us. I looked quickly at Marshall.

"He shouldn't be able to walk." I said.

"He's not alone," said Marshall. "It's in him, the evil spirit."

"No evil spirits here." said Dusty in a dual voice that absolutely made my skin crawl. "I'm a servant of God. All fags must die! God hates queers!" His voice alone seemed as if it was enough to kill. It so filled me with terror that I felt like I couldn't move.

I stared at Dusty, feeling with my mind what was within him. I looked at Marshall, then back at Dusty.

"I know who you are." I said. Dusty glared at me with eyes that seemed not his own. "You're that guy who was the leader of the 'God Hates Queers' group. The one who killed himself." As I spoke the fear in me turned to disgust and contempt. "You are no servant of God. You were a wicked man full of hate and malice and now you're an evil spirit filled with the same."

Dusty screamed at me with two voices and rushed at me. I darted around the heavy kitchen table, keeping it between us.

"Don't piss him off dude!" yelled Marshall.

Marshall didn't understand. That thing was already intent on killing me. Making it madder wouldn't change that. It might make him more reckless however and give us a chance to knock Dusty out cold. The evil spirit didn't seem able to do much with an unconscious body. I looked at Marshall. He was eyeing Dusty, waiting for his chance. I knew he'd try to bash him in the head when the opportunity arose. I'd do the same if I got the chance. I wasn't worried about hurting Dusty. He'd helped kill my friends and he couldn't blame it on an evil spirit. Both Marty and Ken had been murdered before the "God Hates Queers" guy killed himself. Rev. Devlin had nothing at all to do with the first two murders and maybe not with the third.

"I know why you killed yourself." I said. "I know what the police found when they searched your motel room. You're not only a liar, you're a hypocrite. I know about the photos, and the video tapes. I know what was on them. You're nothing more than a child molester."

Dusty grabbed a meat cleaver and vaulted right over the kitchen table. I hadn't counted on that. Apparently the possessed had more than ordinary strength. I fell on my back and watched as the cleaver hurtled down. I jerked to the side and the cleaver bit deep into the floor, splinters flew into my face. I rolled away and jumped to my feet as Dusty wrenched it free.

I grabbed a frying pan and used it to bat away the cleaver as Dusty swung at me. I didn't dare take my eyes off him for a moment. He swiped at me yet again and I couldn't quite get clear. The cleaver ripped through my shirt. I felt the cleaver cut me, but I knew it had barely touched me. Dusty smiled at me. It was an evil, wicked smile, a smile from the depths of hell.

I was breathing hard, half from exertion, half from sheer terror. I tried not to think about what would happen if Dusty managed a good swipe at me. He kept trying, kept coming at me. I dodged and parried, leaped and ran, I fended off the blows with the skillet, but he just kept coming. He was relentless.

Marshall was busy, but there didn't seem to be much he could do. He cracked Dusty across the back with a broom handle, actually snapping it in two. Dusty cried out in pain, but it didn't even slow him down that much. Marshall nailed him with whatever he could find to hurl at him, but Dusty just shrugged it off like a mosquito bite. Pain didn't seem to affect him. Marshall aimed a blow at his head, but Dusty jerked down and to the side. I used the opportunity. I leaped in and caught Dusty up side the head with the skillet. He sank to the floor unconscious.

"Rope!" said Marshall.

I frantically searched through the drawers and came up with some heavy clothesline. Marshall bound Dusty with it, tying both his hands and feet. When he awoke, the evil spirit would be in control of a bound boy.

"We don't have much time," said Marshall. "We've got to get rid of that thing before it comes back."

"And how do we do that?" I asked.

"We have to perform an exorcism."

"Are you out of your mind?"

"You have a better idea?"

I didn't have any ideas at all.

"Doesn't that take a priest?" I asked.

"No. That would be better, but we don't have the time."

"What do we do?"

"First, get a white candle and light it."

I grabbed one of the candles we'd used for the séance and set it in the middle of the kitchen table. It was a big thick one, about four inches across. I lit it.

"Get a big bowl, something you can start a fire in."

I jerked a thick crock bowl off the counter. My mom would shit when she found out what I did to her precious antique, but I'd worry about that later. I had bigger troubles on my mind.

"Now put a tablespoon of powdered garlic in it."

I was rushing around the kitchen like some kind of cook gone mad, searching for the ingredients. While I was getting the garlic, Marshall went on.

"We'll also need a tablespoon of ground cloves, a couple handfuls of sage, a tablespoon of peppermint…"

Mom didn't have ground cloves, but I found a little spice jar with whole cloves. I dumped them on the counter and smashed them with a heavy meat mallet.

"Sage, sage, I know there's some here somewhere."

I couldn't find any with the other spices, then I noticed mom's dried herbs hanging on the wall. She liked to decorate with them. I wondered which one was sage. I sniffed each bunch until I found the one that smelled like the stuff in sausage. I knew that sage was in sausage, so that had to be it. I dumped the sage in the bowl, then rifled through the cabinets looking for peppermint.

"There's no peppermint!" I said.

"Um, how about peppermint tea." said Marshall.

"Got that!" I said as I grabbed a box of peppermint tea and dumped the entire contents in the bowl. "Its that it?"

"No, we need a little dried thistle."

"Thistle? I know there's no thistle in here. Will this work without it?"

"No." said Marshall, "We've got to have all the ingredients."

"We're screwed." I said. Marshall and I just looked at each other. The kitchen was deathly quiet. I felt like I'd just written our epitaph.

I felt something wash over me and flow into me. I wanted to warn Marshall, but I couldn't make myself speak. Something was preventing it. I fought it, but I couldn't keep it out, it was far too strong. It was like trying to stop a forest fire with a thimble full of water.

I casually walked over to the refrigerator, against my will. I knew that thing was in me, controlling me. I fought against it, but I couldn't break its hold on me. I was screaming inside. I knew what it had planned. I knew Marshall would never see it coming. He was going to die by my hand before he even knew what hit him.

I opened the refrigerator door. It was such a simple and innocent move, so common, but this time so evil. I reached in and pulled out two bottles of root beer, then turned to Marshall. I wanted to scream at him to run, as he'd warned me, but I couldn't do it. I couldn't do anything but look at Marshall as if all was well. I couldn't even warn him by rolling my eyes. I had no control whatsoever over my own body. I fought with all my might to do something, anything, to warn Marshall, but I was powerless.

"Uh Sean, this isn't exactly the time for a break. We've got to get some thistle!"

I prayed he'd pick up on the illogic of my actions. I prayed he'd see the strangeness in the out of place normalcy. Who in his right mind would be stopping for a drink when he should be scrambling to save his life? I directed my thoughts at Marshall projecting "Think Marshall think! Get away!" It was no use, nothing I tried made any difference. I wanted to scream, I wanted to cry, I could do neither.

"Root beer?" I asked Marshall just as casually and friendly as if I was asking him if he'd like something to go with his pizza. There was nothing casual about it however. My arm involuntarily hurtled the bottle downward, striking the base on the table. It shattered leaving me holding the jagged bottle neck. I made a lightning fast swipe at Marshall's exposed throat as he jumped backward. It all happened so fast I don't know how he got out of the way in time. I thanked God that he did however.

I felt a smile form on my lips that was not my own. I took another swipe at Marshall, but he was ready for me. He dodged out of the way. I kept coming at him, kept slashing for his throat, but I couldn't quite make contact. It was worse than my worst nightmare. No matter how hard I fought against it, I couldn't stop my body from trying to kill my friend.

Marshall gaped at me with a look of both fear and understanding. He knew it wasn't me who was trying to kill him. It was that thing. I fought against it as hard as I could, but it was too powerful. It made me feel weak and impotent. I was completely controlled by another. The thing inside me laughed at me. If I could have willed myself dead at that moment I would have done so. I was crying. I couldn't bear the thought of hurting Marshall.

A terrible vision forced its way into my head. I don't know if it sprang from my own mind, or if it was placed there by the evil presence within me. I saw myself wandering the streets of Verona, lurking, waiting my chance. I saw myself murdering my friends, everyone I cared about. I couldn't bare the thoughts, but I couldn't stop them either.

Marshall was keeping himself just out of range. He was quite a gymnast it seemed. He dove and rolled and vaulted. Being assaulted by a possessed maniac seemed to inspire one to tremendous athletic feats.

When the evil one was in Marshall and after me, I'd found myself doing things I never thought I'd be able to do.

Marshall grabbed up a heavy rolling pin. I knew what had to happen if he was going to survive. The thought of the pain made my heart clutch in terror. I could almost feel Marshall crushing my skull. Maybe he'd be able to keep from killing me, but maybe not. Either way, it was going to hurt bad.

The fear of pain wasn't the least of it. I didn't want to die. I'd never really feared death, but I wasn't ready, not yet. I especially didn't want to die like this. I didn't want Marshall to face the guilt and I didn't want the evil bastard within me to win.

Using my force of will, I tried to leave myself open so Marshall could take a swing at me. I tried to lower my defenses. I couldn't do it. For the first time ever I wished that I was physically weaker. I wished that I had less muscle, less strength. I wanted Marshall to be able to take me. No matter how hard I tried, I couldn't weaken my own defenses. I couldn't even throw off my balance for the merest of moments. I felt that thing laughing at my futile efforts. I was humiliated.

Marshall never got the chance to knock me out cold, or to kill me. The evil presence within me learned fast. It knew our game.

I threw down the bottle neck and grabbed up a large knife. I didn't slash at Marshall. Instead I took it by the blade and threw it at him. He dove for the floor just in time as the knife buried itself in the wall behind him. I grabbed up another knife and threw it at him with deadly accuracy. Marshall bolted out the door leading outside, barely escaping the butcher knife that I hurled at his head.

I screamed in rage, but the scream was not my own. My hand flung out and smashed the candle and the bowl to the floor. The bowl did not break, but the contents were spilled. I turned to the counter and violently raked everything to the floor with my arm. I trashed everything that had to do with the exorcism. I fought it as hard as I could, but I was impotent and powerless.

My hand grabbed the bottle neck and picked it up. I watched as I held it out in front of me. I knew what was going to happen. The evil spirit taunted me from within, forcing horrible images into my mind of what would happen to my body as it forced me to slash and disembowel myself. I couldn't even scream. I had no control at all.

My free hand grabbed my shirt and pulled it up, exposing my abdomen and the lower part of my chest. I swallowed hard. I wanted to close my eyes, but the evil presence within me would not allow it. It forced me to watch. I couldn't even turn my eyes away from my hand as it held the broken bottle.

I watched in horror as my hand rose then stabbed the jagged bottle neck toward my abdomen. In the same instant I saw Marshall hurtle himself through the kitchen window and fling himself at me. Broken glass flew all over the kitchen as the window shattered. The bottle flew from my hands and exploded into a thousand pieces on the floor. Marshall's full weight fell on my chest and knocked the wind out of me for a moment. My head snapped back on the floor and I was dazed, but only for a moment. I raised myself up, reaching for Marshall's throat with outstretched fingers, but he backhanded me and broke free.

Marshall dove for his backpack and I saw him pull something small and silver out of it. I rushed at him, but he held a small cross up in front of himself and I felt my body brake and scramble backwards. I screamed in agonized terror, but I knew it was the evil one within me who shrank from the cross.

Marshall advanced on me, holding the cross in front of him like he was in some kind of vampire movie. I backed away from him, the evil spirit within me enraged but powerless against the religious symbol. My back was to the kitchen wall and Marshall closed on me relentlessly. My body writhed and clawed the air. The evil within me spouted horrible curses from my lips, but I was oddly calm and without fear.

"Leave him!" said Marshall in a commanding tone I'd never heard issue from his lips before. He spoke with a dual voice as before, but it had not the sound of evil in it. I was certain that Marshall was indeed possessed as I was, but not by a spirit of evil, rather by one of good.

"Leave him!" shouted Marshall more loudly.

The cross was before my eyes and they were wild with terror. Marshall reached out and ripped my shirt, exposing my chest. He pressed the cross directly over my heart and screamed at the evil one.

"Get out you fucking bastard!"

My lips screamed and I felt a rush as the evil spirit fled from my body. I sank to the floor, exhausted. Marshall grabbed what was left of my shirt and pulled me toward the kitchen table.

"Stay close, it will be back," he said. "Take my hand. Whatever happens, don't let go!"

Marshall slapped his hand against my own and held it tight. I could feel the cross between us. More than that, I could feel a tremendous surge of energy flowing through us and I could feel the presence of others within me. We were not alone. I felt no fear from within however. I knew who was there and I knew they would do no harm to either of us.

With our free hands we scooped up the spilled contents of the bowl and placed them back within it. We set the bowl and candle back on the table. We re-lit the candle.

"What about the thistle?" I said.

Marshall pulled some withered plants from his pocket and tossed them into the bowl.

"Good thing your yard is overgrown." he said.

We felt something surging around us, like a powerful wind, but more than that. Its mere presence filled me with terror. The force of it whipped my hair around and threatened to rip my torn shirt from my body. It was that strong. Pots and pans started flying around the kitchen, hurtling through the air. Glass was breaking everywhere. It was like being inside a whirlwind. Despite the wind, the candle remained steady, it didn't even flicker. The evil force could not touch it. I felt it pressing against us while the energy within us repelled it with terrifying force. I felt like I was standing in the midst of an ancient battle between good and evil.

"Don't let go of my hand!" yelled Marshall, shouting over the wind.

Marshall lit a thistle blossom in the candle and thrust it into the bowl. The contents ignited with a great flash and smoke began to fill the room. Marshall began to speak in a steady chant.

"In the name of the Eternal Lady and Lord, I bid thee part. I consecrate and clear this space. Let nothing but joy linger here."

We heard a great wail and felt a rush as the evil fled. There was a great force of wind rushing from the room as we were left behind in its wake. Still holding my hand, Marshall led me into the next room and repeated "In the name of the Eternal Lady and Lord, I bid thee part. I consecrate and clear this space. Let nothing but joy linger here."

I could detect the evil presence no longer. I could detect no energy within me. I felt like it was just me in my body. Marshall led me from one room to the next, chanting the same words in each, never releasing my hand. When we had gone through the entire house (no small task I assure you), including the attic and the crypt, we returned to the kitchen. Marshall set the bowl beside the still lit candle and we watched as the last of the mixture burned out. We took the ashes outside and sprinkled them over the yard. Only then did Marshall release my hand.

"This has been one fucked up night," said Marshall. "But I wouldn't have missed it for the world."

I smiled at him for a moment. "You are so weird Marshall." He laughed.

We limped our way to Marshall's house, both of us had taken quite a beating. We called the police and pretty soon the red lights of squad cars and ambulances were bathing the neighborhood in flashing lights.

Dusty was carried out on a stretcher. He had a punctured lung and couldn't even move. He'd live for his trial however. Justin was carried out in a body bag. I put my arm around Marshall's shoulders and held him close as the black bag was slipped into the back of an ambulance. Marshall was pretty torn up over having killed him, even though he knew he had no choice. If Marshall hadn't done it, it would have been my body in that bag. Still, it was something that would take him a long time to learn to deal with.

Kyle was brought out in handcuffs last of all. He glared at us with pure hatred and malice. I wondered how he'd been able to hide all that hate from me for so long. It just didn't seem possible. As he passed he spit at us.

"I'll get both you fuckers! Just you wait! Especially you faggot!"

I was sure saying that would really help him at his trial. It probably didn't matter. I was sure there would be more than enough proof to put him away.

Marshall and I were stuffed in a squad car. We were taken to the police station where we made our statements. We told about everything that had happened, but omitted all references to ghosts and evil spirits. Most people didn't believe in stuff like that. We didn't get home until the early morning hours. I didn't even remember walking up to my room. I was asleep before my head even hit the pillow. I slept the sleep of the dead.

Chapter 29

The Return of Friends

Marshall was at my house early the next afternoon. The two of us had a lot to talk about.

"That wasn't just you near the end was it?" I asked him.

"No." said Marshall. "I'd like to take credit for being so brave, but I didn't really have a choice. The second knife you threw at me would have got me, but I felt something come into me just then, something that took over my body and hurled me out the door. I felt like someone just picked up my body and tossed it, but yet it was my body that was doing it, it just wasn't me in control. It wasn't even me who grabbed up the thistle and shoved it into my pocket. It all happened so fast I didn't have time to even think.

"The next thing I knew I was crashing through that window. The only thing I was thinking right then was how I was going to be cut to ribbons, but I didn't even get a scratch. It was like being a spectator, except unlike before, my body was doing things I wanted it to do. It was them, it was Taylor and Mark that were in me."

"Yes," I said, "I could feel them when you took my hand. I wasn't afraid anymore after that."

We were both silent for a moment.

"I guess they're gone for good now." I said. I looked at Marshall, hoping he'd tell me I was wrong, hoping he'd tell me that the exorcism didn't force them away too.

"I guess so," he said.

I felt like crying.

* * *

A few nights later I was sitting up in bed reading when I heard a noise outside my door. I wondered if Edward and his father would come rushing in. I had not seen the ghostly reenactment of the murders since the night I'd almost been killed. The whole house had been very quiet since then, as if all the ghosts were either gone, or at peace at last.

Two figures stepped through the door and I recognized them immediately. I jumped from my bed and ran toward them smiling. I felt like I was seeing long lost friends.

"I thought you guys were gone forever!" I said.

"No," said Taylor smiling, "exorcisms only work on evil spirits. We'll be sticking around. This is where we belong. We've only been resting. Nights like the other one take a lot out of a ghost."

I laughed. I was so relieved to see them.

"Seriously though, thank you both, you saved my life."

"Hey," said Mark, "There are enough ghosts around this place already, we don't need you haunting Graymoor too. Besides, Tay and I had a score to settle with that particular evil spirit."

"What do you mean?" I asked.

"You've read what I wrote. Remember Devon? The boy who beat me up so bad he almost killed me? The boy who made our lives a living hell?"

"Yeah," I said, "but that evil spirit was Rev. Devlin, I just know it."

"Yes," said Mark, "Rev. Devon Devlin."

"Holy shit!" I said.

"Yep,' said Mark, "one and the same."

I was astounded. I'd never expected that for a moment. Then again, why would I? Who would have made the connection between the eighteen-year-old boy of some twenty years before and the thirty-something leader of the "God Hates Queers" movement.

"I'm so glad you're back. I said.

I paused for a moment, looking around me. "I feel terrible that you have to stay in this horrible old place though." I said. I thought those two boys deserved to be somewhere beautiful.

"Remember," said Taylor, "that it isn't the same for us here as it is for you. Take my hand and I'll show you."

I reached out and grasped both Mark and Taylor by the hand. I was amazed when I discovered they were both solid, and warm. They felt every bit as much alive as I did. I didn't have time to wonder about that however as my surroundings were transformed in an instant. The room was no longer dark and gray and dingy. It was bright and beautiful, a paradise. It was the same room, with the same furnishings, but everything was so clean, so warm, so beautiful. It looked as I imagined Graymoor must have looked when it was new, only better. Everything had a golden glow. I felt as if I had stepped into Heaven.

I looked at Taylor and Mark and saw them as they really were for the first time. They were no longer bluish gray and transparent. They looked like any flesh and blood boys, but even more beautiful and radiant than they were in their photo. It was as if they were as they had been in life, only perfected. They were so beautiful I almost couldn't look at them, and yet I didn't want to stop looking. I could feel such kindness and warmth from them that I felt again I was in the presence of angels. I guess I was.

They took me from room to room and I marveled at what I saw there. Everything was bright and beautiful. I recognized much of what was there, but there were other things too, pieces of furniture that had long ago disappeared from Graymoor, but were once again there for Taylor and Mark.

"Your dream came true didn't it?" I said, turning to them. "You wanted to live here forever and ever, together in a place where no one would bother you."

"Yes." said Taylor as he hugged Mark close to him.

"Is this Heaven?" I asked.

"It's our Heaven." Mark answered. "Have you ever read in the Bible, where it says 'My father has many mansions?'" He asked.

"Yes." I said.

"This is one of them." Suddenly, I understood. I had no need to worry about my friends. They were beyond all harm and hate, nothing could ever hurt them again.

"The friends you lost are surely in a place like this too, their own place." said Taylor. "Someday you can join them if you like, but don't hurry."

"I won't." I said smiling. Coming so close to death had made me really appreciate my life. I intended to live it as long as I could and get as much out of it as possible.

We walked outside and I was amazed to find we were in the full light of day, although I knew it was night.

"But how…" I began to ask.

"Day and night are kind of relative in our world," explained Taylor. "As are the seasons and even the years. It's all a matter of perception and we wanted you to see our world in the light of day."

"Oh my gosh." I said, looking at Graymoor. It didn't look like the creepy old mansion that I'd come to know. It was an elegant, stately home just as beautiful as it could be. At that moment I decided I'd help my parents with the renovations. I knew Graymoor would look just like what I was seeing when my parents were done with it.

We walked through the streets of Verona. Most of it was familiar, but there were homes and buildings there that hadn't been there before.

There were also places that were missing. The boys could tell I was a little confused.

"This is what it was like when we were alive. This is what Verona looked like twenty years ago," said Mark.

It all made sense then, the appearance of the town that is. One thing didn't make sense at all however.

"Why would you want to stay here?" I asked. "After the way everyone treated you. After the horrible things they did and said."

"This is our home," said Taylor. "It's familiar and comfortable. Unpleasant things happened here, but wonderful things happened as well. You're remembering only the bad, where we tend to remember only the good. We suffered here, but we also experienced the best times of our lives here. There were those who were cruel, but also those who showed friendship that was without bounds."

"I think I understand." I said. I guess if I died right then, I'd have wanted to stay right there too.

We walked on to the soccer fields. Somehow I knew that's where we'd end up.

"We spend a great deal of time here," said Mark.

"I didn't know ghosts played soccer." I said smiling.

"Actually we play it quite well." said Taylor.

There was a soccer ball there, although I hadn't noticed it before. Mark took a position in the goal and Taylor and I passed the ball back and forth until we could take a shot. I wasn't very good at soccer really, but that didn't matter, it was fun. Taylor rifled the ball right past Mark's head.

"He never was a very good goalie," said Taylor laughing.

"Hey!" yelled Mark, as if he were upset, then he laughed too.

We played for several minutes. We played until I completely forgot that the boys I was playing with were "dead". As soon as that realization came to me, both Mark and Taylor looked at me.

"You understand now don't you?" said Taylor.

"Yes." I said smiling. I did understand. I understood that there was nothing to fear from death, nothing at all. It was just like life, only without the problems and pain. I had no need to grieve for Marty and the others. If this was what death was like, then they were happier than ever. Death was nothing less than dreams coming true. I'd understood when Taylor and Mark explained it to me, but it really became clear when they showed it to me.

There was even more to it than that however. If there was nothing to fear from death, what was there to fear from life? I suddenly felt very free. I felt like I could do anything. More than that, I knew I could. I smiled at the boys. I realized what they'd done for me.

"It is time to take you back," said Mark. "Keeping you here is not allowed and no one goes against the wishes of the big guy."

"I bet not!" I smiled.

In an instant, we were back in my room and all was as it had been before.

"Will I see you again?" I asked.

"As often as you wish." said Taylor and then the two of them disappeared before my eyes.

Chapter 30

A Boyfriend at Last

I got up the next morning looking at the world with new eyes. There seemed to be so much more there than ever before. The world hadn't changed however, I had. The fears that kept me from living my life as I should disappeared like fog in the sun.

I showered and dressed, then rode my bike out to the farm. It was summer at last and I was working full time for Ethan and Nathan. It was hot work, and sometimes hard, but I loved it. I helped Ethan repair a tractor for about an hour, then joined Nathan and Nick clearing the fence rows. We were just about done with that task. We'd been working on it for what seemed like forever, but I was still amazed that we'd cleared out literally miles of fencing in such a short time. I enjoyed working side by side with Nathan, and especially Nick.

I'd had my eye on Nick since the first day I saw him. Even when I was lusting after Kyle, I was beginning to fall for Nick. I felt something when I looked at him that drew me to him, and I'm not talking about sexual attraction, although that was there too. Something in my heart responded to him. I felt for him. I didn't even realize what it was for a long time. It was only after Kyle was revealed as a monster than I came to understand what I was feeling for Nick. I was falling in love.

That realization had hit me only days before and it filled me with indescribable happiness as well as sheer terror and dread. I loved someone and had the possibility of a boyfriend before me for the first time. I knew the danger however. Nick most likely didn't go for guys. I was falling in love with him when he could very well be a straight boy. If he was, my hopes would be crushed and I could even lose him as a friend.

I looked at Nick as he hacked a small sapling out of the fence row. He was smiling and joking around with Nathan. I loved him. I was in love with him. There was no denying it. Those feelings had kind of slipped up on me and taken me unaware, but they were as clear as they could be. For the last few days I'd been looking at Nick, watching him with both love and fear in my heart. My time with Taylor and Mark had changed me however. I knew that whichever way things worked out, everything would be okay. My fear was either gone, or powerless.

Nathan looked up at me and our eyes locked. I looked at Nick, then back at Nathan. There was the barest hint of a smile on my face as my feelings for Nick showed through. Nathan smiled at me.

"I hate to leave you boys, but I need to run into town. You'll survive without me won't you?"

"I think we can manage," said Nick.

Nathan gave me a look that clearly said, "go for it". I wondered how he could read me so easily. Was my interest in Nick that apparent?

Nathan departed and it was just me and Nick. We worked for a bit more while butterflies started flying around in my stomach. I wasn't afraid, but I was a bit nervous. I was far more bold than I ever had been before however. I stopped working and just looked at Nick, admiring his beauty. Nick wasn't wearing a shirt and there was plenty to admire.

He paused and looked at me shyly. He knew he was being observed. I stepped closer to him and took his hands in mine.

"I have something to tell you Nick." I said, looking into his eyes. He gazed back at me. There was no fear in them, no revulsion. He didn't draw back, which was a very good sign. A gay boy had just taken him by the hands and he didn't flinch.

"I love you." I said. The tone of my voice made it clear I meant it with all my heart.

I stood there waiting for his reaction. I had a good feeling within me, but even if he told me he didn't love me back, somehow I knew that would be okay too. Somehow I knew we'd still be the best of friends. I stood there without fear in what should have been one of the most terrifying moments of my life.

Nick didn't say anything. Instead he wrapped his arms around me and gave me the most passionate kiss I'd ever experienced.

I was ready for a lot of reactions, but Nick took me completely by surprise. He held me tight and kissed me so forcefully he took my breath away. When he pulled his lips from mine I felt weak in the knees.

"It sure took you long enough to tell me." he said.

His words took me by surprise even more than his kiss. Nick looked at my astonished features and laughed.

"You really thought I didn't know, didn't you?" he said.

I didn't know how to answer. I had no idea I'd been so obvious. I felt faintly foolish, but for some reason, I didn't mind.

"If you knew then why didn't you say something?"

"I figured you'd appreciate me more if you had to suffer a little." Nick smiled wickedly.

"You little bitch!" I said laughing.

I pounced on him and wrestled him to the dirt. The dusty soil clung to our sweaty bodies. In mere moments I was on top of Nick, holding him down. His firm, young body was spread out full length beneath me. I pressed my lips to his and kissed him with hunger and passion. He returned my kiss with fierce intensity. I felt within him the same needs that overwhelmed my own young body. I wanted to rip his shorts away right then and there, but I knew waiting would only make it better. Besides, kissing him and feeling his well-muscled body beneath me was more arousing than anything I'd ever experienced in my entire life.

It was several minutes before we pulled ourselves out of the dirt and got back to work. We kept smiling at each other. Our hands touched whenever we were near. I was so much in love with Nick that I thought my heart would explode. I knew he loved me too. We could go no more than a few minutes without stopping to kiss. It was the best day of my life.

When it was almost time for lunch, Nathan came walking toward us with a big bag.

"Here, I thought you guys might like to have a picnic." he said.

He looked at our muddy bodies and smiled. I'm sure he knew just how we got so dirty.

"If you follow the path through the woods," he said pointing to the line of trees in the far distance, "there's a great spot for a picnic by a little lake. It looks like you two could use a swim."

I could tell he understood everything from the way he looked at us. I almost felt like he was responsible for it. I didn't think that he and Ethan had adopted Nick so I could have a boyfriend, but I had a feeling that they'd done something. I had no idea what it was, but they'd done something. Those two had done so much for me. There were almost as much like angels as Taylor and Mark.

"Thank you," I said, kissing him on the cheek, "for everything." I could tell Nathan understood.

"Don't worry about hurrying back." said Nathan. "It's too hot to work anyway, so take your time."

"Thanks." said Nick, giving Nathan a kiss on the cheek as well.

Nick and I took the bag and walked toward the line of trees, holding hands. I was happier than I had ever been. My head was swimming. I actually had a boyfriend.

We walked between fields of growing corn, the sun beating down on us without mercy. Little trickles of sweat flowed down Nick's torso and back. It made him sexier than ever. Before we even reached the trees, we couldn't resist stopping to kiss once more. I couldn't go without the taste of his sweet lips for more than a few moments.

We finally forced our lips to part and walked on. We found the beginnings of a little path and followed it into the woods. We were hidden from the scorching sun, but it seemed a little humid under the great canopy of leaves. It was almost like a jungle in there. I looked at Nick and though of him as a wild, jungle boy. I liked thinking of him like that.

We came across an ancient log cabin and stopped to ponder it for just a moment. We didn't linger long however for the cool waters of the little lake were near and called to us. We ran hand in hand down the grassy slope and jumped in, not even bothering to take off our shoes. The water engulfed us in blissful coolness that seemed like Heaven.

It didn't take me long to pull Nick to me and wrap my arms around his firm, young body. We kissed each other fiercely, as if we couldn't possibly get enough of each other, which was true enough. I'd been wandering through a great boyfriend desert all my life and I couldn't help but gulp when I found someone at last. My lips and tongue devoured him.

We waded closer to the shore until we were only thigh deep in the lake. We tossed our soaked shoes and socks to the shore. The muddy bottom of the lake felt good squishing through my toes. I tugged at Nick's shorts and he made no move to stop me. He responded my pulling mine away as they fought to cling to my wet skin. In just a few moments we stood naked in the lake. Nick was so beautiful he made my heart ache.

I kissed his full, sweet lips yet again, then nibbled and kissed my way down his neck. I couldn't keep from kissing him over and over. I knew if I kissed him a million times that it would never be enough. I was more aroused that I ever had been in my entire life, which is saying quite a lot, and yet, what we were doing was about far more than mere sex. Now that it was actually happening, the sex was secondary, it was a mere expression of our love.

I lathered Nick's torso with my tongue, then sank to my knees before him, up to my neck in the cool water's of the lake. I looked up at Nick and he was smiling at me. I thought my heart would burst with my love for him. I leaned forward and Nick softly moaned as we both experienced love making for the first time.

Chapter 31

Wounds of the Past Healed

Ethan and Nathan sat nervously on my bed in Graymoor. I could tell they were ill at ease about being in Verona's most notorious haunted house. I smiled to myself. I understood well how they felt. It had not been that long since Graymoor had given me the creeps as well. All that had changed however and the ghosts of Graymoor held no terror for me, even the murderous father who still rushed into my room some nights to hack his son to death.

"They're coming." I said quietly. I could feel more than hear them. I'd grown very sensitive to those from the other side.

Mark and Taylor quietly entered the room. I think they knew that Ethan and Nathan were on edge. One could hardly blame them. It wasn't every day that one was reunited with friends that had died twenty years before.

Ethan's eyes grew wide and he squeezed Nathan's hand. The two of them gazed at the boys before them, utterly astonished.

"There is nothing to fear," said Mark. He smiled. "How have you been Ethan?"

"I, uh…I've been fine." He was bewildered, but that was understandable. He looked closely at Mark.

"It's really you," he said.

"It's really me," laughed Mark.

"Mark, Taylor, I'm so sorry." said Ethan. "I'm so sorry I wasn't a better friend when you needed me the most. I'm sorry I didn't have the courage to stand by you, and stick up for you. I've regretted it all these years. Maybe if I'd done more…"

"You were a great friend Ethan," said Mark. "You and Nathan talked to us when few others would. You accepted us. I can't even begin to tell you how much that meant."

Ethan was crying.

"I've just felt so…. All these years I've felt…."

"Let it go Ethan. There is no reason for you to be haunted with that pain. You stood by us as best you could and that's all anyone could ask."

Nathan was looking at the boys in awe, but most of all at Taylor.

"You look just like I remember you," he said. "You're still beautiful." I had the feeling that Nathan had once had quite a crush on Taylor, one that still wasn't quite dead.

Taylor smiled shyly and brushed his hair out of his eyes.

"And you look better than ever." he said to Nathan.

"Hey," said Ethan, "no hitting on my boyfriend." That made everyone laugh.

I sat and watched as the four discussed things that happened before I was born, but I didn't feel like an outsider. I was among friends. Ethan and Nathan talked to Mark and Taylor long into the night. I fell fast asleep on my bed before they were done.

* * *

In just a few months, everything concerning the murders was pretty much wrapped up. Kyle was found guilty of the murders of all three boys. Dusty was sentenced for his part in the deaths of Ken and Tony. There was more than enough evidence to convict them. Their sneakers matched the prints found at the site of Ken's murder and minute traces of blood from all three murder victims were found on Kyle's clothes. Traces of Ken and Tony's blood were found on Dusty's clothes as well. As soon as that evidence was presented, the boys admitted to their crimes. I looked at Kyle just before he was taken away. I wondered how I'd ever fallen for him.

The last day of the trial, what was left of the "God Hates Queers" group quietly disappeared from town. There weren't that many of them left. Some of them were in jail, while a great many others seemed to have wised up and broken away from the cult. I think many of them had finally realized how they had been wickedly misled. I found it hard to fathom how anyone could see hate as a good thing, but at least some of them wised up in the end.

The group's only part in the murders had been their negative influence, but as far as I was concerned, they were every bit as guilty and Kyle, Dusty, and Justin. It was their message of hate that had brought all this to pass. I learned during the trial that Kyle had been a member of their church back in Colorado. He had brought their hate with him to Verona and they had followed.

I walked out of the courthouse, leaving behind all the troubles of the last several weeks. At last, it was truly over.

Everything returned to boring normalcy in Verona, and for once I was glad. No longer did I wish for excitement. I'd had quite enough of that. Boring would suit me just fine for a while.

* * *

I stood on my knees before the flower bed in front of Graymoor, gathering flowers. It was a bright sunny day and I felt quite comfortable in my shorts and tee-shirt. I smiled, my whole life seemed bright and sunny now that the unpleasant business of the last few weeks was over and I had a boyfriend. I think the boyfriend part had the most to do with it. I was in love and it was all the more special because I never thought it would happen to me.

The object of my love pushed open the gate and walked toward me. He stood smiling down at me, looking so fine in his sexy sleeveless shirt and white shorts.

"You ready?" asked Nick.

"I'm ready."

We walked to the cemetery. I placed flowers on the graves of Marty, Ken, and Tony. I'd miss them all. I knew I'd miss Marty the most. His absence left a void that could never be filled.

I placed flowers on the graves of Taylor and Mark too, even though I felt odd doing so. To me, Taylor and Mark were still very much alive. Marty, Ken, and Tony were too. The sting of death had left my mind on the day that Taylor and Mark showed me what it was really like. I knew it wasn't an ending, but only a transformation. There was nothing to fear. There was no sorrow. I knew that Marty and the others were alive and well, and that someday, I'd see them again. Kyle and others had sought to destroy them, but had utterly failed.

I looked up to find Nick gazing at me. I drew closer and pressed my lips to his, kissing him with all the love I felt for him. I took his hand in mine and we walked to the park. I didn't care if anyone looked at us, or what they thought. I had nothing to fear from death, so what had I to fear from life? Besides, I had a boyfriend at last and I wanted the whole world to know that I loved him.

About the Author

Mark A. Roeder is a full-time writer who lives in a small northern Indiana town. This is his third published novel.

CPSIA information can be obtained at www.ICGtesting.com
228974LV00004B/108/A